1

My Job Sucketh

"It's election year, 2020. This November, the American people will vote in the most competitive election this country has ever seen. As we look out on the landscape of this divided nation we ask ourselves: Will the Democrats pull out a victory against the Republicans? Will America elect its first female president? If Sunako Wainwright has anything to say about it, then yes! Elected as a Congresswoman for the state of Alaska at the tender age of twenty-five, Suni served two terms in the House before winning her Senate seat at thirty. She's the youngest woman ever elected to Congress and the Senate. And now, as a thirty-five-year-old seasoned politician, she's poised to take the presidency. If the polls are correct and all goes as predicted, then our first female president will be Suni Wainwright. Let's give an enormous cheer as Suni joins us live in the studio. Welcome, Suni!"

Suni struts in as her campaign song "Sunny," the 1976 Boney M. disco version, blasts through the studio. Her hair is perfect, black and shiny. Her turquoise suit against her tan skin gives just the pop she needs to stand out. Her long, delicately beaded Alaska Native earrings complete the ensemble. She's captivating. She gives Linda, the studio and the cameras the best watts of her smile. Something about her is intoxicating. It's hard to look away. There's no doubt she'll win.

"Thanks for having me, Linda," Suni coos. "It's so great to be here."

The smugness behind her smile irritates me. If anyone on the planet knows what a phony Suni is, it's me. I can't take anymore. She hasn't said a lot, but I've already seen enough. Besides, I know all her talking points by heart. I grab the remote and turn off the television with a jerk. The violence of the motion upsets my cereal bowl. Almond milk and homemade granola splash all over the front of my work clothes.

Crap! I'm already late! I peel off my outfit and throw it on the kitchen stool next to me. I trudge into the bedroom and grab my black shift dress, it's the last of my clean clothes. I sigh when I see my reflection. The dress bubbles out awkwardly in the front. I look six months pregnant. I'm hating this day already.

I take a breath and try to summon my positivity. Being in this house always brings me down. There's no furniture, and my bed is a mattress on the floor. I mean don't get me wrong, the house isn't a dump. The finishes are nice, and everything's new and top of the line, but I never really moved in. I didn't plan on living here. This house was supposed to be a flip, and then life happened. But I'm making progress. Last week I ordered a couch.

My phone's buzzing. I know who it is without even looking. I don't have time for this! I grab my messenger bag and slip on the super comfy ballet shoes everyone says 'look orthopedic'. The dirty cereal bowl and the trail of mushy granola is still on the counter, but I'll get that later. Everything else looks good. Alarm set, that's it. I'm off.

It's spring in our nation's capital. Purple crocuses push their way through muddy patches in people's yards and the sky is a crisp, clear blue. The wind is always blowing. My hair tangles immediately. I reach back, twist it around itself, and tuck it into a bun. My standard-issue camel colored trench blends into the throngs walking like zombies towards the Metro, too lost in their phones to even look up, let alone speak.

I turn my phone off, and tuck it in my bag, it's an unusual move. I just need this last twenty minutes of peace, time before the storm, the space to think. The Metro stairs are slippery. I hold the rail on the way down and run as soon as I hit the platform. I make it onto the train just as the doors are closing. I find a seat by a window, clutch my bag to my stomach for warmth, and lean my head against the hard plastic. I hope I don't get lice.

I close my eyes and drift. Bed bugs and lice. I deliberate about them a lot these days. Crazy people are releasing them in stores like little critters of mass destruction. I open my eyes and look around. I spot the guy asleep across from me, mouth open, hygiene clearly not his thing. It's not such a far leap to feel like everything's contaminated.

Even the almond milk I drink is slowly killing the bees. There's just nothing benign about existing—it's exhausting. Everything I do causes some chaos, some earthly disturbance. Trying to be eco-conscious, to

2

wear, eat, and travel without harm is super time-consuming. We need more apps, and different services that will help the mainstream consumer be eco-friendlier. And when I say mainstream consumer, I mean me. Hey! I want to help the planet too and do my part. I just need a pathway in.

I'm constantly coming up with inventions I think could make a difference. I write them in a little notebook. I like how paranoid it makes people when you carry a little notebook, whip it out, and write random things. Mostly it's nothing, like must buy reusable eco-friendly alternative to plastic wrap. News flash—there isn't any! I mean, not really. I want a roll of vegetable cellulose I can just unravel, stuff like that.

I shift in my seat, open-mouth guy is awake, staring at me. I have this habit of gesturing when I'm deep thinking. The kind of thing people do when they're talking, except I'm not saying anything, so I know it looks weird. There's no way to really play it off either. If you enjoy talking to yourself, you can just pretend you're on your cell, but making a bunch of random hand moves weirds people out.

Ugh! I wish I was going anywhere but work. I don't want to sound like a brat, because I'm really grateful to have a job in the first place, but… I hate my job. I hate commuting with the thousands of other dark-circled, drained people who are all just trying to get through another day. I hate that I hate my job. I should love it. I should celebrate it. Whenever I tell people what I do when I'm at a bar or a cocktail party, they always get really excited, lean in conspiratorially, and ask a thousand questions. I used to love what I do. It's just lately there's been something off. I don't know if it's the job or if it's me, but all signs point to me.

To me, and my breakup and freaking Kyle, who after three months I already can't get a hold of and who before he left opened a cell account in my name. Holy handbooks of Satan! What was I thinking getting involved with such a bag of scum? Why did all this happen to me? I know why it happened. I'm not dense. I take responsibility for all my actions. I just have this compulsory need to keep asking, hoping the answer will be different.

I've always been smart, not particularly outgoing, but I had my place in the grand scheme of things. Drama and acting in plays in high school, political action groups in college. And then I met Kyle. I was a newly minted adult, with a promising future, and a good degree. Traveling was all I could think about. Then I went to a party at my friend Ashley's. Kyle was on the other side of her gate when I walked into her yard. And the rest is history. Horrible, rocky, what—was—I—ever—thinking history? The kind that eats years and leaves behind nothing.

It's my stop. I rise and scramble out while mouth-gape guy eyes my legs. Ugh! Repugnant! Why is it that some men think they have a right to check any and every woman out? As though they're doing us some kind of favor. As though we women would wilt without the attention of strange men we'll never see again leering at us. Keep telling yourselves that, boys!

I pick up the pace, dodge, weave, scurry, go, go, go! I pump down the hall, and fly into the office, head low, head low, no eye contact, no eye contact, safe. I dump my bag on the floor, plop into my desk, and take a minute to breathe behind the cubicle wall. Not that it offers any protection, you can hear every cough, every shift, every conversation. There's no such thing as privacy.

"Suni isn't happy." Beth's nasal tone echoes in the quiet hush of my cube.

I snap my head up like a startled bird. "Oh, wow, you scared me. I didn't know you were there."

"You seem not to notice a lot of things these days," Beth says, crossing her thin arms over her bony chest. I squirm in my chair, and she knows her jab has landed. She tosses her sand colored bob and smirks down at me with glittering eyes. She's in her element. She loves wielding her authority. A little smile splays across her lips as she speaks. "Suni will be back in the office by one. You better spend the rest of the morning making it make sense."

4

I resist the urge to mouth off, to tell her to stuff it. I don't have time for her sycophantic drivel right now, she's a total robot. Nice enough, I guess, if you like the super up tight, sweater-set wearing, perfect little Miss type. I don't personally have a problem with her. I can get along with anybody. But lately she's been on this kick to get us to do all kinds of team-building exercises and stupid activities.

"I think I've got this Beth." I don't even look up. I just slump over and start digging in my bag. It's a totally passive aggressive piss on her fire.

"Just make sure everything's correct this time. That means a check and a recheck."

"I know how to do my job Beth."

"It's not about doing your job, it's about making sure everything is perfect for Suni. Why is that so hard to understand?" Her voice reaches a hysterical octave. "What may seem like one small mistake to you is something that could snowball for Suni. I—"

I cut her off. "Beth, let it go. I've got this. Trust me. Nice headband by the way," I say, trying to change the subject. It's a little snarky to mention the headband since the wide black velvet seems to overpower her small head and make her skin seem even more sallow, but she kind of deserves it after her swipe at me.

"Yeah, nice dress." Beth's eyes scan the big front bubble that's even more prominent now that I'm sitting.

"Thanks," I say with a rakish smile, smoothing out the fabric as best I can.

"All right, well, enough of this, I have things to do." Beth purses her lips and huffs down the hall.

I know Beth's mad, but I don't care. She picked the wrong one today. Besides, all this really isn't my fault—it's Suni's. Unfortunately, pointing out the truth would amount to treason. We're all supposed to act like Suni is the pinnacle of perfection, that the sun rises and sets with Suni. Goodness only knows it's the image she's sold to America and we're gobbling it up like hungry wolves. And I can't really blame us, I mean Suni is the best candidate we've had in years.

5

Suni, that's who I work for. I'm the media content manager for our future youngest and first female president. Well, at least we hope, but her campaign looks great, and all the polls put her in the lead. She's just the kind of candidate Americans can get behind. She's young, athletic, well spoken, with a history of breaking barriers and a good track record for her political career. Plus, she's pretty, a kind of steel-toed delicate pretty that allows people to admire and fear her at the same time.

I grab my cell, turn it back on, and groan when I see three messages from Barbara. She's my mom. I've always called her by her first name. Don't ask.

"You really steamed the edamame with this one, didn't you?" Brett slides into my cube and installs himself in the chair positioned next to my desk. He puts his coffee cup right on top of a stack of papers I've been meaning to look over. I watch as a fat drop plops onto the white, leaving a big brown splotch. Great. This is just what I need. First Beth and now…

"I don't think that's a thing. Steamed the edamame?"

"You tell me. You're the millennial." Brett gives me a smug smile like he's won some epic battle.

"Yeah, but I'm pretty sure you just made that up."

"Did I? Or are you just not down with the lingo of your generation? Ask yourself that, Maverick." Brett slaps my desk like he's one-upped me bigly, winks at me, grabs his coffee cup and wanders off to find Maisy. She's a new intern from Idaho with long blonde hair, clear green eyes, and a laugh like a donkey's bray. He's been hitting on her relentlessly. I don't know how she can stand it.

I'm not in the mood for Brett's antics this morning. He's nice, but he's a man lost in a world of frat parties and which chick is the hottest, even though he's pushing 50. He's a Gen-Xer, who despite his intellectual command of language, can't seem to understand or incorporate modern day slang—or maybe he's right? Maybe I'm not down with the lingo of my generation, who knows.

Brett has his good points, but I feel sorry for his family. His wife is nice, mousy, but nice. All he ever does is complain about her and his

6

kids and hit on new young interns. Brett's brilliance is his saving grace. He's one of the best speech writers of his time. Suni always starts out his material calm and slow. Then she raises the tempo until it's frenzied. She crashes the crescendo with a whisper that everyone rides like a wave. It's super inspiring, so it plays out really well. She's also being hailed as one of the best orators of her generation, thanks to Brett.

You probably noticed my name. You're right, that's my name. Maverick Johnson Malone, my dad named me. I was born November 11,1986, *Top Gun* and Magic Johnson were cultural icons of the time. And yes, my dad really did that to me. He combined his two favorites and viola, hence my name. Most people don't get the wordplay, but some do. They say things like, "So, your dad put together the Maverick character from *Top Gun* and Magic Johnson to come up with your name? Wow. Just wow. No words. You have my sincere apologies."

Barbara calls me Mavie. I've told her again and again I hate that nickname, but she never listens. It seems to be a reoccurring theme in our relationship. She criticizes me, violates all my boundaries, and then calls it motherly love. I go by my full name, but lately Suni's been calling me Rik. I don't like it, but I don't have the energy to fight another battle with her.

Suni was the one who insisted we use the picture that got us into hot water. Hence why she's mad at me. Usually we try to create our own visual media, but this time we used a stock photo, and one of the interns tagged the picture incorrectly. Apparently, despite all the other things I do, I was supposed to notice the mistake. Be omniscient, but I wasn't, so we gave credit to the wrong photographer.

Not usually such a big deal, a quick apology, a sidebar making people aware of our mistake, but this one's different. This guy is kicking up a big stink, and seeking mainstream media channels to air his grievances. He's accusing Suni of copyright infringement and at the same time bashing her politically. It feels and smells like a setup. It's all about publicity, his chance to piggyback on someone more visible than himself, get his name out there. Who knows, he may even be getting paid by the opposition, a culture vulture I call him.

I grab the papers stained by Brett's coffee and quickly read through them. They're off-the-cuff ideas, slogans, topics for Suni's, Instagram, Twitter, Facebook feeds. I mainly manage the posts and write the content of what we put out there. We have two interns who do most of the actual input, but the buck always stops with me for any mistakes, or discrepancies, and Suni demands one hundred percent accuracy and beyond.

Our Senate office isn't sexy. It's hot in the summer, and cold in the winter, just barely passable right now. With the campaign, and Suni's Senate duties, we hardly have enough space for the flow of people in and out. I haven't worked here long, a little over a year. The office has high turnover rates. It's no mystery why Suni turns every situation into a bigger deal than it should be.

I read over the statement about the picture and get ready to hand it off to Beth. She'll make sure it gets published, it's my atonement. I shift in my chair and think back to how this whole thing got started. It was while I was getting my Masters of Arts in Politics at Catholic University. I came to Suni's Senate office to observe for a paper I was writing. It was about women in politics and the social norms we expect them to uphold. Not my best piece of writing, but I still got an A. It was while I was here that it happened. They were all sitting around thinking up slogans for Suni's at the time 'possible' run for the presidency. I was at the copy machine.

"I need something good, something catchy. A name for my fans and stans that incorporates them, me first, but them too." Suni tossed back her shoulder length black hair as she spoke and adjusted one of her long-beaded earrings from cock-eyed crazy back into the lobe.

"What about The Sunako Group?" Beth, ever eager to please, was the first to come up with an idea.

Suni crinkled her nose and shook her head. "Sounds like I'm drilling for oil."

Brett flicked his pen and straightened his hideous tie with a portly hand. "What about The Sunako Collective?" he beefed out.

Suni considered a moment, cocked her head to the side, looked up at Brett from under long dark lashes, and smiled a cinnamon smile. I could tell she'd already dismissed everything he said. She was only humoring him. "Mmm, maybe, we'll save that one for later, it kinda sounds like a funeral home."

"What about Suni and Co.?" I'd stupidly interrupted. "Phonetically it's almost the same as your name. It's a play on words—get it? Sunako—Suni and Co.?" I was instantly mortified. I'm always doing that, blundering into things, talking when I should be listening. I can't help it. It's a habit.

Brett and Beth looked at me with cool superiority and curled their lips at my audacity. I was just visiting and they even let me use the copy machine—How dare I? The room was so quiet you could have heard a pin drop. I couldn't help but agree with Beth and Brett. I should have kept my mouth shut.

Suni's eyes assessed me. "What did you say your name was again?"

"Maverick, Maverick Malone."

I wasn't sure what to make of her. I could tell that she liked to intimidate people, but she didn't intimidate me. She had a natural authority, a way that made you feel like if you crossed her you'd be sorry. Even when you're on the good side of her, it all still feels elusive.

Brett laughed and buffed up. "Sounds like a kid's T.V. show. Suni and Co.? I don't like it."

Beth did a weird giggle snort. "Like you're going to come out dressed in one of those puppet suits or something."

Suni put a hand up, silencing them. "No, I like it, it's simple and clever. Maybe that's just what this country needs, a modern-day 'Mrs. Rogers'. That could do a lot for my image. Sweet and ethical, but with a hard bottom line. Maybe I'll even faux-bake some cookies. Right now, I'm polling as cold, slightly distant. People don't like that I'm not married and don't have kids. I need them to see something domestic. Yeah, this could work."

"But you don't know how to bake!" Beth had blustered all red faced. "I make all those muffins you bring to your committee meetings.

Besides, she doesn't even work here," she'd spluttered, pointing towards me like some dramatic witness on the stand.

Suni gave Beth a withering look. "I guess we'll just have to change that. I need someone new to run my social media accounts now that Leslie's leaving."

And that's how Suni and Co. was born, and how I got the job here. Suni liked the way I thought. Liked the prolific way I wrote, not a lot of need for rumination, just a straight shot on the page. At first it felt like a dream working for Suni. She's only a few years older than I am, already been in the halls of Congress and the Senate for years, an impressive track record. What's not to like? It turns out it's Suni; I don't like. She's a total fake.

I sigh and start our next Instagram post. Something about this day and women's rights. Ugh, I need a vacation. I could, should be able to work from home, and come in to the office occasionally, but Suni likes all her people present. She's a micromanager. Luckily, she travels a lot for her campaign. She live streams everything. Thank goodness I'm off the hook for that.

I shake myself and think about grabbing a coffee. I try not to get caught up in my general sense of millennial ennui. Everything just feels so heavy, with Kyle leaving, and the messy break up. I hacked his account exactly three months ago. It's not the most ethical thing to do, but he was acting strange. I confronted him first, and asked if he was cheating, lying? Like most gaslighting toads, he denied everything. He made me feel like I was losing it. Crazy! I hadn't been at the job that long with Suni. I was finishing up my degree. He strung me along for months before I cracked his passwords, and slid into his DMs, saw everything.

Oh, crap! I just remember why Barbara's calling incessantly, it's my dad's birthday. I'm supposed to pick up the cake on my way over tonight. Great, dinner with the fam, just what I need. I hunch over my laptop, block all else out, and get to work. I let the hours roll by without thinking about them, about dinner tonight, about Kyle, and all the debt he left me in. Life is good, but sometimes it sucks.

10

Bashir rolls by my desk at one, and whispers, "She's baaack." He makes a face like *The Scream*, before scurrying to his desk at the front.

"Thanks for the heads-up, Man Bun," I call. I hear his laugh echo down the hall.

Bashir is cool people, he answers phones, gives tours, is the friendly face of our operation. I like him. He's twenty-five with long dark straight hair he wears up and deep rich eyes that are already furrowed with laugh lines. He laughs more than he talks. I call him Top Knot or Man Bun, depending on my mood.

I sense rather than hear Suni enter the office. There's an immediate edge, the feeling of calm dissipates, a kind of dodgeball ambiance takes over. We collectively hold our breath, make ourselves small, each of us hoping we don't get bopped on the head by the ruthless side of Suni, the one the public never sees.

Beth scurries past me. "The conference room immediately," she barks. She's carrying a tray of cookies. I envision Beth in her apartment after work, swilling red wine, still in her sweater set, a potholder on one hand as she whips up batch after batch of cookies for Suni. She's definitely Suni's devoted little lackey. Bashir called her, 'Suni's Batter Biatch' one time. I laughed my freaking head off.

I grab my laptop, a pen, the little notebook that strikes terror in the hearts of so many, and head to the bottle filler in the hall with my stainless-steel water bottle. I joke that it doubles as a weapon when it's full. I refuse to be the first one into the conference room so I can grovel at Suni. I'm good at what I do. If one mistake means she terminates me, so be it—I have my principles.

Of course, these are noble thoughts to have, but I'm mostly just grandstanding, because if push comes to shove, I'll have to do what needs to be done to stay on the good side of Suni. Which isn't easy and involves lots of bum kissing. Which I'm naturally resistant to. What can I say? I've always been an instigator. Why stop now?

I definitely need this job, though. What with money being the way the world operates and all. Plus, it's not like I have lots of savings, or really even any money. I poured what little I had into the rowhome Kyle and I bought by Gallaudet, the College of the Deaf.

Every time my brother Brandon comes to my house, he makes the same tired joke. "I see deaf people. They know they're deaf, but I don't know what they're signing." Funny, not at all funny, but I laugh each time, more out of pity for Brandon, not the Deaf. The Deaf have sound minds. I can't say the same for my brother.

Brett's suddenly behind me with his reusable water bottle. "Suni's all gangsta rap show on this one Maverick, you better hurry to the conference room."

I grab my bottle, give Brett major side eye, and head to the conference room. I walk in with my shoulders square and look Suni directly in the eyes. The only way to win with her is to show no hesitation, no fear. I'm the only person on her staff who challenges her. The rest are too afraid.

I'm daughter of Barbara, the biggest, guilt-trippingest, narcissistic bully on the planet. These are survival skills, baby! I know how to cope and the first rule of dealing with a narc is don't back down, and Suni is definitely a narc. All the signs are there. That's why every time I walk into a room with Suni, Tom Petty's "I Won't Back Down" plays in my head. That's my theme music, Suni!

I don't give Suni a chance to speak. I address it curtly. "It's already taken care of." I nod my head, sit down, and open my notebook. I start to write a list of ingredients I'm going to buy on my way home even though I'll probably be too tired to cook. Oh yetzpa! It hits me again, the cake, my dad's birthday, this day just gets better and better.

Brett blimps into the conference room. "What's up playas?" he says in his 'it's all cas' tone. He winks at Suni and takes the seat next to me. I feel like my all-natural deodorant is failing, my pits are a little sticky. I stop writing, look up at Suni, open my laptop as a screen, and pretend to listen as she speaks.

"Our poll numbers are great, and the interview I did this morning was fire. I think we can all agree on that." Suni beams around the conference room with expectation.

12

It's a familiar cue, and everyone acts accordingly. A low roar rips through the staff, followed by fist pumps. Suni smiles, satisfied. I give a half clap, and eye the pitcher of water and glasses that are in the middle of the table, they're another one of my ideas. When I started working for Suni, I noticed that at all the committee meetings, hearings, anything where political figures gather, there were always plastic water bottles.

For the American public at home, watching politicians sit in meetings with single use plastic water bottles at their elbows and then lecture us on recycling and climate change isn't a good optic. Suni immediately agreed, brought attention to the issue, and passed a bill. Brett said, "Suni really 'Thunberg'd' it out on that one." And he's right. But not once did she even acknowledge the idea came from me. That's when I think I started to sour.

Beth passes around her cookies, everyone takes one, just like nursery school. I pass. I'm trying to rid myself of the evils of sugar. I just watched a Netflix doc that said sugar was more addictive than cocaine when they tested it on a bunch of lab rats. So, meh, no thanks. I'm always reforming my diet, trying to be healthier, better, heck, just plain old nutritious. I'm pretty much open to anything not too crazy on the food spectrum.

"Let me guess?" Brett's breathy whisper moistens my ear, yuk. "You're all sugar free, gluten-free, organic princess, right?"

"More like I'm trying to rid myself of toxins, that goes for people too." I raise my eyebrows, narrow my eyes, and dare him to challenge me.

"Is this what they call clapping back? Am I getting a standing ovation?" Brett winks like we're sharing some great joke.

I'm horrified. "Seriously, do you even have command of the English language?" Brett laughs. Suni looks over. She squints at us at the end of the long table. We stop, unknit our heads, and pay attention. No one crosses Suni.

"Like I was saying, I'll be in Iowa tonight and tomorrow. Then I'll be in Baltimore through the weekend at the Kick Off the Summer with

Suni venue. You know what the goals are. You know what's at stake. I expect everything to run smoothly. All right, time to wrap this up, let's go around the table and share one thing we've learned during this campaign."

I do my inward groan. I always get flashbacks to Brownies when I do activities like this. Trying to sell all those cookies—ugh—it was too much pressure for me. Plus, this girl kept showing me her thumb without a nail on it, it was all open pink stuff, exposed and meaty, disgusting, it's no wonder I'm a vegetarian. It's my turn.

I say, "I'm really glad this campaign will bring exposure to areas of need in our country."

It's true. Suni's Kick Off the Summer with Suni barbecue venue is the first of its kind. I hate to sound like a broken record, but it was my idea too. Before I got all jaded, I asked in a meeting why candidates don't go, and I mean really go into inner cities? Kyle, even though he's White and I'm Biracial, used to be down with people from the city. He grew up poor. I grew up privileged. He could code-switch like you wouldn't believe. People in 'the hood'—I'm using air quotes here—loved him and recognized him as one of their own.

Besides, 'the hood' is a manufactured derivative of our screwed-up history. A blind, so we have permission to throw away an entire sect of people, but that's another topic completely. So, Kyle and I were always going to visit someone in some part of Baltimore or D.C. The kinds of places Barbara was sure I was going to get murdered. Long story short, I learned that America weaponizes race and the old tired stereotypes are all just lies. Black Americans have a valuable voice and perspective that America needs. And if anti-Blackness isn't stopped it will bring this country to its knees. Plus, the idea of race is bollocks, it's all about money, like everything.

Suni saw the potential of what I was saying right away. She loved the idea of going into majority minority inner cities. She's Alaska Native herself, she knows about stereotyping. Before I knew it, she had summer barbecue venues lined up in cities like Baltimore, Detroit,

14

Chicago, and Albuquerque. People loved it. They love her. What more can I say?

Suni's finally finished talking. I stand and start to exit the conference room with everyone else. I'm just about out the door... almost safe.

"Rik." Suni's voice is sharp and commanding. I can't even pretend I didn't hear it. "Don't leave just yet, have a seat."

I turn, walk back, slide into my chair, toss my stuff on the table, cross my arms, and wait while she talks to Brett.

"The Iowa speech, I don't think it has enough oomph. You know what I mean?" Suni smiles. "It needs more of an everyman thread going through it. Think about deep-fried butter, open friendly faces as white and windswept as the moon. People who eat corn and beef and have big trucks even if they live in cities. Those are the people I'm trying to capture. Can you do that, Brett? Can you make it happen for me? And do it quickly, I want to run through it with Jessica, and see what she thinks."

Jessica Ingleman is Suni's campaign manager. A small boxy bull of a woman, who wears flat shoes and no make-up, she's super no nonsense. I like her. You can tell she feels like she's doing exactly what she was born to do by the way she never lets up. She's Suni's biggest asset, and Suni knows it.

"You're the boss." Brett gives a mock salute, snatches up his pen, and some greasy-looking papers. "Laters Maverick." He gives my upper arm a playful air punch, makes a hangman's face Suni can't see, and leaves.

Suni looks down at her phone and scrolls through whatever she's looking at. "Bear with," she says, putting up a pretentious finger. I swear she saw that line on a British T.V. show. I bite my lip, rest my elbow on the table, and put my head in my hand. I should probably start looking for another job. I only close my eyes for a second. When I open them, Suni is sitting opposite me, staring at me with some mind game she's gotten under way while I was micro-napping.

"You ready?" her voice is caustic.

Whatever. I stifle the urge to roll my eyes. "Sure." I grab my water bottle, unscrew the cap, and take a swig.

"I don't think you and I need to mince words. So, I'm just going to put it all out there and say—I don't feel like you're showing us your best right now and I'm concerned."

I set the bottle down on the table a little too hard, and water sloshes out. "That's funny because the data from traffic to your social media accounts says otherwise. Our posts are reshared, retweeted, reposted more than any other candidate. You want to talk about fire? Fire is the social media campaign I've put together for you. I'm not sure what else you want, but I have spread sheets to back up all the data right here." I slide the papers across the table fast, they fan out in a whoosh, and settle between us.

Suni's nostrils flare. She looks at me with disdain. "You're right, the numbers are definitely with you, but this conversation is about your attitude. You think I don't see it? You think all of us don't see it? Your eye rolls at our team-building activities, smug faces, snarky remarks. You're not as witty as you think you are, Maverick. You need to remember that your job is about me, your time is mine, and I am the only thing that should matter when you're here. If I say 'jump,' you need to ask 'how high'?" She leans in close and makes her voice soft. "See, there's something you need to understand." Her tone changes it's full blast. "I am the boss and no one speaks when I am speaking!" Her fist pounds the table hard, her face is red, her hair explosive.

I've never seen her this heated before. I almost expect her head to start spinning. Oy, this is not a good look for her.

Suni takes a breath and calms herself. "You've hatched a lot of good ideas while you've been with us Maverick, but I need more than that. I need you to be loyal, obedient, and willing to do anything I say. What I don't need is someone who's a know it all upstart. Got it? Otherwise there are going to be some very hard decisions to make, and you know I'm very decisive. It's something people love about me, but as the polls show, most Americans love everything about me. I can make or break anyone in this country. Is that clear?"

Despite my best intentions, I snap, push back. "Don't patronize me, Suni. I'll amend my attitude, but you need to realize that this team works hard for you and the last thing any of us want to do is extra team-building activities, nights and weekends in what should be our time off. And I'm not an upstart, what I am is honest." I think I'm done, but then this little gem pops out. "You know who else demanded total allegiance, Suni? Hitler."

Oy, now that I didn't mean to say, well, at least not out loud. We sit in shocked silence for a minute, before Suni's eyes flick to mine, a threat disguised as warning in them. I know instantly that someday she and I are going to go *millennial a millennial*, and it won't be pretty. No point in arguing with her now, though.

"Look, I apologize for the misprint. I'll make sure it doesn't happen again. That's all I can give you, Suni."

Suni runs her tongue across her teeth. "This isn't a fairy tale Maverick, but I still want the happy ending. Get my drift?"

"Completely."

"Great." Suni rises to her full height and looks down her nose at me. "In the future, when we have little chats like this," she smooths her turquoise power skirt as she talks. "I expect your mannerisms to be a little more deferential. You need to remember that you are addressing the future first female president. Do you understand?"

I just nod, there's nothing else to say.

"Perfect." Suni looks down at her phone and zombie walks out of the conference room.

I grab my stuff, head to my cube, and try to shake off the whole conversation. I'm not trying to make Suni angry. I don't enjoy confrontation with my boss. I guess it's just a personality clash, maybe we're just too different, not capable of seeing eye to eye. I don't know, but I do know Suni's not the only one who has some decisions to make.

I drop into my chair and stare at my blank computer screen. I always write out future posts ahead of time, even for events that haven't happened yet. I've got some great ideas for the Baltimore Summer with Suni barbecue. My write up intersects the history of the neighborhood

Suni's going to visit with the social justice angle that Suni's followers demand. They love the fact that Suni's outside the box. With her they can actually believe there might be change, and hope is a mighty powerful thing.

At four I grab my phone, head to a quiet nook in the hall, and call Barbara back.

"Finally." Barbara doesn't say hello, she gets right to the point. "Did you already pick up your father's cake?" She doesn't let me answer the question, she just mows on. "Be here by seven, there's someone coming over I want you to meet, and I want to make sure you look decent. Don't forget to get your father a nice card. You know how he likes a nice card. Brandon already got him one of those high-end massaging chairs. You know the leather kind that aren't too hideous. We put it in the den. Your father's been sitting in it all day, but don't worry Mavie, we know you can't afford nice things so just a card. Write something clever on the inside. You always do so well with your clever little words, and for heaven's sake don't forget to bring the cake. Oh, I've gotta go, Brandon's FaceTiming me. He's just so hysterical. See you tonight."

I hang up and look down at my phone. Someday I'm going to dial Barbara's number, put the phone down and just walk away, let her have one of her nit picking, Brandon loving, conversations with herself. It's not like she ever lets me get a word in, and when I do, she takes it as a challenge. She takes everything I say as a challenge. It's Greek tragedy level drama; maybe someday I'll turn it into my own mommy issue play, but for now I tell her nothing of import, and keep the contact to a minimum, it's the only way we get along.

Brandon on the other hand is the golden child, the one who can do and say no wrong. He'll be forty this year. He's unmarried, and he calls Barbara every day, sometimes multiple times a day. He still brings her over his laundry. It'll be interesting to see who finally ponies up and marries him, or if there's even a woman who can crack his mama's boy code. I have my doubts about it.

Genesis, one of our interns, is at my cube when I get back. "Suni wants to see a rough copy of your Baltimore write-up." Her face is all apology as she asks.

All Suni had to do was text and I would have sent her what I had. This is a power play, a move to put me in my place, and let me know who's in control. Good thing I'm always two steps ahead of Suni.

"No problem, just a sec." I plug in my flash drive, hit print, and hand Genesis the pages, careful not to smear the wet ink.

Gen glances at the pages, then at me. "Suni said she's going to mark these up, then she wants me to bring them back to you. Are you going to be here for a few minutes? Cause if not, I can scan and email them to you."

"It's no problem Gen. I'm not going anywhere."

She nods and lets out a sigh of relief. I hate to see her caught in the crossfire. She's a nice kid, idealistic and savvy. I can tell if she stays true to herself, there's nothing she won't accomplish.

"Great." She lifts the papers at me like a cheers, and trudges down the hall, the hem of her pants drags on the carpet.

Our office is diverse. Suni says she wants her constituents to 'see the rainbow', so everyone represents a certain sect of Suni's constituency. We're the most multi-racial staff in the halls of the Senate. Suni, let's everyone know it. Suni doesn't do things unless everyone knows it. Suni isn't Suni, unless everyone's watching.

I prefer a quieter existence, people not to notice me, but it's an impossibility. I think I'll get noticed until I'm an old woman, or at least until my hair dulls. It's *Flaming June* red and hangs down in big beach curls to my waist. I have deep dark eyes like shots of espresso, and so many freckles you could map constellations on my face. My skin is that nice after the summer tan that White people try so hard to achieve.

I confuse everyone, and more than one person has wandered up to me and asked. "What are you?" with a scrunched-up face full of confusion.

I have all kinds of devious answers to this, like sometimes I just say, "I'm a mermaid," or I say, "I'm American."

Then they say, "But what country are you from?"

And I say, "America."

Then they get a little frustrated and say something like, "No, what is your ethnicity?"

That's when I pull out all the stops. I call it my Jessica Simpson act, with a dash of Britney Spears, thanks for the inspiration ladies! And I say stuff like this, "Oh, okay, got ya, I'm A-m-e-r-i-c-a-n." I say American really well pronounced and slow like English is their second language, it's a hoot! I really lay it on thick for this next part. I use my Wisconsin soccer mom voice for this. "Where are you from, somewhere exotic or overseas like Canada? Oh, I've always wanted to visit, but I'm just so afraid of getting on a plane, especially flying over oceans."

It's usually the last straw and they give me a weird look before they huff off. I'm not being mean, it's just that if my racial makeup is always to be questioned, I might as well get something out of it too. And it's pure amusement. Try it sometime. This tactic can be applied to the questions of any nosey parker you encounter.

Lately, I've been trying out a new one, I just start speaking Russian. The minute I say, "*Privyet, droog moy,*" people get really freaked out. Then I say in my best Boris voice, "Greetings, my American friend." I don't usually have to say much more, people usually look around all sketchy and just kinda take off. I laugh myself silly at the reactions.

This need people have to place others in a box is strange to me. I never give people's racial makeup much thought when I'm out and about. I'm usually thinking about giving people genuine smiles and offering help if it's needed, making sure my fellow citizens are all doing okay, and just enjoying myself. I don't want to waste my time trying to figure out what people are. It's who they are that counts to me, and I like nice people, people you can just be yourself with.

Besides, I have lots of goals for what I want in my life and I'm pretty busy. Like right now, I'm teaching myself Russian through a combination of YouTube and language books, and I love speaking it. Before he left, Kyle was thoroughly freaked out by the whole thing. He used to say, "You're gonna have the Department of Homeland Security breaking down our freaking door with all your weird Russian search history and random YouTube feeds. I swear they monitor that stuff."

It's not that I want to learn Russian to add to the optical confusion of my appearance. I'm obsessed with Tolstoy, and not just *War and Peace*, his later works. His mid-life crisis stuff that questions the source of everything, examines life and what it means. Someday I plan to go to Russia, to visit Tolstoy's home, Yasnaya Polyana, to walk the meadows and sit by the streams as he once did. I want to feel the echoes of his greatness even in the time I'm living. It's super complex. Deep. Kyle didn't get any of it.

"Who's this guy again?" he asked when I told him of my plan to go to Russia.

I could tell by his tone he was semi-jealous. Which was weird since he didn't care about the plaid shirt wearing neighbor down the street who couldn't seem to get enough of staring at me and was always trying to trap me in conversations whilst giving off total lurker vibes that jarred me. I always had one finger on the trigger of my pepper spray when I saw him coming.

"Don't worry Kyle, Tolstoy's been dead for over a hundred years." I'd said, annoyed that he was more jealous of a dead guy than protecting me from some neighborhood perv.

"Yeah right, I know."

I seriously doubt he did. "So, what's up?" I'd asked.

"I'm just wondering, you know, why you like him so much?"

"I guess I relate to his journey of self-discovery. He was never a fixed equation, he explored, changed his mind, and opinions, he grew. That's deep."

"The meaning of life." Kyle smiled his deep dimple smile, thrust his hips in his low-slung jeans. "That's what you've got me for baby." I wince at the memory. Why did I ever date such a douzzleberry?

Genesis is back. She hands me the marked-up pages. I can tell she wants to make me feel better. She and Bashir are good friends, they hang out after work all the time. "Bashir and I are going to get a drink after work, it's karaoke night. Bashir say's we're going to try a never heard before rendition of Lizzo's "Truth Hurts." She tucks a lock of chin length curly brown hair behind her ear, and pushes up her black-framed glasses with her index finger, she's all *Ugly Betty* cute.

I wish I could just tell my family to get stuffed and go out and actually have fun, but—oh crap—it's quarter to five, the cake! I grab my bag and start stuffing things in. "Thanks Gen, but I've got a family thing tonight. It's my dad's birthday."

"Fun?" she asks with raised brows.

"Not fun," I say, stuffing the scarf that's been thrown over the back of my chair for a couple of weeks into my bag.

"Well then, you know what to do?"

"What?" I ask, turning off my desk lamp and shouldering into my camel trench.

"Drink," Genesis says with a laugh.

Playing Happy Families

My family home isn't actually in D.C., it's more the Chevy Chase, Maryland area where I grew up, and am Ubering to right now. I have a car but I mainly Metro and Uber around the city, traffic and parking just aren't worth it. I use the car when I go on long weekend getaways. Head up to places like Burlington, Vermont, hit Church Street in the hopes of getting a glimpse of Bernie Sanders, stuff like that.

I made it to the bakery right before they closed. My dad's cake is on the seat next to me, vanilla cake with vanilla icing. Dad's favorite. He doesn't exactly have an adventurous palette; his tastes are mostly bland. He retired from being Director of Human Resources with the U.S. Treasury last year. Barbara insisted he retire at exactly the age of sixty. She's never worked, other than raising us, and she wanted him to be free to travel. The only problem is they mainly don't go anywhere. I think Brandon would go into a toxic shock meltdown if his mommy went too far away from him.

"This is the place?" the Uber driver pulls up to my parent's house.

"This is it." I hit the app and give him a big tip. He and I went round and round after I hopped into his car. He was so happy to see me, he was convinced I was from his country. His command of the English language isn't that good, and I tried to explain to him that I'm Biracial, that's why I look the way I do, but he didn't seem to get it. He kind of clucked and gave up talking to me.

Sometimes the international crowd thinks I'm from their country. They get disappointed, like I'm in some funk of American denial when I politely explain I'm from this country. But I appreciate them trying to include me. Maybe one day I'll just say "Yes," and we can celebrate whatever country it is we're from. Oh, well. I grab the cake, say "Thanks," slide out of the car, and hit the sidewalk in front of the house.

Our house isn't some crazy mansion or anything, it's a respectable four-square colonial. I call it the bread box. The front garden is full of perennials just starting to bloom. Barbara has a knack for color and gardening, so the house has major curb appeal. I open the wrought-iron

23

gate, careful to balance the cake. I notice that Barbara bought new solar powered sidewalk lights. They look nice. A burst of giggles comes from the house, and I know Barbara and Brandon are huddled by the front door, watching me approach on the security monitor. Nice.

"Maverick Johnson's on the court," Brandon says through the speaker. He flicks the outside lights and sends out a couple of whoops. "Maverick dribbles down the center, she fakes right, left, she shoots, she scores! The crowd goes wild." The sound of Brandon doing the 'aaahhhh' for the crowd, and Barbara laughing hysterically, floats in the gloaming. Barbara's voice breaks through my last shred of serenity. I feel my shoulders tense; she has that effect on me.

"Mavie, can't you ever do anything with your hair?" I can practically hear the glass of wine swirling in her hand as she speaks. Part of me wants to throw the cake down on the walkway, turn around and leave, but this is their bag. They're always goading me to see how I'll react, while my dad just sits disembodied in the background. Family get-togethers are nothing short of excruciating, which is why I keep them to a minimum.

"You guys done yet?" I'm at the door. I kick it with my foot, the least they can do is open it for me, they know I have the cake. The door swings in, Brandon and Barbara have their arms slung around each other in the glow of the hammered steel Moroccan hall light. They're both statuesque blonds. Brandon got Barbara's chiseled features, while I got my dad's rounded ones. Brandon's hazel eyes, and café au lait skin, are really striking. He and Barbara would make a cozy picture if they weren't so toxic.

Barbara sets her wine on the marble-topped hall table, snatches the cake box out of my hand, and whisks down the hall with it to the big open kitchen. I kick off my shoes (Barbara doesn't allow footwear in the house) and traipse after her. Brandon grabs her wineglass and follows. My dad is nowhere in sight, but that's nothing new. Barbara's already peeled back the cake box lid and is foisting it onto a crystal cake stand. Everything looks good. The frosting didn't get smeared in transport, so I'm pretty happy with it.

"I guess it'll have to do," Barbara says with a sigh. She retrieves her wineglass from Brandon, pours herself some more, and takes a seat at the white quartz breakfast bar. "So, Mavie, Brandon has something exciting to tell you, and I think you should be really grateful to him because he went out on a limb for you with this one."

"Is this about the person you want me to meet?"

Brandon laughs. "He's not just anyone, he works at the DOJ with me." Brandon's a lawyer, and a Georgetown graduate, he works it into most conversations, you could play a drinking game to it. "Ry guy is the best."

Oh, Tutankhamun, it's worse than I expected. "Ry, guy?" Genesis was right, I'm gonna need wine for this, a lot of wine. I plod over to the china hutch, slide my fuzzy socks across the smooth pine floorboards, grab a wineglass from the collection, and pour a hefty dose of the chardonnay Barbara has on the counter. I take a deep swig—ahh—that's nice.

Brandon sticks his hands in his pockets, pleased as punch with himself. "That's a little joke between us, he calls me Brando, I call him Ry guy. You know. Bro stuff."

I almost choke on my wine. I toy with the idea of suddenly claiming stomach cramps, a vicious bout of diarrhea, anything but this. "What time is he getting here?"

"You've got about fifteen minutes, little sis. And hey, you can thank me later because if I'm right about this—" Brandon swipes his phone, opens his Spotify app, starts to blare out Billy Idol's, "White Wedding," and head bang around the kitchen. I wince. How dare he desecrate a song I love with his bad dancing? I take the last gulps of my wine, and head to the powder room in the hall. I plan to hide out for at least the next fifteen minutes or maybe the whole night.

I catch a glimpse of myself in the mirror as I pace the tiny floor. I look a little washed out. It's something I've noticed since becoming an over thirty. My skin doesn't seem to have quite the luminosity it used to. I tried to remedy it by tanning for a natural glow, but that just gave me more freckles. I've never been one of those people who hated their freckles. I've never really thought much about them. When Barbara is your mom and you're trying to grow up and navigate the world, you have matters that are much more pressing.

I hear the doorbell ring. This is it. Please let this guy not be a raving weirdo. Oh well, here goes! Brandon is opening the door, giving someone, I can't see a one armed, broseph hug. Ugh, he's such a brosepher.

"Ry, my man, come on in."

I walk fast across the hall, back into the kitchen, and grab more wine. I can hear Brandon introducing his friend to Barbara.

"Ryan Yamamoto, this is my mom, Barbara."

Barbara gushes, wineglass still in hand, I'm sure. "Ryan, I've heard so much about you, come into the family room and have a seat. Brandon grab the wine. So, Ryan, you're an attorney?" Their voices fade as they move into the family room. I'm at the breakfast bar when Brandon walks in.

"Ry's here." He slaps the counter as he goes by, grabs another wineglass, and a new bottle out of the wine chiller. "Mom's right about your hair, you're over thirty now, maybe time for a little snip, snip." He laughs at his own joke. "Seriously, let's go. It's Dad's b-day, and Mom and I thought it would be nice if you finally met somebody."

I say nothing, but the irony of Brandon, the ultimate singleton, telling me I need to meet someone doesn't escape me. I don't move though. I'll come when I'm ready. I'm not going to let Brandon command me.

He notices my lack of enthusiasm, and his quick temper flares. "You're such a brat, you're always doing stuff like this. Mom and I try to be nice, but you don't make it easy. Geez, tonight's about Dad, okay, not you. You put us all through hell by dating that loser Kyle and when we try to introduce you to a nice guy you sulk. Well, suck it up buttercup and get out there, cause Dad just came out of the den to meet Ryan and everybody's waiting on you." He stalks out with the wine, all full of self-righteous indignation. What a tosser.

26

I grab my wineglass and move through to the family room. Ryan's on the couch with Brandon, my dad and Barbara are in wing chairs on either side of the fireplace. I smile at Ryan, and sink into the sage crushed velvet loveseat that used to be Prudence, my grandma's. She died a few days after Thanksgiving last year. I miss her every day.

"So, Ryan, you work for the DOJ?" My dad, Stan, is popping almonds into his mouth, crunching them with veracity. Dad's tall and skinny. He's where I get my super-fast metabolism from. He wears glasses and button-down shirts with sweaters and reads a lot of newspapers. He likes to keep up on politics. He loves Suni. He loves people who are ambitious and able to move through the upper echelons of life like him. He's not a narc like Barbara, but he's a total snob. It's something I find quite surprising about him.

I was shooketh when I realized the extent of Dad's snobbery. For some reason his Blackness always felt like the mantle of a saint to me. Like he would eschew judgement of other people because he understands what it's like to be judged himself, but underneath it all he's just like everybody else. That's why I say the invention of race is bullocks, it's all about money. And both my parents think highly of people with money and degrees, people like themselves.

Ryan clears his throat and takes a sip of his wine. He's wearing an open neck white shirt. His hair is short on the sides, long and spiked in the front. He has tan skin, perfect teeth, and a lanky muscled body. He's definitely hot, drool-worthy hot. Our eyes catch for a minute, and I blink. It's like looking into the sun. Sweet baby Jesus, maybe I will owe Brandon a thank you after this.

Ryan answers my dad's question. "Yeah, I work in Computer Crime and Intellectual Property, I love it."

All that, and smart too, I resist the urge to fan myself. Instead, I take a deeper sip of wine than I should.

"That's how Ry and I met, I needed some info on a cyber heist and everybody told me he was the man." Brandon puts it out for a fist bump and I almost gag. Ryan looks in my direction, obviously aware of the lack of cool he's about to display, but he bumps fists with Brandon anyway, laughs it off, and I'm piqued.

"So, you're originally from California, Ryan?" Barbara crosses her long legs, and looks down at her shoes. She doesn't really care how he answers, she just wants to be involved in the conversation. I'm pretty sure she's not listening to him, anyway.

"The Pasadena area. I miss the weather there every winter, but I love it here. I like having seasons." We catch eyes again, hold it longer this time. Even though I'm across the room, I feel myself lean into him. He's not like Brandon and Barbara at all, he's nice. I wonder what he's doing here?

"Are we going to eat anytime, soon?" I know the grilling of Ryan could nonchalantly go on for hours and I just want to get right to the main event. Shoot, I forgot the card I got for my dad on my kitchen table. I wonder if there's any paper and a pen in the den?

"Little Mavie piggy bottom," Barbara sings. "She always wants to eat and eat. Ryan, you wouldn't believe the appetite on that one. Where does it all go? She's all gristle and muscle, but some men like that. The dining room's this way."

A fine lace tablecloth is thrown over the mahogany dining table. *The Lady and the Unicorn* tapestry chairs add warmth, the chandelier glows, everything is just so. Barbara knows how to entertain. She puts on quite the spread. We all fall into our usual seats, Ryan takes the odd man out chair next to Brandon, across from me. Barbara offers up a toast to my dad and we all raise glasses, toast to his health, to longevity, and happiness. It's a nice moment.

Barbara dishes up plates of steak, potatoes, and green beans from the sideboard and Brandon passes them around. He plops a plate with a baked potato, green beans, and a big blob of what looks like bear scat, with corn and some other bits swirled through, in front of me.

"Oh, Mavie." Barbara settles into her chair, and takes a swig of wine. "I made you a vegan steak, it's mushed up black beans, corn, and a bunch of other stuff I threw in there. I thought you'd like it."

"It looks like a pile of ish," Brandon snickers, spearing a bite of steak he's just sawed off the bone. "But that's the kind of stuff Maverick eats, she's been a vegetarian since we were kids. She was always doing autopsies on everything we ate until my parents just couldn't stand it anymore. She's got a weird brain, but she's good people, you know what I mean?" Brandon stuffs a piece of roll into his mouth and I feel like popping him one.

Ryan looks sympathetically at me. "It's cool, having a plant-based diet is proven to be healthy in so many ways. I've actually been thinking about trying it out myself. I just don't know how to cook anything."

"Oh, Ryan," Barbara laughs. "How do you eat?"

"Mostly, Uber Eats," Ryan confesses. "It's not that bad, plus I work a lot."

"He does." Brandon is in talk with his mouthful mode. No one ever corrects him. I hate it. I know if I gnashed my food like that, Barbara would have a heart attack. "This dude is a beast, you should see the hours he puts in, but there's big talk about him, he's definitely going places."

Ryan blushes, it's cute, sweet. I like him even more. My dad nods his head, bends over his food. His mind is probably on politics. I give it two minutes before he brings up some random world news topic.

"So, do you have siblings?" Barbara's table manners are impeccable, but she drinks more than she eats. She's all about staying, being, achieving skinny, it's her thing, you know? She loves being tall and blonde, with a svelte body. She's always resented that I can eat what I like and don't have to worry about gaining weight. She's naturally competitive with everyone but Brandon. But it's okay, I'm used to it.

"A sister," Ryan nods. "She's only fourteen. She was a surprise baby for my parents. She ice skates, there's talk of the Olympics, it's a pretty big deal."

"Wow." Barbara is genuinely impressed. "With her tall, thin body we tried to get Mavie involved in ballet, but she was just too gawky. Every time she danced, it looked like a chicken squawking. Oh

Brandon, remember that Christmas recital in ninety-five? Oh, it was hysterical. I think we have the video somewhere."

Brandon folds his arms to his sides, does a wing flapping impression, and cranes his head forward like a chicken. He and Barbara melt into hysterics.

My dad snaps his head up. "Did you know that Jimmy Carter is a speed reader? I think he's on record as having read as many as two thousand words per minute. Can you imagine the level of literacy he brought to the White House? Those were the days..."

"Oh, that's cool. I didn't know that. Interesting." Ryan's the only one to answer. The rest of us are silent; it's not that we don't care, or even know the information, it's just that we're used to my dad jamming some random fact into the middle of a conversation. Barbara is highly scornful of my dad's habit of this, and lately she's been Google fact-checking everything he says, and bullying him if he makes a mistake. He's always prided himself on being smart, but I've noticed his confidence start to slip a bit. But that's what happens when you spend 24/7 with Barbara.

"All right, time for cake." Barbara whips away my dad's plate. Brandon takes Ryan's. The big slab of poo beans Barbara made is still on my plate. I took a small taste, but it was rank. I'm not sure what she put in there, but it's not an experience I want to repeat. I grab my plate, head to the kitchen, and scrape it into the trash before she can notice. She's too busy flaming up the cake with candles. Brandon comes back from the hall with a stack of presents.

Barbara's flabbergasted. "More stuff, Brandon, you shouldn't spoil us like this."

Brandon beams, he laps this kind of stuff up. He looks at me like the cat that got the cream. "Where's your gift, Maverick? Want me to carry it in for you?"

"Actually," my neck flushes a little, "I have a card, but I forgot it at home. Is there some paper in the den? I just want to write Dad out a quick IOU."

Barbara curls her lip. "Oh, really Mavie, it's not like you're in third grade anymore, that stuff's just not cute."

"Looks like someone could use some lessons on adulting," Brandon jeers.

I wish I could slap the satisfaction right off Brandon's face. "Look, it's been a rough day, Suni, and I got into it, and I had to get the cake. I just forgot, okay."

Barbara turns sharply, and looks at me. "You got into it with Suni? This is the best job you've had so far, Mavie, you better not screw it up now because if you get fired or leave without a reference—" She makes a throat slitting motion with a candle. "Besides, I don't know what your problem with Suni is? I'd be delighted to have a daughter like Suni, and she's only a few years older than you. Everything she's accomplished, seasoned Congresswoman, Senator, and now this first female president. I still think you should introduce her to Brandon. I just know they would hit it off. Can you imagine the wedding? It would be a royal/presidential extravaganza."

My eyes feel like they're about to explode as they bug from my head. She's right about one thing though, Suni and Brandon definitely deserve each other. They could out narc themselves all day and all night. "Look just direct me to some paper and a pen and give me five minutes."

"The den somewhere." Barbara turns back towards the cake, lights the last candle, and smiles in the flush. "Come on, Brandon."

Brandon grabs the pile of presents. They sing "Happy Birthday" as soon as they hit the hall. I head to the den, spot a pen on my dad's desk, grab some paper from the printer, sit in the red leather club chair and quickly write a few words.

"Is it always like this?" Ryan's peering in at me from the hall.

"Normally." I try not to get all messy, not to smile at him like someday I may be his stalker. I want to play it cool, but the obsession is real. I'm struck. I wave him in.

Ryan takes a seat in the other club chair. "I kinda already knew that. Brandon swings by to visit me at work, a lot. Does he have any friends?"

"You mean other than my mother?" I pause for a moment to consider. "No, that pretty much locks it down. He and Barbara have been BFFs since he was born. I don't think there's even room to get another person in there. I thought you and he were friends? Before you got here, he was all glowy about the state of your bromance. Is that not a thing?"

"Oh, it's a thing. It's the thing that happens every Wednesday. Ever since he consulted with me, Brandon shows up and asks me to lunch every Wednesday. I'm not gonna lie, a few times I've been ahead of the game and ducked out when I saw him coming down the hall. Does he know every derivative of bro? I've been called, broseph, brojito, bronana, brotato, that's personally one of my faves. Bropepita, that one was just weird, we both felt awkward after that."

"Eh, cringey, but that's Brandon. He's an emotionally stilted man child, with classic Oedipal stylings."

Ryan laughs. "I mean don't get me wrong, he's not that bad, or I wouldn't be here tonight. Though I mostly came..." he pauses.

I finish the thought. "Out of pity, a sense of duty for a likeable dullard. I know just how you feel. I don't want to drag Brandon, but he can be a real pip."

"Pip, bringing back the old school sayings. I like that."

"My Grandma Prudence used to say it. I always liked it."

"Yeah, Brandon was really broken up when she passed away last year."

"We all were. Grandma Prue was a beloved figure."

"I know what that's like." Ryan pauses before he asks, "So, are you going to stay here for a while or do you wanna UberPool out soon?"

I cock my head to the side and look at Ryan. Our eyes, like flint and steel, create a spark each time they meet. I can tell we both feel it. "Definitely, definitely. Let's just nosh some cake, tell my dad happy birthday, and then let's go."

"Yes, let's," Ryan says with palpable relief.

"A new watch." My dad shoots out his arm like a glamour model from *The Price is Right* as soon as we walk into the room. Dad likes stuff, so I can tell he's pleased as punch with all Brandon's offerings. I think it's great. I mean, don't get me wrong. I'm not jealous of Brandon in any way. He and my parents occupy one wavelength. I occupy another. I need more substance, more depth to the things that excite me.

"Wow, that's nice, Cartier, luxury, good job Brandon." I can tell Ryan's being sincere in his compliment. He's the kind of guy who ends up being friends with everyone because he's so genuine, accepting, nice. Just the kind of person I need after the Kyle debacle.

"The cake's a little dry." Barbara serves us each a piece. "But if you add ice cream, it kind of evens it out. Mavie, two scoops? I know strawberries, your favorite." She plops the two scoops without waiting, and hands me the plate. "Ryan you probably don't eat as much as Mavie, nobody does." She plops him one scoop, and hands him the plate.

I'm hungry after the pile of steaming excrement Barbara called a vegan steak. So, despite my no sugar or dairy vow, I shovel the cake and ice cream in pretty quick. I wince when the cold hits me and I get a headache.

"I always said she would be a natural at competitive eating." Brandon swings his spoon at me as he speaks. "It's always the little ones who can shovel all that food in. Have you ever noticed? Of course, you have to wonder if they walk around with bloated stomachs for days afterwards. Like those *Save the Children* commercials? But I think there can actually be some good money in it. Hey, maybe if Suni fires Maverick, she can get a sweatband and start training for the next contest. I bet they'd let her eat carrot dogs instead of hot dogs."

"Is Suni mad at you?" It's the first time my dad has talked to me, maybe even noticed I'm there all night.

"No, not really, there was a mix-up with a picture that got tagged incorrectly. The photographer kicked up a brouhaha. But it's nothing. It's already solved. Anyway, I've told you how Suni can be."

My dad comes to Suni's defense. "Of course, she's under immense pressure. Can you grasp the enormity of what she's doing? First and youngest female president, Harvard graduate, and she came from nothing. Where did you say she grew up again, Mav?"

Mav, my dad calls me Mav. "In the bush outside of Fairbanks, Alaska."

"And she didn't have any formal schooling until her senior year of high school, right? Didn't her parents homeschool her, and then one night their cabin burned down and they both died in the fire but Suni survived and moved into town with friends and became a cross-country ski sensation and graduated top of her class that same year, am I right?"

"That's Suni." I say all false hope and cheer.

"It's a remarkable story," Barbara pipes in. "So much inner fortitude, just like you Brandon."

I give Barbara a stealth, 'what you talkin' about Willis' look. "Yep, she's great." My voice sounds all chirpy and fake. "Speaking of Suni, I need to get home. There's a write up I need to do before tomorrow. A few things I have to post. Dad happy birthday. I have a card for you, it's at home, so here's an IOU. I'll slap a stamp on the card and drop it in the mail. Barbara the meal was great as always. Brandon, see you soon bronana." Brandon gives Ryan an eyebrow lifted, 'what have you two been talking about?' look, while I give air hugs all around.

"Yeah, you know I think I'll head out too." Ryan stands and stretches. "It's been great Mr. and Mrs. Malone, wonderful food, amazing company, thanks for the hospitality. Brandon, see you at work. I'm going to Uber out with Maverick. I've got a couple of projects I'm working on. Things I need to do. But again, thank you, this was fantastic." Barbara glows with the praise. My dad slaps Ryan on the back and shakes his hand while looking down at his shiny new watch.

Brandon gives Ryan a quick fist bump. "Want me to walk you out, Bro? Need me to walk you out?"

Ryan waves his hand. "Nah, I got this."

I press the Uber app, punch in my info, pass my phone to Ryan for his; two minutes away. We make for the front hall. Dive into our shoes. Pull on our coats as we bolt out the door and shut it behind us. We don't let out a breath until we're safely in the back of the Uber, speeding away.

I scrunch back against the seat and sigh. "Well, I'm glad that's over."

"What?"

"Playing happy families."

"I know the feeling."

I sit up a little and look sideways at Ryan. "You've been saying that a lot tonight. I think it's time you spilled the tea."

"You want the tea? All right. Well, I'm Ryan Yamamoto. I've got a little blonde," he does air quotes here, "'tiger mom' at home, or at least that's what she calls herself. She's White, my dad's Japanese. So obviously I'm Biracial, like you. Though I usually read Asian man to people, which comes with all kinds of confusing stereotypes. My sister, Pear—don't ask it was the single digit two-thousands it was all a little cray and fruit names were trending—is the golden child, just like Brandon is in your family. My mom absolutely lives through Pear, and my dad just kind of sits back and watches westerns on T.V. in the den. Sound familiar?"

It's my turn. "I know the feeling. Narc moms are the best," I say sarcastically. "Let's compare Biracial notes. Do you get a lot of 'where are you from? What country are you originally from?' Like me? It gets super precious when someone I know meets Barbara for the first time. There are usually two reactions. They'll ask me, 'That's your mom? That's really your mom? Why didn't you tell me you were adopted', and when I say 'Because I'm not,' they blurt out things like, 'Where did you come from'?"

"Now that," Ryan taps my shoulder, "deserves side-eye from hell."

"I know right, or here's my personal favorite." I lightly touch his arm. "I say 'This is my mom Barbara', and they say, 'Oh, oh, wow, you two look exactly alike'. That's when I like to scrunch my face right up close next to Barbara's and say, 'Don't we'?"

35

Ryan laughs. "Thank god you don't. I get the 'Where are you froms' too. And when I say 'Here', they say 'But where is your family originally from?' and when I say 'Here', they say things like, 'Well you speak very good English', to which I usually reply, 'I hope so I've lived in California my whole life.'"

We collapse against each other in hysterics. You could say it's going very well. I'm in semi-shock that I have Brandon to thank for this. Sometimes you just never know. The Uber stops, it's my place. Man, the ride went super-fast. There's no way I can invite Ryan in. I don't want him to see the way I currently live.

"Well, this was fun." I put my hand on the door handle and get ready to pop it open.

"You up for lunch tomorrow?"

I scan my brain for tomorrow's schedule. It's doable, and even if it's not, who cares! There's no way I'm turning Ryan down. I'm suddenly glad I discovered what a lying scum bag Kyle was three months ago. Cause it means right now I'm free, and the nicest guy I've ever met is right here in front of me. "I'd love to name the time and place."

"Smithsonian's, Mineral and Gem collection, twelve-fifteen."

"Is this something you already have all planned out?"

"A little bit, a little bit."

"Is this something you do with all the girls you meet or…"

Ryan shakes his head. "No, just you. Let's just say it's something I've always wanted to try, and I may be flying too close to the sun. So, are we good?"

"Oh, we're better than good, we're spectacular."

"Great, till tomorrow than." Ryan takes my hand in his and kisses it.

"Till tomorrow." I slide out of the Uber, close the door softly, and put a hand up as the car drives away.

"Who was that?" I turn around. Jade or Jay as she prefers to be called, my next-door neighbor who is all of ten, is sitting on the stoop. She and her mom have the basement apartment in the rowhouse next to mine.

"Just a friend."

"Well, if you plan on seeing him again, try not to look quite so thirsty next time."

"What? What are you even talking about? Where's your mom?" Jay's mother is notorious for disappearing, she's still young herself, just turned twenty-three. I can't imagine becoming a mother when you're only thirteen, but she does the best she can. Jay is unusually smart and perceptive for a child of her age. Sometimes she makes me feel like a bumbling idiot with her quick common sense. I have a feeling she'll be a natural at adulting when she gets to that stage.

"She's out." Jay slides her iPhone into her pocket. "You know how it goes with Dream, most days she's a nightmare." Jay calls her mother by her first name too, I think it's just a natural occurrence for some mother daughter combos.

"All right, well, I need to get some work done. Do you want to come in? Maybe have a little something to eat?" This happens a lot. I find Jay kind of milling around and invite her in with me. We both seem to like it. I think.

"Is it avocado toast again?"

"You said you liked my avocado toast. You said it was the bomb."

"Okay, no one says the bomb anymore, it's not the early 00s. Your avocado toast is the GOAT. I was just asking because I think it could use a skosh more Himalayan sea salt."

"Who are you? You're ten and use words like skosh."

"Hey." Jay follows me up the steps to my house. "It's not like the olden days. We don't have to go to desktop computers and use dial up to surf the net. I'm part of the information generation. We can learn anything we want with the tap of a finger, of course I know words like skosh."

"I'm not that old," I say, turning the key in the lock, and disarming the alarm as we step in.

"Over thirty, that seems pretty old to me."

"Trust me, you don't have that long till it's you standing here baby. Time goes faster than you think."

"Well, let's just hope I have some furniture when I'm your age," Jay says looking around. "Did you finally order a couch?"

"I did actually." I turn on the lights, grab the cereal bowl that's still on the counter, and mop up the now disintegrated granola. I go to my messenger bag that's dangling over the back of a bar stool, open the flap, and dig for my flash drive. I want to check something from the piece I need to post tonight. I scramble in the bottom of the bag, but keep coming up empty.

"What are you looking for?" Jay is beside me, curious.

"My flash drive."

"Uh, you're so old-fashioned with these things. I told you to save all your work in the Cloud."

"I don't like the Cloud, it's just a cauldron of intellectual property theft waiting to happen."

"And that's why you have situations like this." Jay shakes her head and folds her arms.

"Do you want to come with me?"

"Where?"

"To my work."

"Can we get Baskin-Robbins on the way back?"

"Sure. Why not?" I hit the Uber app.

Why Am I Always the One?

"Just drop us off here." The Uber pulls up to a door where I can swipe my badge and get into the office building.

"You work here?" For the first time Jay seems genuinely impressed.

"I do." We walk fast across the courtyard and swipe in. The halls are calm and quiet. I know somewhere there are cleaning crews and security guards, but not here. "This way." I walk fast. I want to get in and out. I unlock the main door to our offices and usher Jay in. "Just wait here. I'll grab what I need and be right back."

I navigate through the dark quickly, succinctly. I grab the flash drive from the spot, I always leave it on my desk. I feel my shoes spark against the carpet as I zoom out.

"Success!" I hiss to Jay. "Who needs the Cloud when you've got this?" I hold the flash drive up victoriously. I give it a jaunty little toss, but fumble on the downward delivery. I drop it and accidently kick it under the front desk.

"Still you, it would seem," Jay sighs. I get down on my knees and try to fish out the flash drive. Jay comes to help. "It's right here." Jay's long skinny arm finds it immediately. She slaps it a little less than graciously into my hand. "Well, that was fun not fun, now can we get ice cream?" she asks.

"Sure," I say, smoothing back my hair. We lock up the office and repeat our pattern in reverse. We Uber to Baskin-Robbins and get waffle cones with two scoops each. I get the vegan chocolate chip cookie dough to atone for my earlier cake and ice cream sin. It's delish.

"That was fun," I say, when we're back in front of our houses. I fumble for my key. "Do you want to come in? Maybe watch a movie? I only have a little work to do."

Jay swipes her screen. "No, I'm reading *The Communist Manifesto*, it's fascinating. Plus, I have a spelling test tomorrow. I need my full eight hours."

"Sometimes you scare me. Are you sure you're a child and not an adult with a kid body who works for the CIA?"

"Oh, I'm a kid. I'm generation Alpha and we intend to live up to our name. I plan to be a woke princess who achieves world dominance through humanitarian work and an eco-friendly fashion line, #princessofwokeness. You're never too young to start branding. There are kids younger than me who already have their name out there, but I figure I have until sixteen to make a name for myself. I mean Greta Thunberg is kind of geriatric in the current kids save the world trend. Don't you think? Her cuteness definitely has an expiration date. If I can make it now. I'll have years."

I'm at a loss for words, she's so witty, ruthless, and marvelously cunning. It makes me feel totally inadequate, a little afraid even. "Wow, now I feel like a major slacker. When I was your age, it was all Tamagotchi's, and Cabbage Patch Snacktime kids, super creepy, good fun, stuff like that. Well, I guess we millennials better watch ourselves with generation Alpha nipping at our heels."

"Oh, you millennials are already canceled. You just don't know it yet. Goodnight." Jay skips down her steps, takes out the key she keeps on a chain around her neck, and unlocks her door.

I kinda hate letting her go into her apartment alone. What with all the weird, random things that might happen. I wish she could spend nights like this with me, but I don't even have a couch. Although that's about to change.

"Are you sure you're okay?"

Jay crosses the threshold and waves back at me. "I'm okay, see you tomorrow."

"Tomorrow." I climb my steps, go into my dark house, and hit the lights. I change into my cozy clothes, pour myself a glass of water, and think about Ryan. So much hope wells inside of me. I wish...

I fire up my computer. It's time to get some work done and then sleep. What am I going to wear tomorrow? Focus, focus. I plug in the flash drive and scroll through the files. What the...? None of them are mine. A76, R/45, it's super weird and random. I'm about to click out. This is probably some strange gaming thing of Bashir's. After all, he's the one who man buns the front desk—get it! —but then I see it, 11/11Suni. I can't help it. I'm all kinds of curious. What is it? I open it.

The video is grainy, like it was shot from a distance. The sound is muffled, but I can make it out. It's Suni, she's on some kind of stage in a dimly lit room dense with people. She's speaking Russian. I catch a phrase, pause the video, and grab my phone. Maybe I can use Google translate to get the rest of what she's saying? I recognized her 'Hello, good evening', but that's as far as my basic Russian can take me. I hit play again and go through the video line by line. I try to enter the spelling as best I can in the translator app. I write down each word and line as I go. The video's twelve minutes long. I sit in shock when it's done. I can't believe what I just stumbled on. No way is this flash drive Bashir's unless he's in on it, and Suni is definitely in on it. I think.

The video doesn't say anything too incriminating. Suni just welcomes them all as friends and associates. Then she talks about their common mission—although she never spells out what their common mission is—and the hope that she will soon be in power. That her election prospects are looking good, and that she won't forget the people who helped her get there when she reaches the top. Nothing flaming. She doesn't ask for dirt on other candidates, or declare her allegiance to 'Mother Russia' or anything like that. But for some reason the hairs on the back of my neck are standing at total attention and I'm thoroughly creeped out. Suddenly it's me who wants to go down to Jay's apartment, knock and see if I can stay there. The whole thing gives me the heebie-jeebies.

I scramble around, do some posts, pace back and forth, and hash out all kinds of theories on Suni. I can't really tell if I want to peg her as a Russian operative because I don't like her or because she is one. Either way, it doesn't really look good for her. My house has a built in safe. I lock the flash drive in it for the night and leave the family room and kitchen lights on. I go to bed and fall into a restless sleep.

I'm a bundle of nerves on my commute in the morning. I keep expecting the cops, FBI, or Homeland Security to stop and frisk me, throw me against the wall, and question me about the flash drive. But nothing happens. I almost stroke out walking into the office. I try to keep my cool as I pass Bashir at the front desk with a friendly smile, a teasing, "What's up Top Knot?" that makes him snort laugh. Everything seems as it should. Except I'm totally uneasy, on edge.

Suni flew out to Iowa last night, so Beth and Brett are both on high alert. Suni makes lots of remote demands when she's out of the office. I'm sure she'll have Brett tweaking her speech until the last minute. Even though he can be a pill, I don't envy him his job.

I hear Beth talking to Brett in his office when I get to my cube. He's one of the few of us who has an actual designated space with walls of his own. You can still hear every conversation, but at least there's the illusion of privacy.

Beth is full of self-importance. "Suni wants you to go down to the capital and take pictures of tourists with this life size Suni cardboard cut-out. You need to ask them about their Suntastic Suni Highlights. You know, like which parts of her campaign really resonate with how they think, feel, believe? That kind of stuff."

Brett blusters before rebuffing Beth's orders. "That sounds like something Maverick should do. That's more her bag, collecting little snippets for the Twitterverse. I write speeches, remember? I need to be on standby for Suni in Iowa."

"Actually," Beth's voice is cold, even from my cube I can feel the chill. "Suni has that covered, and she specifically told me she wants you to do this."

Brett isn't going to be commanded that easily. "What do you mean Suni has that covered? Not without me, she doesn't. Look go tell Maverick or heck one of the interns to do this, while I talk to Suni myself."

Beth is curt. "You can't, Suni's not available for comment right now. Just do what I'm telling you while you still have a choice, okay?"

"What do you mean? Why should I?" Brett demands.

"Because I'm voluntelling you to do this, that's why. Later, I'm just going to command you. Do you understand?"

"Whoa, I'm getting some serious misandrist vibes from you right now, Beth. So, I would watch my language if I were you. I don't want this to turn into a manbellion."

"Mis what? Man who?"

"Yeah, that's what I thought. You balk when faced with the truth. Misandrist Miss, that's you. So, I'll do this thing Suni wants, but not because you voluntold me, but because Suni asked. But once I finish this, I want to get to the bottom of this whole thing, capeesh? I'm Suni's speech writer, not her lackey. There are plenty of other candidates who would love to have me work for them, trust me. I've had plenty of offers. So, you can just voluntell Suni that for me, all right, Beth. Thanks."

"Right." I hear Beth stomp down the hall, in seconds Brett is at my desk.

"What was all that about?" I don't even try to play it off like I haven't heard. We all have.

Brett buffs up, and tries to reclaim some of his dignity. "I don't know, but this whole asking people questions, taking pictures, seems like more your bag than mine."

"I know. Right?" I can't disagree. "I wonder what Suni's up to?"

"Look, I'm going to do what she's asking. I think I'll take Maisy with me and we can get this done and wrapped in a few hours. Just know I'm not doing this to step on your toes."

"No worries, Brett," I say and I mean it.

If this is Suni's way of making me feel insecure about my job, it's not going to work. Even with his superior skills of verbosity, there's no way that Brett's cut out to manage her social media accounts. I suppress a giggle at the thought of him trying.

"Look Brett, try to have fun with the whole thing. I'm going out for lunch. So, if I'm not here when you get back, you can tell me about it later. Okay?"

Brett raises his eyebrows. "Skrt, what's this? No tuna sandwich, brown bag lunch for Maverick? Who is this guy? How did you meet him? Is he a smokin' papasito? Does he slay?"

"Okay, never say any of what you just said—ever—again. And yes, he's really nice, and I don't eat tuna. I told you that was a mock tuna salad sandwich."

"Why don't you just call it what it is? Smushed up chickpeas with some other bits on bread. Have fun with your Hansel. Maybe you can throw down some bread crumbs for him, girl, and lead him along that trail."

"Okay, that was the witch who lead Hansel and Gretel along, not the love interest."

Brett throws up his hands. "Just sayin'. Stay woke, Maverick, all this realness is leaving me shook. I can't believe you have a date. I'm dead right now."

"Did you fall down some kind of modern-day slang rabbit hole? Because all this..." I take my index finger, and draw an imaginary circle around his whole body, "Is too extra." Two can play the slang game. Even though I'm really not in the mood.

I've been counting down the hours until lunch with Ryan and my chance to show somebody else the video from the flash drive. I'm holding my breath, waiting for someone to say something to me, to bust me for having one heck of an incriminating piece of evidence against Suni, but still nothing.

What do I have? I still don't know. I mean, the most I can see her doing in the video is speaking Russian, which in our current political climate is highly suspect, but still, it's not like she asked them to hack into our elections and steal it or anything.

Brett looks like he's buffering, searching for random Millennial-esque things to say. I cut him off at the pass. "All right, class dismissed. See you later, Brett. Good luck."

"Now that's just low key extra. Don't be ratchet, Maverick. It's all Gucci. Have fun on your lunch date."

I roll my eyes. "Bye Felicia." It's so old and tired, it actually seems funny. It gives me a zing.

Beth is two steps behind Brett. She stops at the exact spot by my desk he just vacated. "Lunch date?"

44

Dear sweet sauce of mercy, now everyone knows. I might as well just call Barbara and Brandon and inform the whole gang. "It's not really a date, it's just a thing." I feel my neck start to itch and I know it's flushing red. It's the tell for when I'm lying or embarrassed. I look Beth in the eye and ignore the betrayals of my body. "So, what's up?"

"Well good. I'm glad you're not busy because Suni wants you to be on standby for the Iowa speech."

"Me?" Now I'm thoroughly confused, that's definitely Brett territory. What's Suni playing at?

"Yes, you." Beth doesn't even have a modicum of patience, she gets like this every time Suni is away. I think she starts to fiend after a few hours.

"Is there something Brett and I should know about?" I smile to ease the tension.

Beth shakes me off like I'm totally overreacting. "No, everything is fine. It's just a little switch up."

I don't have the energy to pursue it. "All right well, I have my thing at 12:15 but that shouldn't take long."

Beth sighs, she looks a little less than effervescent this morning. "Fine, just make sure you have your phone with you at all times."

I resist the urge to salute as she clomps back down the hall into the conference room where she's set up a war room of sorts. I click the rest of the hours by. Hit the Metro at the earliest time I can. Get to the natural gems before Ryan. Huddle on a bench in the hall. Watch tourists wander by.

"Hey, you're super early." Ryan looks a little anxious with the deviation from the plan.

"Look, I know you have something special planned, but can we shelf it? Maybe save it for another time, it's just that…"

It doesn't take more than that. Ryan's on the bench next to me in seconds, his knee centimeters from mine. He leans in as close as he can get without seeming lecherous. "Yeah, sure. Say no more. What's up? You look really upset? You know what? There's this Greek deli around the corner. It's where we were going to eat. Want to grab a bite and you can tell me everything?"

"Sounds perfect." My stomach's been in knots all morning, and I haven't eaten anything. I get hummus on pita. Ryan gets a gyro. We get spanakopita and baklava to share and make the whole order to go. We wander over to the Mall, find a bench under some shade trees, put the food between us, unwrap our pitas and take hungry bites. We wash it all down with fizzy drinks.

"So, what's going on?" Ryan asks between bites.

Suddenly I feel shy, and a little silly. I take a deep breath. "I found this flash drive at work last night. I dropped mine under the main desk and got what I thought was the same one back, but it wasn't. And there's this grainy video on it. In the video Suni's speaking Russian to a room full of people, saying things about their mission, and how she'll be in power soon. It's really weird and suspect. I can't stop obsessing about it. I thought maybe you could watch it and tell me what you think."

"Okay." Ryan is calm and level-headed. "It does sound super shady and given what I do I've seen all sorts of nefarious things happen in all walks of life. Suni seems to be pretty above board though. I can't say she's my favorite candidate, but she seems pretty legit."

"Just watch it and give me your opinion." I slide my laptop out of my bag, set aside my pita, plug in the flash drive, and put the whole operation on my knees. Ryan watches the grainy twelve minutes without comment.

"I see you what you mean. It's weird, awkward, and even though I only caught a few words here and there, it definitely is highly suspect, but this video alone proves nothing. It's not a crime to speak a different language. Maybe it was a group of newly minted Russian-Americans and Suni was addressing them in their native tongue so they could understand. Who knows in clips before or after this one she could have been telling them about her plans for Universal healthcare. So, I don't know Maverick. I agree it's shady, but that's not enough to turn Suni in or anything. I mean, you could offer it up to the court of social media.

I'm sure there are lots of conspiracy theory nuts who would run with this, but it's probably nothing. At least, I hope. I don't want a Russian operative in office any more than you do, that's the last thing this country needs."

I clear my throat and take a sip of fizzy drink. I'm not sure what kind of reaction I expected from Ryan. I mean after all he did just meet me, and it does seem a little crack pot conspiracy theory to go all unhinged just because I found a video of Suni speaking Russian, but there's some inkling in my brain telling me not to let this go, not to let it slide. "What if I wanted to pursue this?"

Ryan shifts in his seat, picks his gyro back up, and contemplates a minute. "Then I'd say you have to find a lot more evidence than that."

"You're probably right." My phone buzzes. "Speak of the devil. Hold on just a minute, it's Suni. I'm her stand by speech writer for the moment for some reason." I give him my apology face, answer the call, and step away. "Suni?"

Suni breathes rapidly. "Maverick, I need you to help me with this bit. Brett has me saying when it comes to my political track record no one has better receipts. At first, I thought it was cute, but now I'm worried that a lot of Boomers won't know what that means. What do you think?"

I'm a little surprised Suni is even asking my opinion on stuff like this. I mean normally I chip in my two cents, a random thought here or there, and we keep it at that. I've always gotten the impression that Suni doesn't like me to shine too much. Oy vey, how did I get sunk into a hotbed of narcs? Barbara, Brandon, Suni, but not Ryan. I look over at him. He waves playfully at me from the bench, picks up a piece of baklava, pops it into his mouth, takes his fingers kisses them, and mimes falling over in bliss as he chews. It takes everything I have not to hang up on Suni, claim a bad connection, ditch everything and just go sit on the bench with Ryan.

Suni's voice brings me back. "Maverick, are you there?"

"Oh, yeah, sure. I agree. I think it's too casual to use language like that in your speech. You need to seem cutting edge, but you don't want to seem immature. I would just say, no other candidate possesses a proven political track record coupled with exemplary results that speak for themselves, or something like that. Something off the cuff, but not stuffy, witty, the kind of stuff you say naturally all the time."

"All right, yeah. I'll pencil something like that in for myself. What's with Brett lately, anyway? Have you noticed any odd behaviors? Drinking on the job? Sexually harassing the interns? He spends a lot of time with Maisy. The last thing I need is some big #MeToo scandal coming out of my office. And look, I know the two of you are friends, but I'm not asking punitively. I'm genuinely concerned, he just seems off, and if something is going on, I'm here to help." Her voice is sweet as honey, but behind it is a horrible sting.

So, this is the plan, triangulate, and then mob Brett, a classic from the narc's playbook. I go all gray rock and give her nothing. You can't hoover a scapegoat. I'm impervious to all narc techniques. "No, everything's great, Brett's great, we're great." I want this conversation to end, now. "Good luck Suni."

"Yeah, right. Thanks." Suni clicks off.

I can tell even through the dead airwaves I've made her angry. No one rages like a narc.

"Was that her?" Ryan lets out a little hiccup due to the fizzy drink.

"Yep, none other."

"Anything important?"

"Nah, just your everyday attempt at sabotaging someone's career, commonplace back stabbing, you know, the usual."

"Been there, had that happen to me. So, what's your plan now?"

I grab the rest of my pita and wrap it up. "I guess I better get back. I hope I didn't come across all crazy?"

"No, no way, if I'd found that video I would have the same concerns. And don't think for a minute that I'm dismissing your theories or anything like that. I'm just saying I don't think that's enough evidence to pursue anything. I mean, if it got out would it look suspicious that Suni is fluent in Russian? Mmm, maybe, or maybe she would play it off as an asset since she can directly communicate with Russia's government officials in their language. I don't know. I just think you need more proof."

"You're right, no, I totally agree. Thanks for lunch, and everything, this has been fun."

Ryan stands and brushes stray crumbs from his grey chinos. "It has. Dinner Saturday night?"

"I'd like that."

"Eight o'clock? I pick you up at your house like a proper gentleman?"

"Wow. I don't think I've ever been out with a proper gentleman before."

"Well, then it's about time we remedy that. Don't you think?"

"I do."

We lean in for a hug, it's just natural, and affectionate, the prequel to what I know will be mind-alteringly sexy. It's hard to leave, but I do. I want to get back to the office. A thought occurred to me while I was telling this whole story to Ryan. Somewhere underneath that desk is my original flash drive and I intend to find it before anyone else does. Plus, if more proof is what we need, more proof is what I'll get.

I've never been good at playing cool, or nonchalant, and I'm not the kind of person who's naturally sneaky either. It takes a lot for me to fly under the radar. I wear guilt like a neon sign, it's always been easier for me to just walk the straight and narrow. My stomach cramps a bit the closer I get to the office.

My plan is to act normal, like nothing's up for the rest of the afternoon, and then strike when the opportunity comes. I don't know when that will be or what exactly I plan to do, but I figure it'll come to me if I trust myself. I pass an intern friend of Maisy's, who has the music in her earbuds so loud I can clearly hear the bass beat of Billie Eilish's "bad guy." It jumps into my brain and plays on repeat.

When I sail in, Brett and Maisy are in Beth's office laughing about the snippets they got from the tourists. I hear Beth tell them, "It's great stuff," and for Maisy to post it online right away. I try not to feel cheesed off that my job is getting fobbed off on other people, especially since Suni is trying some kind of flip, angling to put me in the driver's seat with her speeches. It's not that I don't think I could do it, or that I wouldn't be interested in doing it, it's that I have more loyalty than that to Brett. I respect him, and unfortunately even understand him. I mean, he's just a future projection of exactly who Brandon is going to be in about ten years. Oy, it never stops.

"We got great stuff. Maisy's posting it now." Brett's at my desk, looking all shifty. "So, did you hear from Suni?"

"Yep, you?" I'm not about to play my hand first.

"Yeah, she wants me to do some more stuff with the social media campaign. It was weird. What do you think is up?"

I sigh. "With Suni, who knows?"

Brett runs a finger along the edge of my desk. "Hey, are you going out with us tonight? We're all going to celebrate Suni's success in Iowa. She really knocked that one out of the park."

"I'm sure she did," I pause. I'm not really into going out, but it could help me pump some of them for info, see what they know, or think they know about Suni. "Mmm, maybe I don't know, hit me up later."

"Can do. You should definitely come though, there's gonna be beer and you know how much I like beer, funny things happen when I drink beer. It's gonna be a boof up you don't want to miss."

"I don't know, it sounds like a geriatric frat party with rapey notes. We'll see. Now be off, I have work to do."

"Chow sister." Brett wanders down the hall and says something to Maisy. I hear her bray giggle loud and clear before they drift out of the office. I heard Beth shuffle around and leave when I was talking to Brett. She usually grabs a late lunch, takes a few laps around the block at a brisk pace, and then comes back. Bashir and Genesis are at lunch. I have to do it now!

I can feel my heart thud in my chest. My skirt is sticking to the back of my legs when I stand up. I haven't even done anything and I'm already a sweaty mess. It's a hang-up from growing up Catholic; confession and everything. Even when you're not guilty, you feel guilty, it's a real mind warp.

50

I walk swiftly to the front of the office, both carved wooden double doors are open. I think about closing them, but wonder if that would look way more suspicious. Instead, I step into the hall look right and then left, kinda awkward but I want to make sure no is coming by. I sink to my knees and fish under the front desk. I feel around for what seems like ages—nothing. Crap! I hit the flashlight on my phone and search the black space, nothing. It's really gone. My mouth goes dry, criminy, this could mean trouble, or I could just say I dropped it on my way out one night. Now for Suni's office.

I close the door to Suni's office. I figure no one will think much of it since she's gone, that way if someone comes I can wait until they've passed, and come out undetected. Suni's office is full of pictures of herself and her dog Bosco, he's named after the famous dog mayor of Sunol, California. Suni liked that the town, Sunol, was kinda like her name, and that Bosco defeated two people to become mayor and served until he died. He was also a black lab mix like her Bosco, so the whole narrative just really fit. Suni adopted him at the beginning of her campaign and we posted each step including the explanation of his name on social media. People ate it up. Suni has this fashionista, justice warrioress thing that the public adores down pat. I've got to admit, she's slick, especially since Bosco mainly lives with her aide Melanie and her family, Suni just trots him out for photo ops.

I start with her desk. I carefully pull out each drawer, trying not to make too much noise. I've seen enough cop, spy, mystery, T.V. shows to run my hand along the bottom of each drawer. I check the sides for anything out of the ordinary too. Nothing. I hit her bookshelf next. I open each book, fan it out, and wait for things to drop. Nada. Pictures, I check behind each one, and feel around their frames. Empty. I'm starting to feel a bit crazy, the reality of what I'm doing hits me. I'm just an ordinary person, trying to suss out some what? Russian operative who is trying to infiltrate our system as president so they can destroy our Democracy? What are the odds?

Kyle always accused me of being a bit of a fantasist, although not exactly in those terms, more like "You think some crazy ish, Maverick."

51

Of course, he turned out to be a lying sociopath and despite all his pumped-up denials, I was right about him all along. It spurs me to trust my gut. I look around a little harder and see the carpet pulled back just a skosh in the corner.

It looks more like it's unraveling than anything when I go over to examine it. Goodness knows our offices could use a well-deserved make over, but still. I get on my knees and pull the carpet back a bit. There's resistance, but it's not glue, it's Velcro, someone has gone to great lengths to secure this corner. I keep pulling and it comes up in my hand, a perfect square, an illusion, a carpet patch. Underneath is something that makes me gasp. A built in safe. It can't be for petty cash, Beth keeps things like that in a locked filing cabinet in her office.

I remove the metal cover, it's blue, a nice color. I look helplessly at the dial. I feel like I'm back in middle school trying to remember the combination to my locker. And the dial direction, right, left, right? I get a little flush and sink back on my haunches. This could be a total invasion, something of Suni's that's deeply personal, and I could be totally crazy, and way off base. Except, there's nothing deeply personal about Suni, nothing beyond veneer, like trying to find the heart of a plastic onion, you just keep peeling but it's all the same underneath.

I grab my phone and Google how to crack a safe? Thank goodness we live in the modern age. I follow the directions and pictures to a T. I'm not gonna act like I don't have to read the directions more than once, or that it doesn't take me ages to figure out what all the lingo and diagrams mean, but the office is kind of empty for a Thursday afternoon so I have time. I get lucky. The much need stethoscope is on Suni's trophy case. It's from St. Jude's. She gave them a huge personal donation and starred in one of their commercials. Suni knows how to angle things.

I hold my breath as I listen for the two clicks, it all takes forever and I end up having to keep a record of all the clicks on my phone. I grab some paper off Suni's desk and do a line graph. This is starting to feel like Algebra homework. I finally set the dial clean, and right, left, the combo I've figured out. If this isn't it, I give up, and am going to the conference room to eat jelly donuts.

I'm astounded when I hear the familiar click. I turn the lever and open the safe door, there's not much. A few old newspaper clippings of Suni, when she was a cross-country ski champion in Fairbanks, her run at the Olympic trials. She was highly favored, everything was on her side, she had a shot at the Olympics, a knee injury took her out, and something else.

A slip of paper, a scrawled address, somewhere in Alaska, two words, Russian again, Babushka, Dedushka, grandma, grandpa. I put everything else back in the safe, slip the paper into my pocket, close it up, and wipe it clean. You can't be too careful and I've seen the forensics shows. I put the carpet back like it was before, except I make sure the frayed edge doesn't stick up and that it all blends.

I take one last look around. A *Suni Shines on America* campaign banner hangs above her desk. I hate to be on repeat, but that was my idea too. Maybe somewhere under all that wine and narc Barbara is right. Maybe I'm jealous of Suni because she has the hutzpah to put herself out there in a way I'm too scared to do, maybe secretly I feel like it should be me. I mean, Brett and I are the ones who thought up most of the clever slogans and campaign bits. Oh well, I put it aside, I'm trying to spy, not analyze myself. I crack the door and eyeball the hall, it's safe. I slip out and try not to run back to my cube. I breathe a sigh of relief when I'm back in my chair.

Once everything's settled down and everyone's back in from lunch and other sundry things, I slip the paper out of my pocket. I Google the address, it's forty miles outside of Fairbanks on the way to Denali. I look at the satellite image on Google maps. It looks like nothing, just forest, strange. I've never been to Alaska before. I've watched all those reality shows about it. Alaskan life looks all outhousey hard.

I mean, Suni's family had a generator for back-up, but they lived without electricity, and didn't have indoor plumbing. Suni used to bathe in a copper tub that they filled with water from the creek that they'd boiled. The ground was too full of arsenic from the gold mines that used to be there for them to have a well. Suni did say using an outhouse wasn't all bad, that there were nights she saw amazing northern light shows on her way to the john, but still.

For heat they had a woodstove, that's how Suni's parents died. The flue got blocked one night, and the cabin caught fire. Horrible. I can't even imagine. I look at the address again. This could just be some friend of Suni's, someone important to her. A plan is starting to rapidly hatch in the recess of my mind, as hard as I try to push it back it keeps coming.

"You're down with tonight, right?" It's Beth, she's at my cube, she looks halfway human. I wonder why she wants me to go?

"Um, probably not. I'm probably just going to call it an early night. I don't feel that good, my throat hurts. I'm sure it's nothing, but I think I'll just drink tea and curl up with a good book." It's all a lie, the formulation of the start of my plan, but Beth doesn't know that.

"Oh, that's too bad. Yeah, there's stuff going around. I think it's the weather. Well, if you change your mind definitely come, this is a good chance for us to bond and team build. Bashir said something about karaoke, and that's always a good time."

"Who doesn't love the 'raoke?" I say, in an attempt at peacemaking. I mean after all I like Beth she can't help that she's half robot, half human. I wonder what her parents did to her to make her so obedient to a dominant personality? I grab a tissue and swab at my nose for affect.

Beth plows on. "Well, as you know I'll be heading out on an early train to meet Suni in Baltimore for the barbeque this weekend—"

"I hope you baked enough cookies," I interject without sarcasm. I have no doubt that back at Beth's apartment there are Tupperware stacks of waiting cookies. I've seen it before. Suni likes to hand out little tokens of esteem, and Beth's sugar cookies are melt in your mouth good, the icing supreme, Suni has her shape them into little suns. Personally, I would tell Suni to hire a bakery, but Beth does it all without complaining. I don't know if she's a psycho or a saint.

Beth laughs it off. "I think I did. We'll see. Anyway, you don't have to worry about covering the barbeque over the weekend. Suni already asked Amy from Delaware to do it, so you're home free. All right, well hopefully we'll see you tonight and if not rest up and I'll see you on Monday."

I try to keep the irritation from my voice. "Yep, see you on Monday. Have a safe trip."

Amy from Delaware? That biscuit, she's been after my job forever, and I have to admit her content is clever, but still. The amount of backstabbing, sucking up, climbing up and down the greasy pole in politics is almost too much for me. If Amy wants my job so badly, she can have it. I have bigger fish to fry this weekend, anyway. I shuffle some papers, do a few more things, pack up my stuff, and get ready to head out.

"You coming tonight?" Brett has on his ball cap. His backpack is slung over one shoulder. He's all *Fresh Prince* cool.

"Nah, I actually don't feel so great."

"That's too bad, drink some ginger tea with lemon and honey. My wife always makes it for me when I'm sick. It'll help you feel better and boost your immune system."

For a minute I'm stunned, Brett sounds almost human, caring even. "Thanks, I'll try that. All right, laters."

"Laters." Brett makes a gun with his index finger and thumb, winks and clicks his tongue as he shoots it at me. Now that's the Brett I know.

The stoop is deserted when I get home. I wonder how Jay did on her spelling test and if she got the full eight hour's rest she needed to make it great? I schlep myself inside, throw my bag over a bar stool, grab my phone, and lean against the counter. I'm going to need a cheap flight; goodness knows my credit card is nearly maxed out. Kyle went on a spending spree right before I dumped him. Lumpy mashed potato bastard! I want to scream.

The fastest and cheapest flight is ten hours and fifty-five minutes. I'll fly from Reagan International into SeaTac, and then on to Fairbanks. It's perfect. I want to bump myself up to business class, but I stick to coach.

The total cost of the ticket makes my eyes water a little, but I figure it'll be worth it.

What am I doing? I have no idea, it's just that I have suspicions and once I have suspicions, they're hard to let go. It was the same with Kyle, and I already said how that turned out, so... I'm going for it. I take a deep breath and decide to call Ryan to tell him my plan. I fly out early, and I need to pack and at least attempt to sleep.

The phone only rings once before he picks up. "I knew you couldn't stay away. Netflix and chill?"

I laugh. "I wish, but no that's not why I'm calling. I'm actually going out of town for a few days so I won't be able to make our date for Saturday."

Ryan sounds disappointed. "That's too bad. I was really looking forward to it. We can do it another time. Next weekend, maybe? Nothing serious happened, did it?"

"No, no, nothing like that. And yeah, next weekend sounds great, for sure. Actually," I chuckle. I wonder if I'm about to sound crazy and deranged, but here goes. "I'm flying to Alaska. Fairbanks, in fact. I found some stuff after I got back to the office, nothing incriminating. I just have this feeling in my gut that I can't shake. I need to investigate this a little. Something about this whole thing is off. I can feel it. I know it sounds crazy, and it's not like I'm some *Bourne Identity* on some mission or anything like that. It's just if I'm right about this, if this is what I think it is, I have to do something."

"So, you're the one." Ryan responds, totally catching me off guard.

"The one what?" I ask, not sure if I want to hear the answer.

"The whistleblower," Ryan says with gravitas. "Well, if it's what you feel you have to do, I support you one hundred percent. You've got a good head on your shoulders, if there's something there you'll find out. I wish I could go with you. I hate the thought of you traveling all that way alone, but I have a huge meeting tomorrow. I've been preparing for it for months, all the big mucky mucks, and such. You know what I mean?"

"Perfectly." He's such a gentleman, so understanding, but I'm curious about one thing. "How do you know I have a good head on my shoulders?"

Ryan laughs. "Maverick, I've met your family. If you weren't a person of strength, of true character, you would have cracked under the burden of being the scapegoat of that nut house long ago. Besides, we're pretty similar in most things, so that's how I know you'll be okay."

"How did I get so lucky? And introduced by Brandon, of all things."

"I know." Ryan laughs again. "Who would have thought the thing that happens every Wednesday would lead me to you. All right, well, travel safe, and keep me posted, maybe even allow me to see your location. Someone needs to keep tabs on where you're at."

"I will for sure. All right, goodnight Ryan."

"Goodnight, Maverick. Good luck and Godspeed."

I pull out my black watch plaid rolling duffle and start to pack. I'll wear my heavy coat and boots on the plane that way they won't take up space in my bag. Even though it's spring, it's still cold there. I mean really, no matter the temperature, it's Alaska, I'm sure it'll seem cold to me. Luckily there are still rooms available at a hotel on the side of town where Suni's old high school teacher lives, she's my first stop.

Her name is Mrs. Gustafson. I saw an interview she gave in one of the articles about Suni; it seemed like the two were really close. I dug deep into Suni's background this afternoon, searched her out online relentlessly, followed every thread. I'm still not sure what I'm looking for, speaking Russian, hidden addresses, none of these things are crimes.

Still, every time I think about Suni the hair on my arms stands at attention and I get this super creepy sensation. Who knows? I take a shower and curl up on my mattress on the floor. I hope I'm not crazy. For the price of the Alaska ticket, I could have gotten a bed. Oh, well. I roll over and fall into a deep sleep.

I have to wake up so early that I don't hear my alarm until fifteen minutes after it's already gone off and been beeping. I lunge out of bed, speed around, and manage to find myself at the airport in pretty good time. The plane is huge. It feels like I walk half a football field just to find my seat. I picked an aisle seat. That way I can make a quick escape if I need to.

The plane is mainly filled with retirees. It kinda feels like the sequel to *Cocoon*, and that scares the hell out of me. Brandon made me watch that movie when I was six or seven and for some reason it left a lasting scar on my psyche, that and *E.T.* Who thought a pot roast headed alien, riding a bike, coming at people with a glowing finger was a good movie for kids? I shudder to think of it.

I get to my seat, a couple are already in the window and middle, they look excited, chatty, friendly. I throw my bag into the over-head, along with my heavy coat, slide my phone into the pocket of my sweater and make a big show of putting in my earbuds, but it's too late. The woman of the couple is right next to me, and she's already turned in my direction, talking.

"We're Hal and Carole Allen from Virginia. We're on our way to Alaska because our daughter is having our first grandchild. Her husband is stationed at the base there, Fort Wainwright, and we're just so excited. A trip to Alaska and a new baby. Oh, it doesn't get any better than this. Bette, that's our daughter, we named her after that song, you know." She starts to sing "Bette Davis Eyes," in a really high voice. It's an interesting choice for a namesake, but okay. "She says that March is the best time to see the northern lights. Did you know that now is the best time to see the northern lights? Bette says the days in March are so clear and sunny you get amazing northern light shows. You know, the kind where the lights turn colors and rain down on you. Did you know that's good luck? Some cultures believe that conceiving a baby under the northern lights will bring it extra wisdom. I think it's the Japanese culture that believes that. I guess there are a lot of tourists who come to Alaska to make babies. Can you imagine if you black-lighted those hotel rooms?" She elbows me as she says this.

"I'm pretty sure from what I read the whole sex under the northern lights thing for the Japanese is just a myth spread by ignorance. Just like

58

everyone else, they're going to see the northern lights." I smile to lessen the sting of my words. I'm not tolerant of stereotypes about anyone. "Congratulations on the baby," I say as sweetly as possible before popping in my right earbud.

Carole isn't dissuaded she just keeps talking. "You look about the same age as Bette, do you have a family? Are you flying to Alaska or stopping in Seattle? Is your husband in the military too? Bette says everyone on base is really great, and there's a real sense of comradery because everyone's so far away from home and all. Of course, this isn't Bette's first time being away from home. She traveled to South America during college. Hal and I were so worried when she said she was going down there to volunteer at orphanages with a group from her school, but it turned out great. She's got such an adventurous soul. We're just so proud of her."

I'm not sure if I have to answer or if she even wants me to answer. It's a revelation to hear someone speak so highly of their daughter though. Barbara's talk about me is usually laced with scorn and debasement. "Very nice," I say. I turn on my playlist loud enough so I know Carole can hear it. I smile and pick up the book I brought for this very reason.

The rest of the flight is pretty nondescript, Carole talks to me some more when they bring around the refreshment carts, and I mainly just smile and nod. They're on my flight again when I land and then re-board in Seattle, but thankfully they're several rows back from me. The flight from Seattle to Fairbanks is only three hours and I'm glad because I'm tired of being cramped and I don't feel like sitting.

The air is cold and crisp when I trudge outside to get my rental car. Even though it's late in the evening, it's still light outside. The sun won't set for another few hours. My hotel is located on the same road as the airport so I'm there in a jiffy. I lug my bag up to my room, contemplate running out and getting something to eat, but settle on making myself content with the nuts and granola I packed for the plane.

My phone's been off the whole time I was traveling and I turn it on to alert Ryan that I'm here, and that I made it safely. I'm shocked when I see my voicemail is overflowing. I click the first message; it's Beth. I wonder what's up? Maybe Amy from Delaware couldn't hack it after all.

"Maverick, I know you're at home sick today, but I was just calling in case you hadn't seen the news. God, it's awful. I can't believe it, no one can believe it, and Suni, well she's just beside herself with grief. All right, I just wanted to touch base with you. Call if get a chance otherwise, see you Monday. Oh, by the way, we're not going to be working in our offices. They'll have some temporary accommodations available for us, but we'll get all the details on Monday. It's just so terrible, I can't believe it." I can hear a bunch of breathy sobs before Beth continues. "All right, bye Maverick. I hope you're okay."

I'm shaken to the core by the message. This doesn't sound anything like our Beth; the one who's always marching around voluntelling people what to do. What the heck is going on? I grab the remote and flick on the news. I start to scroll through the news cycle on my phone. The headline blares out at me: *Two Killed in Horror Attack*. Brett and Maisy's pictures are under the byline. Apparently after they partied with everyone else last night, Brett and Maisy headed back to the office and surprised an intruder. They were both shot at point blank range.

It's so awful I can't catch my breath for a minute. I sit on the edge of the bed, stunned. The FBI has already released the footage of the suspected attacker. I click the link and watch the video with intensity. The hair looks like it's tucked into a cap; the person is wearing coveralls, so there's not much to the shape, 5'10, it could be anyone except something in the gait reminds me of Suni. I shake my head, it's impossible. She was on her way to Baltimore last night. She spent today at the barbeque and is supposed to be in Baltimore through the weekend.

I can't believe this is happening. I'm sure the police will want to speak to me, to all of us. I check the other message, five are from Ryan. I feel guilty I should have kept in better touch with him. It's just that my battery runs down so fast these days, I need to replace it. Plus, truth be told, I just wanted a few hours to myself, suspended in air, time to think. I hit Ryan's number, it's late there, but it's Friday night. I swear the phone doesn't ring at all this time before he's on the line.

"Are you okay? Your mom and Brandon are going crazy. I told them you were fine, that you went to Baltimore with Suni. A lie, but a white lie. I hope you're not mad at me."

I let out a huge sigh. "No way, more like super thankful. Thank you, and yes, I'm fine. The flight was okay, and I'm already checked into the hotel. I just turned my phone on and found out about this whole thing with Brett and Maisy. It's horrible. I feel so sorry for their families. Why would anyone attack them? And what was someone doing with that kind of weaponry in our offices after hours?"

"Good questions. I think the FBI is working on it. So far, the media is saying that it looks like a break-in. Someone trying to get dirt on Suni, who was startled in the act and took lethal action against your coworkers. Why did they go back there at two in the morning, anyway?"

I rack my brain. I can't think of anything. I mean the usual stuff. Maybe Maisy was smitten by Brett. It makes me throw up in my mouth a little to even have the thought and I shoot it down immediately. Maisy had no shortage of admirers among the intern crew her age. She wouldn't have to fish for someone like Brett. And as much of a player as Brett pretended to be, he wasn't one. For all his talk and flirting, I doubt he ever cheated on his wife. The only reasonable explanation I can think of is something to do with that footage of tourists they shot for Suni that they'd been working on together.

"I don't know why they went back," I say. "But this has Suni written all over it and when we get to the bottom of this, I bet we're going to find out that she's behind everything."

"Look," Ryan's voice is low and stern. "I support whatever you want to do, but this whole thing is getting scary. All this weird stuff you found and now two killings in your office. Just be careful. This thing is no joke, and if it is Suni, if she is some kind of Russian operative trying to infiltrate our Democracy, she's going to have people helping her, a lot of people. If this is what you think it is, then this thing is big, really big, bigger than both of us big. So just don't try to be a shero. Don't take any chances, okay? Because we haven't even gotten to go on a proper date yet, and I have one heck of a good one planned."

"I'll be careful. I promise. I'll call you in the morning. I'm going to shower off some of this plane funk and try to get some sleep."

"All right. I'm going to call my friend Jake at the FBI and see if I can get some dirt on this thing at your office. I'm also going to see what I can dig up from the cyber world about Suni. Sleep tight, Maverick."

"Thanks Ryan."

I take a long hot shower and let the water run over me. I cry like a baby. I feel so bad for Brett's wife, his boys, and Maisy's parents. I can't even imagine it. I bundle into my robe, wander over to the window, pull back the curtains, look out into a deep dark sky, and it happens. Swirling streaks of color fill the night and rain down on me. I smile. It's a blessing. I'm going to need all the luck I can get.

A Chip Off the Old Communist Block

I make the mistake of turning on the news first thing in the morning, while I eat the yogurt, bagel and coffee I got from the downstairs breakfast. I'm not surprised when a clip of Suni, dressed impeccably in black, her face just the perfect touch of sad, vulnerable and strong, makes a statement to the camera.

"First, I want to say that everyone who worked with and knew Brett Tucker and Maisy Adams is incredibly bereft. The world has lost two wonderful talented souls and we all shine a little less bright without them. Especially me, Suni." She hangs her head here, struggles with palpable emotion, clears her throat, blinks, and recovers. "I want the American public to know that this crime will not go unsolved. Multiple government agencies are working on why this occurred in my offices and foul play is suspected."

Suni looks directly into the camera for the folks watching at home. "I'm seeking election for the highest office in this nation, because I want to be your president, because the time has come for a new form of leadership, the kind I will provide. But the cost of losing two lives, two valuable beings who were loved and needed, is too high of a price to pay. I want you to know that every person in this country is important to me, and you are not just a statistic, or a gender, or a race, I truly see you. And you are valuable, needed, and loved."

Suni pauses again, takes a breath, and shuffles her notes. "We ask that anyone who has any information concerning these tragic events please come forward. For our part, we are going to continue to serve the citizens of this great nation in the best way we can. We have decided to go ahead with our Summer with Suni barbeque today, because that's what Brett and Maisy would want. They believed in us, in our strength as a nation, and in our resilience in times of trouble, turmoil or grief. Today and every day forward I will honor them with my vow that poverty, despair, drug addiction, homelessness, prejudice, racism, and violence will no longer be a part of our America. From this day forward, we will transform and become a new America. A better America. An America that honors the suffering woven into the fabric of our history, and the hope for our future by how we live in the present. So, I, Suni Wainwright, pledge my life to live in memory of Brett and Maisy and all of you."

Her voice cracks and she wipes away a tear. "A candlelight vigil is planned for Monday night on the steps of the Capitol for our two slain friends and coworkers. The defense of democracy is no small thing, and these two brave patriots gave their lives trying to protect ours as I promise to give my life upholding it. Thank you and take care America. Don't forget Suni Shines On even in the face of tragedy."

She's a genius, even though I know she's probably a double-crossing secret agent, and she doesn't really mean anything she just said, I have tears in my eyes from her speech. Damn, she's good. I turn off the television and start my mental notes for the day.

It's Saturday. I couldn't find Mrs. Gustafson's number in my search, but I have her address. I plan to drive around town, get a feel for it, and go past some sites mentioned in the articles about Suni over the years. I'll give it until eleven, before I stop by her house, see if she's home and willing to talk.

The sun is shining brightly outside, but it's in the twenties, cold to me. I shiver in my jeans and decide to make the first order of business a swing by a sporting good's store. I could use a hat, some gloves, snow pants, things I should've packed on my trip, but that didn't cross my mind. I'm used to living in our nation's capital, not a snow globe.

I warm up the rental car, while I scrape ice off the windshield. This is fun, just what I thought a cross-country romp to track down a Russian operative would be. I hit Airport Road. I pull over when I see a place called Big Rays. I go inside and find some decent black snow pants, thick socks, gloves and a hat. I ask casually about Suni when they ring me up at the register, but they don't know her personally, it's a dead end.

I put on the warmer things in the car. I pull the snow pants up over my jeans. I feel slightly overdressed when I'm done. A man in shorts and a t-shirt passed me when I was putting on my new ultra thick socks. Apparently twenty degrees is warm to Alaskans. They must have crazy internal thermostats. I don't care if I don't fit in. I just want to survive this whole expedition.

I drive out to some place called Birch Hill next, park my car and hike around the trails people use for cross-country skiing. This is where Suni won her first race. More like I should say this is where Suni annihilated all the competition against her, made her mark dramatically, and caught the attention of everybody.

The trail is white and crisp. The birch trees are beautiful. Peels of their bark lie on the snow like parchment. The experience doesn't provide much other than a nice walk. I get back to the car and it's time for me to start heading over to Mrs. Gustafson's house.

I've been texting with Ryan all morning, checking in. I also turned on the locater feature on my phone so he can see where I am. I text and let him know where I'm heading now. He sends back a serious of emojis that makes me laugh. I'm a little hungry, but I figure I'll wait until after I talk to Mrs. Gustafson to find somewhere to eat.

I head out of town, past the University of Alaska and its beautiful Museum of the North. It's a modern building that reflects the rays of the sun. The way it blends into the white landscape, like a glowing jewel, is breathtaking. Something about how the light diffuses in Alaska fascinates me.

I keep driving. The road gets twisty. I slow down around the curves; I have a line of impatient vehicles behind me at one point. I turn off the main road, and head down a long winding road. There are lots of driveways, but all the houses are tucked back into the trees. The road is dirt, and gravel, packed with snow. I follow the tire tracks; the last thing I need is to get stuck out here in the rental car.

Mrs. Gustafson's house is on the left. Like all the other houses on her street, I can't see anything, just a curving drive. I can tell the house has a breathtaking mountain view from my position at the top of the driveway. I pull up, careful not to block the entrance. I get out and lock my car. I feel a little weird as I walk down the gravel drive.

The house is around the corner, and the view is as spectacular as I thought it would be. The house is beautiful too. It's a barn style log cabin, with a cheerful blue metal roof. A plume of smoke comes from the chimney, big windows show a cozy interior scene. I don't even make it to the front door before a woman who I assume is Mrs. Gustafson is opening it, saying "Hello?" in that tentative way everyone does when a stranger shows up at their door.

"Hi." I have no plan for what I'm about to say. I will it to come, but there's an awkward beat before I find my voice. "I'm with Freedom Patriots magazine, we're doing a feature on Suni, and we wanted to interview some people who knew her before she was the famous politician she is now. Do you think that you could spare just a few minutes of your time to talk about Suni? From what I gather, you were one of her favorite teachers."

Mrs. Gustafson takes a step back and flutters a moment before making up her mind. She opens the door and ushers me in. "Do you want to leave your boots and snow pants here? I have the wood stove burning and you might get a little hot. My husband is out snowmobiling on the Dome and I was just about to spend the afternoon curled up with some cookies and a good book, but you're welcome to come in. I'd love to talk about Suni. Boy, it's been ages since I've seen her in person. Of course, I watch her on T.V. all the time, that stuff at her office…" She brings her hand to her mouth. "Awful, horrible, but Suni handled it just like I knew she would. She's so brave, so well spoken. I just can't praise her enough. A real American treasure is what I call her. I tell all the kids I teach that I taught her for a year, they get a real kick out of it."

I've finally tugged off the boots, and snow pants. It's cold in the entry and I shiver in my sweater and jeans.

"Come on in."

I trail Mrs. Gustafson from the artic entry to the main part of the house. The ceilings soar to the roof, windows line the entire front of the house, the couch faces the amazing view. A red cast iron wood stove burns hot in the corner, a plate of lemon sandwich cookies is on the coffee table. If living in Alaska is like this, I could definitely get used to it.

66

"Have a seat." Mrs. Gustafson ushers me into a blue tapestry chair, bustles to the open kitchen to grab another mug, and holds up the teapot. It's not my favorite, but I nod my head yes. She pours me a cup, grabs honey and cream, and sets it all on the coffee table. I fix myself a sweet soothing cup and take a grateful drink.

"So, what do you want to know?" Mrs. Gustafson asks as she takes a lemon cookie from the plate.

"The usual," I say. "You taught English. Is that correct?"

"Correct. I taught Suni her senior year. She was in my World Literature class. It was AP, of course, Suni was always so smart. I think she was in all AP classes that year, despite having no formal education before that. I remember the first day she showed up at the school. We all knew about her. The local newspapers covered the fire, but I'm sure you already know about that. Oh, it was horrific. She's about the same age as our Michael, and so my heart just went out to her. She didn't miss a beat, though. She walked in with that same inner confidence she has now. That same look at me all you want, I'm bound for bigger things attitude. She was full of opinions and ideas. Did you know she was voted senior class president after only a month of being there? All the kids liked her, well most of the kids, there was one girl who really didn't like her, and seemed to have it in for her. I think it was jealousy, but other than that she was just a joy to teach. And whatever her parents had been teaching her before they died was good. She was very well read, and she knew a lot about current events, happenings in the world. I'm not surprised she ended up in politics."

I've gleaned a tidbit from her whole sycophantic spiel. I pounce on it. "Do you remember the name of the student that didn't like her?"

"Oh, that." Mrs. Gustafson waves a dismissive hand. "Like I said, that was just pure jealousy. Everest Begay, she's up the road at Ivory Jack's a lot. We thought she'd do more with her life than occupy a bar stool. Goodness knows she was beautiful and talented. She and Suni were actually pretty good friends at the beginning until they had some kind of falling out. I'm not sure what happened between them, but it never seemed like Everest could get right after that."

"Did you ever know Suni to speak any foreign languages, Spanish, French, or Russian?" I try to slip it in all casual.

"Well." Mrs. G. looks out at the view. "I can't say, '*we can see Russia from our house,*' but the whole class did learn a few Russian phrases when we read Tolstoy. I wanted to set the mood. I think we ate some Russian food and visited some Russian sights around town. I mean, we did buy Alaska from Russia in 1867. So, you know there are remnants, cultural infusions, but nothing out of the ordinary. Although I did hear Suni speak a different language at her graduation, not Russian, I would have recognized it. This was something else, it struck me as kind of odd, but I didn't think too much about it."

"Who was she talking to?"

"These two elderly people that came bustling up to her after everything was over. Suni was valedictorian, so a lot of people were trying to congratulate her. Ask her about her future plans, and the scholarship to Harvard. She was big time, a huge win for Alaska, we were, and still are so proud. You won't find many who have a bad word to say about Suni in these parts. And look at her now practically first female president." Tears shine in Mrs. G's eyes. "I can't believe she was my student, what an honor."

I can tell I'm not going to get much more out of her, the mystery language, and the older couple, there's definitely some stuff to sink your teeth into there. She said that place Ivory Jack's was just up the road, it's Everest I plan to find next. I thank her for the tea, put my boots back on, but drape my snow pants over my arm.

Mrs. G gives me a pat on the back as I go out the door. "Well, that was nice, I just love reliving old memories about Suni. I hope you got enough for your article. It felt like I was just babbling."

"No, you were great. Thanks for taking the time, and of course the tea. Enjoy the rest of your afternoon, it was really nice to meet you." I give a smile, a wave, and set off up the driveway.

I turn my car around in the cul-de-sac and go out the way I came. My phone gives me the directions to Ivory Jack's, it's not that far away. The parking lot is stacked. It's Saturday at lunchtime, and the place is hopping. I'm guessing jeans, boots, and big snow parkas are de rigueur in Alaska so I won't be out of place.

A wave of cigarette smoke hits me as soon as I walk in. There's a sign that divides the place in half, non-smokers to the left, smokers to the right, but as it's all one cavernous room, it makes no difference. The waitresses are all busy so I head straight to the bar. A stunning Alaska Native woman is sitting on a stool watching one of the televisions while drinking a pop.

I don't know how, but I know right away she's Everest. She's next level beautiful. Next to her, Suni would look nothing more than basic. I'm sure Suni did everything possible to destroy this woman in high school. I just have to play it cool, work the story out of her slowly. I slide onto the stool next to her and give her a nod. The bartender is in front of me immediately. It's too early for a drink so I order ginger ale, and gluten-free nachos with beans but no meat.

Everest is still watching the basketball game on T.V. I can't see who's playing, but it looks like a high school match. Perfect.

"Is that the local team?" I ask.

Everest nods. "Yep, quite the match up. West Valley against Lathrop, big time rivalry, both schools are in Fairbanks. It's basically townies versus Army brats. Even though I graduated from West Valley, I always root for Lathrop."

"I know the feeling. I wasn't the biggest fan of my high school years either. Who is? Only cheerleaders and jocks, everyone else is just suffering with acne and self-doubt. I much preferred college, now those were good times."

Everest gives me a sideways look. I wonder if I sound dumb, loony even, but she coughs up a nugget. "I know right. Actually, high school was pretty good for me, of course there's always something."

"Let me guess." I pretend to ponder for a moment. "Some mean girl who was mad because a boy liked you and not her?"

Everest shrugs. "I wish it was that easy, more like a psycho posing as a normal girl who tried to destroy my life."

Right to the point, just what I was hoping for. "Ugh. I know the type, little Ms. Suzy Sunshine right, but underneath they're all hard as nails without a conscience. Trust me, I've had my own run-ins with those types. She's probably imploding somewhere in a minivan, nagging her poor husband and kids. Those types are never satisfied."

I lay down the bait. Wait for it, wait for it…

"Actually, she's doing pretty well. I see her on T.V. all the time. No regrets for her, she's not the type. She's ruthless under a pretty face."

"Oh, someone famous." I scoot my stool a little closer. "Spill, who is it?"

Everest contemplates me. I mean really scrutinizes me, narrows her eyes and everything, before she decides I'm just some quirky chick who likes to talk. "Suni Wainwright, the one they all say is going to be the first female president. Her."

I nod my head. "I can see it. I know she comes across all woke and help the planet, but there's something about her I don't trust. I've tried to put my finger on it, but I've never been able to, and saying anything negative about her amounts to treason, people just love her. I mean she's from here, right? So, I'm sure most people here are obsessed with her."

Everest shrugs. "That's only because they don't know the real her. They don't see beyond the carefully crafted image, in truth, she's rotten to the core." Everest's food arrives. She takes a bite of her hamburger, stares back at the screen, and watches the action on the court.

I let her chew and swallow, before I throw out my next goad. "I bet you've got lots of good dirt on Suni."

Everest stops eating. She suspends the burger in mid-air and looks at me with suspicion. "Why are you asking so many questions about Suni? I mean, you're not a reporter or anything, are you?"

I pretend to bluster. It scares me a little how adept I am at lying, but they voted me most likely to win an Academy Award for my senior superlative, so maybe it's not lying as much as acting. "Me?" I put my hand on my chest, all flustered. "Of course not. I mean, I have a little blog and everything, but that's just about my life. You know, cooking

70

and cleaning for my husband and the kids. I was just interested, it's fun to hear the good bits of gossip. So many of these presidential candidates are all smoke and mirrors, bait and switch. You vote for one thing and get another. You know what I mean?"

Everest relaxes, and I can tell it's worked, and that I've got her. "Tell me about it," she says. "And Suni, she's no different. Heck, she may think the sun shines out of her butt, but let me assure you it doesn't."

"That would be an interesting campaign slogan," I joke. I take a bite of the steaming nachos that just got placed in front of me, they're good. "She must have done something pretty bad for you to still dislike her so much after all these years. Well, I know one thing she's not going to get my vote, not that she ever had it."

Everest laughs. "Right. Why let mean girls win?"

"I know totally." It feels like we're getting along great. I just let it hang there for a few minutes, munch my nachos, and half keep an eye on the game.

"You know how I said, Suni, isn't who everyone thinks she is?"

I nod my head and let Everest draw out her thought.

"It's even worse than that." She leans in close. "She's a fraud, nothing is like she says it is. I should know, she and I used to be best friends. The fire that killed her parents, I don't think those people were her parents. A well-known homeless couple went missing around the same time. No one thought about checking their DNA, they just went with what Suni said. I mean, she's really convincing, that's how I got drawn in. Before she showed up senior year, I was the most popular girl. Not that I'm bitter about losing my status or anything. This was years ago, it's water under the bridge. I just hate to see someone so dishonest get so far in life."

"How do you know that about her parents?" I ask.

Everest takes a sip of her drink. "There were all kinds of tells, things that were more than curious. For one, she's supposed to be home-schooled. She knows all kinds of information about a variety of things, but is totally sketchy when it comes to Alaska Native food, dress, and customs. Someone half Native, with a Native mom who supposedly grew up in the bush, would know much more than she does. You can't help but know this stuff. You learn the culture almost by osmosis."

"Is that part of the culture?" I gesture towards the beautifully patterned tunic she's wearing.

"Yeah, it's called a kuspuk. Suni knew basic stuff like that, but there was no heart behind it. It was like she learned all her info about Alaska Natives from the internet. It was weird. Even back then, you couldn't say a cross word about Suni without someone shouting you down. She brought a lot of publicity to this town, what with her cross-country skiing ability and everything. People loved her."

"Seems like they still do," I sympathize.

"People like Suni, they only let others see what they want them to see. There was just too much stuff about her that didn't add up and was too convenient. Like how she supposedly lived in that cabin in the bush for seventeen years, but no one out that way even knew who she was or had ever seen her family. I mean, it's one thing to be Alaskan, and to be self-sufficient, but we're talking about nonexistent. Plus, there was this weird thing that I saw. Suni and I weren't friends anymore by the time we were graduating, but I remember that night after she made her speech, and everything was over. She had a crowd of admirers around her as usual, and out of nowhere comes this little old couple, all foreign seeming. They said something to her in a language I didn't know, but it made her really mad. She played it off in an instant, and sent them on their way, but just for a fraction of a second, I saw the look on her face. It was pure murderous rage. I've always wondered about those people. I managed to pick up a few words of what they were saying, '*Dostat daaram*'. I found out it's Dari, a form of the Persian language. It means 'I love you'. I clearly heard her answer, '*Man ham dostat daraam*', 'I love you too', before she sent them packing. The whole thing was just odd, very odd. No one else in her group even seemed to notice the interaction, it was so quick. And her friend Dustin was making a spectacle of himself as usual, playing the clown for Suni, just like they all do."

I look at Everest with newfound respect. She clearly is doing more than just propping up a barstool, and the only thing I've seen her drink so far is pop. I wonder why Mrs. Gustafson went out of her way to slander Everest's name?

"That is super freaky," I say carefully.

Everest takes another bite of her burger and nods her head. I can tell I've gotten everything out of her I'm going to, it's time to move on.

"Well." I finish the last bite of my nachos and slurp my last swallow of ginger ale. "I guess I better take off. I have some stuff to do." I get a bright or not so bright idea. "Hey do you know where this place is?" I show her the address I found in Suni's office, it's already plugged into my phone.

Everest goes immediately cold. "Who are you?"

"What do you mean? Nobody, just who I said I was. It's from a Craigslist add. I'm checking out some puppies for my kids."

"That's not from a Craigslist add. No way. That's the address, the place where Suni's cabin used to be, the spot where her parents died. Like I said, who are you?" She reaches into her jacket pocket and suddenly I'm nervous. She could have a gun.

I decide to come clean. "All right, maybe I haven't been totally honest with you. I work for Suni. I manage her social media content."

Everest takes it all in stride. "Okay, that's a little weird, but what are you doing here, and what do you want with me? I've dealt with Suni enough. You tell her to leave me alone, you hear. If that's what you've come for, you tell her to leave me alone."

I'm startled by Everest's intensity, her naked fear. "I'm not here working for Suni, I'm here working against her. Just like you, I started off liking her, but there have been too many weird things, too many red flags I just can't ignore. I agree with you. I don't think Suni is who she says she is, and the whole story about her past is just too convenient. Like you said, no one knows who she is or has any record of her, her whole life until she bursts on the scene senior year of high school? Highly suspect. I mean I know Alaskan living is all about being off the grid anonymous, but that's just plucked from obscurity convenient, everything about it just seems off."

"Do you have any idea what you're getting into?"

The look in Everest's eyes scares me. "No, absolutely none," I admit.

"Look, I tried to do what you're doing years ago. I called Suni to the carpet and nothing good came of it. And trust me, Suni has some very powerful people behind her, people who can make your life a misery. I can't even get a job in this town, or a loan. I had to save up for the coffee cart I have near the high school for years. She'll use any means possible to keep her secrets, and I mean any means."

"Is that what happened between the two of you?"

Everest sighs. "I've never told this story to anybody, but yeah, you could say that. Suni made sure I would never talk, that her secrets were safe with me." She slips off her shoe and flashes me her left foot with absolutely no toes under the bar.

I'm shocked. "Suni?"

Everest slips back on her sock and her shoe. "Who else? She was over at my house, we were in my room, I had been class president every year for three years and she'd beaten me. I didn't really mind, back then I was gaga about Suni, I thought she was great, brave, that she could do anything. I was asking her questions about her parents, her mom in particular, about her Alaska Native heritage, my parents are really involved with our culture. Suni was stumbling over the answers. I teased her. I told her it didn't even seem like she was really Alaska Native, that she was only half, and with her ambiguous brown looks that she could be anything, spicy White even. She got super mad, angrier than I've ever seen her. I apologized and tried to play it off. My mom called up to me. The woodstove needed feeding, I would have to split some logs. Suni came with me to help. I'm an Alaskan kid we know all about chopping wood, I've never had an injury in my life. I was splitting logs when Suni came up with an extra axe to help. I stood back a little to let her take a whack, except she didn't hit the log. At the last minute, when the axe was barreling down with all her force, she twisted. She made it seem like an out-of-control stumble, but it wasn't.

74

She brought that axe directly down on my foot on purpose. I had on tennis shoes that day, it wasn't that cold outside, and plus I'm Alaskan, if you haven't noticed we barely feel the cold." Everest gestures to the other diners in the restaurant, many in short sleeves. I shudder and pull my sweater more tightly around myself.

Everest continues. "My parents rushed me to the hospital. Suni swore up, and down it was an accident. That her grip slipped. Except if she had really lived out in the bush like she said she did, chopping wood would have been second nature to her, and I saw her. I saw her face and the twist. There was no mistaking the intention. Everyone forgave her, of course. I swear she got more sympathy out of the whole thing than I did. I'll never forget the look on her face just before she brought the axe down, and I can tell you Suni will kill anyone who tries to stand in her way. That's the last time I really talked to Suni. I missed months of school because of my injury, and we drifted apart."

I'm at a loss for words, the whole thing is crazy, it's insane how much blind devotion Suni inspires in people. I pat the back of Everest's hand. "I'm really sorry that happened to you. That just makes me more determined to dig up some dirt on Suni."

Everest points to the address on my phone again. "I just know if you're going out there—" she digs in her bag, and hands me a can of bear spray the size of a small fire extinguisher. "You're going to need this. I think you should reconsider, maybe change your mind, if Suni is capable of doing what I think she is, you may not come out alive."

I slip the bear spray in my ever-present messenger bag. "I know, but I have to do this, someone has to do this."

"All right." Everest motions for me to hand her my phone, and I do. She pulls up my contacts, puts her name, number, and address into it. "I live over by Moose mountain, if you need anything or get in a weird situation, call me. I have plenty of room at my place."

"Thanks." I take back my phone and leave a good tip for the bartender. I shake out my sleepy legs when I stand.

"Be careful." Everest is really worried for me, I can tell.

"I will." I give her a smile, a wave, and truck out to my rental car.

Clouds darken the sky, and big flakes are starting to drift down. Great, this is just what I need, driving in near blizzard like conditions. I pull out of the parking lot, check the map for where I'm going, and turn on the radio to distract myself from the driving. "Danger Zone" by Kenny Loggins, blares out of the speakers loud and clear. It's one of my dad's favorite songs. For the longest time I thought the lyrics were 'highway to the danger's hour' but now it just all seems so fitting, prophetic even. I crank up the radio and navigate my way through a snowy Alaskan afternoon.

I drive as far down the road the house is located on as I can. I'm miles outside of town. I haven't seen another car for a long time. I park the car off to the side at the end of the road. There's a clear-cut trail running through the trees, I pull my snow pants back on over my boots, put on my hat and gloves, and grab my bag. It has a couple of granola bars, my water bottle, and the bear spray Everest gave me.

The cold whips around me as soon as I step out of the car. I shake it off, start out down the path, think better of it, and check my cell for service. I texted Ryan from the bathroom of the restaurant before I left so he knows exactly where I am, the only things is I have no service. Everest's warning rings in my head. I'm about to do something either incredibly stupid, or undoubtedly brave, either way… I start again. I keep a brisk pace down the snowy trail.

It's close to a mile and a half before I see any signs of human life. A plume of smoke rises up above the trees and hangs in the air. I gulp. I look at the black spruce around me and wonder if someone is watching me. It takes every bit of courage I have to keep going, but I do.

I come into a clearing and see a cabin. It's small, but it looks cozy. It doesn't have the high barn style roof of Mrs. Gustafson's house, and there aren't many windows. It's super rustic, but it seems like it would be warm in the winter, and cool in the summer, everything a person could need.

A dog barks from inside. I walk up to the door, pull my glove off and knock. The dog barks viciously. I hear a shuffle inside and know that more than just the dog is in there. The door opens a crack, a withered face looks out, the eyes are unfocused like they haven't been outside yet for the day, and it's their first peek at daylight.

"Hi" I say. I stand back from the door so they can get a good look at me. I can't tell through the crack if it's a man or a woman, but the face looks like a dried apple. "I was just out here hiking and I think I'm lost. Do you mind if I come in for a minute? I'm not from here and I'm really cold. Please?"

I turn on the charm. I give my best, sad stranded hiker face, all repentant and do goody. The crack in the door widens, I'm ushered in. The room is hot. I crack open my parka immediately. It's a man who opened the door, he's small and withered. His wife is in the corner, an amiable smile on her face, she's knitting something. The dog is by her side, resting his head on his paws, waiting for me to make a wrong move.

"Thank you so much," I gush. "I thought I was going to freeze to death out there."

The man seems to be the leader of their union. He nods his head, but doesn't speak. He holds up a teakettle. I nod my head yes, and watch as he puts it on top of the wood stove. He sits down in his easy chair, and motions for the dog to come to him.

"So, have you lived here long?" It's an inane conversation topic, but I need time to think, scope out the place. I look around, suss for anything to latch onto, something to tie them to Suni, a reason to bring her up.

The man nods his head, holds up his hands, flashes ten, and then ten again. For a moment I wonder if he can even speak, he seems to understand me though. He pronounces the kettle sufficiently hot, scrambles up from the depth of his chair, sets three mugs on the counter, pours hot water into each, reaches into a canister and pulls out a tea bag. He unceremoniously plops the bag in each steaming mug for a minute before handing his wife and I our tea.

Interesting. I take the mug and offer my thanks. I'm starting to feel a little exasperated, and then I see it. The mug, it's one of Suni's from her campaign. *Sip with Suni* is emblazoned across the front, *Liquid*

77

SuniShine, is emblazoned across the back with a small cameo of Suni smiling with aplomb, beaming out from the steaming cup. It's the perfect opening.

"Suni." I motion to the picture and pretend to be delighted to see it. "I just love her. Can you believe we might have our first female president? I'm so excited it's happening, and Suni, well I mean she's so qualified. She's been in politics forever. Your state is so lucky to have her." The two of them are beaming. I find it hard to believe that they don't understand every word I'm saying. "I just can't wait to vote for her in November. Do you know her? Have you ever met her? She's from here, right? I'm just up visiting my brother, he's stationed here, he's in the Army, we're from New Mexico, we're not used to all this cold." I wrap my arms around myself and act all brrr for them. "It's beautiful here though. Liam, that's my brother, he loves it here. He says he may never come back home. I thought he was crazy, but now that I'm visiting I can see why. It's a great place and well with a claim to fame like being the birthplace of Suni, America's first female president, that's a huge honor."

I've sparked something in the old man. I can see it working in him. I lean back against the worn loveseat covered by a colorful tapestry. "Suni, ours, our nave," he says motioning towards himself and his wife.

Bingo! I don't know the word nave, but I can guess what it means. I pull out my phone, darn, still no signal. I'm going to have to navigate this conversation without the help of an online translator. I act all surprised and flabbergasted, like I'm the ultimate Suni stan.

"No way, really? I thought Suni didn't have any family?" I add with a pout. "Wow, imagine being related to Suni, that's so lucky. Do you get to see her all the time? She's just so cool."

The old woman considers for a minute. She eyeballs me before reaching into the knitting bag beside her chair. She brings out a worn photo album, and motions me over. I bring my tea and traipse lightly. I'm careful not to act to over eager. I don't want to spoil the mirage of lost ditzy hiker I've created.

One look at the pictures in the album and I suddenly know all Suni's secrets. I can't believe how easy it was to find them. Even though they don't speak English these two have just given away the plot. I sneak a picture out of the back of the album when both their backs are turned rummaging in the tiny kitchen for something.

I collect my parka, and stand to go just as they're turning around with offerings of naan, more green tea with cardamom this time, and some kind of eggplant with what looks like yogurt. It all smells really good, but I smile and clutch my stomach. I tell them I'm already full from a late lunch and that I better find my way out before dark.

I can tell they're sad to see me go. They wave at me from the cabin door until I'm out of sight. I don't just hurry back down the path to my car, I run, like a bear is chasing me, like my life depends on it. Everest was right, Suni's deception is even deeper than I ever could have imagined.

I make it back to the car. I don't even bother to let it warm up. I just hop in snow pants and all and start back down the road. I can't wait to get to the warm comfort of the hotel, to safety. I still have hours before the sun sets, and while I've been inside the cabin, the sky has cleared. Sunshine pours down again, and the sky is blue. It's crazy how fast the weather changed. I decide to take it as a good sign.

I make it back to the main road without incident. I'm cresting the top of a hill, thinking that if everything goes well, I'll be back in Fairbanks in about an hour and thirty minutes. My cell still doesn't have any service, but the closer I get to town the faster that'll change, I tell myself.

I don't flinch when a huge truck looms up behind me. At first, I think it's a semi but I get a glimpse of it in the rear-view mirror and it's just one of those really big, huge, honking trucks that most people seem to have for no reason, but might actually be justified in Alaska. It's a double line but I still make room for them to pass me, I'm definitely driving like a tourist and I don't want to hold anybody up. The truck doesn't pass, it just gets closer and closer to my bumper.

What the heck? I hit the accelerator and let my peppy rental car zoom me up the hill. The truck has lots of horsepower, so they're on me in an instant. I stay as close to the mountain as I dare on the passenger side. Across the lane there's nothing but the gaping maw of a drop off. I try not to look, not to imagine the sounds of crunching metal and breaking glass.

I go as fast as I can. The truck turns its high beams on, and even though it's day, the light still throws me. My arm pits are sweating, I hold the wheel steady. I just keep looking at the road ahead. They ram me for show the first time. I feel the back of the car fishtail, but I manage to get it under control, the second time they put a little more oomph into it, the third time is at a bend in the road, a place where the drop off isn't too bad, but there's no guardrail to keep me on the highway.

I skitter across the oncoming traffic lane; luckily there aren't any cars coming. I launch into the air for what seems like an eternity before I land, skid through the trees, and come to a stop wedged in deep snow. I shake uncontrollably for about fifteen minutes before I calm myself and realize I'm okay. I take deep breaths so I can approach the situation with a level head. I need to survey the damage and think about what I'm going to do next.

After they ran me off the road, the truck drove away at warp speed. The highway is isolated, I doubt many people travel it. I might have to wait a long time before anyone comes, and that's if they even see the tire tracks. The snow is piled up around the doors. I try to open them, but I'm too wedged in. I turn the key in the ignition and the car faintly starts. I roll down the driver's side window and turn the car off. I want to save what's left of my tank of gas, just in case I'm spending the night out here.

I still have on all my hiking gear, so I grab my bag, everything I brought with me, and scramble out of the car. I sink into the snow immediately and start to move like I'm walking through water. I'm eager to get onto more stable ground. I wade out of the deep stuff and onto some walkable territory, there's nothing around, but I just start walking.

When I'm about two miles from the car, I start to feel a little hopeless. I don't want to go too deep into the woods in case I can't find my way back, but then I get this inkling and decide to go just a little further. My reward is a tiny house, and I mean a tiny house, a house so small it looks like a shed. Old cars, tires, machinery, and blue plastic water barrels are all around.

The whole thing is like a set from a serial killer movie, but I keep going. I force myself to walk up to the door. I swear if I put both arms out I could hug the house. I knock despite my reservations. The man who answers the door is exactly who I expected him to be. He has a big bushy grey beard, old duct-taped and patched clothes. I really hope I'm not about to be captured and kept in a cage. The sound of dogs howling, sets up like the wails of a banshee from all around the place, it's truly eerie.

I give the man a twitchy smile. "I slid off the road and crashed my car in the trees about two-and-a-half miles from here. You don't happen to have a phone I could use, do you? I don't have any cell service out here, otherwise I would use mine."

The man throws his head back and laughs. I'm terrified. "Why do you think I moved out here?" he asks with raised eyebrows. "No cell service, total isolation from the outside world, well I figure I've got time to help a stranded lass." He looks me up and down, before throwing open the cabin door. "Come on in."

Stranger danger screams through my head. "No, thanks!" I say as politely as possible.

The interior of the cabin is windowless, a woodstove, a cot in one corner, a bucket that looks like it's used for unseemly things. If I get out of this alive, I vow to myself only to do mundane things from here on out, hobbies like crocheting, painting, yoga, anything but this.

"Do you…?" I pause. "Could I just use your phone?"

"Like I said, I don't have a phone, heck I don't even have indoor plumbing, what we eat is what we catch, don't see many people back here, but sometimes there are a few." He gives me an ominous look. Sweet baby Jesus, please protect me. "You said your car was about two miles from here?"

"Yeah," I look around dubiously at the broken-down trucks, the rusted equipment, tractors that look like they haven't moved in this century. "Do you have something that could pull me out?"

"Oh, I doubt that, I do have something that can get you to town though, assuming that's where you're headed. You can call a tow truck from there, they do plenty of reconnaissance missions for tourists like you that go off the beaten path. I'm assuming you are a tourist."

I decide to stick to my New Mexico story. "Yep, you guessed right. I'm here from New Mexico visiting my brother, he's stationed at Ft. Wainwright." The similarities of Suni's last name and the local Army base don't escape me, she really *Usual Suspected* everybody with her whole schtick, but I'm about to blow her cover completely.

"Whereabouts in New Mexico are you from? I came up here from Arizona in seventy-one, haven't been back to America since. I used to go to Taos all the time. There was this great hippie colony there. I had some good times in New Mexico, and some beautiful women."

The look he gives me alarms me. Oh, pumpkins and donuts, I'm not cut out to be a hillbilly's wife. I flash on the bear spray in my bag. I ease my bag around to the front of my body and play with the flap for easy access. "Oh, yeah, that's great, I'm from the Santa Fe area. So, does one of these trucks work? Do you think you could run me into town? I don't want my brother Liam to get worried, he's pretty into the Army. He likes to shoot things. You know how crazy some guys get when they're really into being a soldier, all shaved heads and pumped up patriotism." I'm really nervous so I can't help the rambling, plus I want this guy to think I have some crazy psychotic *Rambo* brother waiting for me.

"Well, you don't have to worry about me, Miss. I'll get you back to Fairbanks safe and sound, trust me you'll never forget this ride."

As soon as I see his mode of transportation, I know I'll never forget this ride either. The team is made up of twelve dogs, only two of them are huskies, the rest look like different mixes.

"Interesting group you got here," I say eyeing the dancing, prancing dogs in the yard, eager to go on an adventure with their person. "I'm Maverick by the way," I say extending a gloved hand. I figure I might as well get the niceties out of the way before I go on this death-defying ride.

"Maverick, interesting choice, I'm guessing you were born in eighty-six, and your parents were big *Top Gun* fans. I'm Tim Klauss, but none of the other bush people can pronounce my name so they call me T. Klauss like Santa Claus, even though it's Klauss as in rhymes with mouse. I don't mind it though; the team and I go around to all the villages we can at Christmas time bringing little presents. My sister sends me boxes of fresh fruit. She lives in Florida. Oranges especially are a huge hit with village kids; anyone who says there aren't young uns' out there with an appreciation for the simpler things in life has never been to Alaska."

"I can see that. I mean, learning to be self-sustaining is good for everybody. I'm sure Alaskan kids go far in life. They can separate the superficial from real survival, that's a gift. Well, good to meet you T." I gesture to the sled he's hauling out of a shed. "What do you call those contraptions, anyway? And do I have to sit in the front all papoosed up?"

"Only if you want to stay warm, and it's called a dog sled, no reason for a fancy name, the part you're going to ride in is called the basket." He hands me a heavy blanket. I take it dubiously, I have no idea where it's been. "The dogs are what I call Alaskan refugees; every one of them is from America, strays," he pops booties on all the dogs as he speaks. "We've come a long way over the years, haven't we Bears?"

"Bears?"

"I call them *The Bad News Bears*, because when I got them they were the most dysfunctional dog sled team the world had ever seen. Now they work really well together, Harvey and Radcliff are the lead dogs, and the rest just fall in line. Dog psychology is not that different from people really, get the bravest and strongest to agree to it, and the rest will just follow."

"I've seen that theory in play more than once, I work in politics." As soon as it's out of my mouth, I regret it.

T. seizes on it immediately. "What do you mean work in politics? Now that's one thing I stay very far away from. The government is nothing more than a machine conditioned to control the masses. They want to regulate what we eat, think, and breathe. That's why I came up here, to get away. I don't like political types." He eyes me warily.

I backtrack fast the last thing I need is to lose my ride because of partisan differences. "I didn't really mean work per se, I just meant I've been known to volunteer in different capacities, that's all."

T. takes it down a notch. "Good, I don't suppose you've done any work for that Suni's campaign have you?"

I can't tell where he stands on the whole Suni thing, so I just play it off. "Suni, not particularly, why?"

"Just don't like her, that's all, something about her doesn't seem right, all that stuff she posts on Facebook just seems mainly for show. I can't put my finger on it, but there's just something about her I don't trust."

I try not to take his dislike of our social media accounts personally, plus I'm shocked he even knows what Facebook is. "Sure, I could see that," I say.

He runs rigging lines to the dogs' collars, clips the two lead dogs into place, and the rest follow suit. He motions me to take my spot in the basket and I do. "Mush," he calls, and the sled starts to move through the woods, T. stands at the back on the runners, and controls the whole thing. It's exhilarating, but super freaky at the same time.

"You mind a little music while we ride?" he calls.

I shake my head, the wind whips away my, "Of course not."

I'm surprised when T. slips an iPod out of his inside pocket, puts it in some holder he has rigged to the handle of the sled, and starts to blast out "Push It," by Salt-N-Pepa. I can tell it's a regular occurrence because it's like the dogs start stepping to the beat.

We move nimbly through the woods, skim across the path, and rush through the trees. I can't feel my face by the time we fly into the parking lot of the hotel. No one bats an eye at my mode of arrival. I stretch as I step out of the basket.

I take a couple pictures of the team, and T. Just because I'm in the middle of whistleblowing what will probably turn out to be the biggest scandal in our election history doesn't mean I can't acknowledge really cool things. I fish in my bag, grab my wallet, peel off two crisp hundred-dollar bills, and hand them to T.

He puts his hands up and backs away. "I don't expect payment, the Bears and I enjoyed the ride, plus now that we're in town we can go visit some friends. No big deal, save that money for yourself, or something for your brother."

"It's a donation for the kids, so you can have a really good dog sled Santa sleigh full of presents."

T. takes the money reluctantly, lines out the team, gives me a wink and a nod, and takes off down a trail at the back of the hotel. I see him in the distance, going up the side of the highway. I wonder if the friends he's going to visit are as colorful as he is, but I'm sure they are.

I trudge into the hotel. My whole-body aches, but I know one thing for certain. I know I'm not going to stay here for the night. I've stirred up a hornet's nest, and if they can run me off the road, they can come to the hotel at night when I'm asleep and do goodness knows what.

I call Ryan and fill him in on everything. Then I call roadside recovery and give them the exact location of the rental car. They promise to tow it to the hotel for me; the price makes me cry a little, but hey, what choice do I have?

I pick up my phone one last time, press the number, and let it ring. I blurt it all out as soon as the voice says "Hello."

"Hey, some really weird stuff is going on." I throw my slippers into my duffle. "Do you think you could pick me up at the grocery store across the street from my hotel, and I could spend the night at your place?"

"No problem. I'll be there in fifteen, pick up a good wine and some guacamole while you're at the store, will you? It sounds like we have a lot to talk about."

I grab my stuff and head outside. I check that no one is following me. I hit the store across the street and grab a perfect smorgasbord of munchies. I wait outside. I know the truck when it pulls up to the curb. I step inside, and we're off.

The Truth Yurts

The yurt we pull up to is amazing. It has a red outside membrane, with wood accent slats around the doors and windows. It's up out of the trees on a huge deck, I can't wait to get through the double French doors and see the inside. "That's awesome," I gasp.

Everest, smiles. "I know, I love it out here in the woods, not a solitary soul around, just me and the quiet, well and Hunter of course."

I can already hear happy barking from inside. I grab my bag out of the car and follow Everest up the stairs. The inside doesn't disappoint, tongue-and-groove aspen walls and ceiling, a wood stove in the corner, everything running to a huge round skylight at the top. We still have a couple hours before sunset and light pours in through the windows; it's nice, cozy, and warm. There's a big central kitchen living space, and then a loft, with two doors below.

Everest points to the door on the right. "That's the bathroom, the other door is my room; it's ensuite so that bathroom will be all yours, and I'll show you where you'll sleep." Everest motions for me to follow and an ecstatic Hunter comes too, leaping with excitement that his favorite person is home. We walk up carpeted stairs to the loft; a double bed and a couch are up there. "This is the guest room." Everest looks around and makes sure everything's kosher.

I hand her the reusable grocery bag full of treats. "All right," I say, relieved I'm somewhere I can finally relax. "Well, I'm just going to get settled in up here. I need to change out of these clothes, and then we can talk. You were right, we have a lot to talk about."

Everest nods. "We do." She turns and pads back down the stairs. She rattles around in the kitchen and talks nonsense to Hunter while she feeds him his dinner.

I change into comfortable sweats. I pull on different thick socks, put my hair in a bun, and take a few deep breaths. The enormity of what I've been through hits me, and I start to shake a little. I decide my blood sugar is low and I need company. I text Ryan that everything's cool, Everest and I got to her place safe; he sends me his heart in an emoji.

I pad downstairs, Everest is letting an exuberant Hunter out the door. She turns and smiles at me. "You hungry? I laid out all the stuff you got. You didn't have to buy the whole store, I have plenty to eat."

"No, I thought we could just snack, and talk, so much happened today."

We move to the couch, she's set up the whole spread on her round coffee table; the couch is a soft down sectional. I sink into one end; she sinks into the other. I grab the glass of wine she's poured for me, take a healthy swig, and tell her everything. The old couple in the cabin, all the dirt on Suni, the car chase, the sled dogs, everything. When I'm done I collapse back, Everest lets out a big sigh.

"That is crazy, like the kind of crazy that sounds like a Hollywood movie." She grabs her wine and takes a sip. "So, what's your plan now?"

I look at her hard, she's not fazed by any of it. "You already knew, didn't you? Everything I told you about Suni, you've always known, haven't you? Why have you kept quiet all this time? Let her climb so far? Why didn't you blow the whistle a long time ago?"

"Don't judge me too soon," Everest cautions. "I used to be like you. To think that all I needed to do was get the word out there and people would listen, but I was wrong. Suni has people in places you can't imagine, the highest and the lowest corners of humanity, and it's not just Americans. No, the whole Suni thing is international. Why do you think I live out here in the woods? I mean granted I like it, but I used to have a cute little house right in town, I could walk to my coffee stand from there. One night I looked out the window and there was Suni, standing at the top of my driveway with an axe. She must have stood out there just glaring at my house for over an hour. Every time I try to report Suni, to anybody, the cops, those FBI lines they tell you to call if you see something suspicious, I always get played like I'm some kind of unhinged nutter. So, don't accuse me of not trying. I've tried, but I'm not willing to lose my life over Suni."

"She's got to be stopped."

Everest nods. "I completely agree, but how?"

"I have connections, people I know. I can make phone calls. In fact, do you mind if I just step outside?" Everest waves me on. I'm going to call Brandon and see who he thinks I should contact. Ryan's FBI friend had a few nuggets, but not much. Brandon works for the DOJ, surely, he knows some big players.

He picks up on the third ring. "Maverick?"

I can tell I'm on speaker phone, great, it's Saturday night and Brandon has nothing better to do than hang out with Barbara, I should have known.

He starts in on me immediately. "Where are you? Mom and I have been going crazy worrying about you. Ryan said you were in Baltimore, but when we couldn't get a hold of you, we called Suni and she said you told one of your coworkers you were sick. So, we went to your house, and no one was there. When we called Suni to see if she'd heard from you, she was as surprised as we were that you weren't home."

I can see where this is going, so I cut him off, "Look Brandon, something major is going on. It's about Suni, she's not who she says she is, I have proof. I'm being chased by people who are trying to kill me. I need your help, do you know anybody I can call, and report this to?"

Silence thunders down the line, it's Barbara's voice, not Brandon's that comes through. "Seriously Mavie, now Suni's trying to kill you?" she says sarcastically. "This whole delusions about Suni thing has gone on long enough. We know it's been hard for you since Kyle dumped you, but Ryan, your brother's nice, successful friend is actually interested in you and you're off on some fantasy hunt for clues about Suni? You better play your cards right this time Maverick because you're not getting any younger, and Brandon says Ryan has lots of young, attractive, blondes who buzz around him at the office."

Ryan's already told me about the *Legally Blondes* as he calls them. If he wanted to marry a version of his mother, he would have stuck with his high school girlfriend, Paisley. Barbara's words don't have the affect she hopes, but there is one thing. "I dumped Kyle," I say, "he didn't dump me."

I did dump him; he left the same day I dumped him with all his stuff in trash bags. Everything was in my name anyway, the house, the bills, everything. He had no choice but to leave when I kicked him to the curb.

"Poor Mavie, sure you did, look wherever you are, whatever you think you're doing just come home. You're not right in the head, sweetie. I mean, you never have been, but you've finally had that break with reality we were afraid of. You've always been so jealous of everyone else's success, Brandon's, Suni's, you just can't be happy for people. It's selfish, and so is what you're pulling right now, and besmirching Suni's good name in the process just because you're not in her shoes is shameful. You'll never have what other people have Maverick, you're just average, nothing special, and the sooner you accept that the better your life will be."

I've had enough. "Don't talk to me like that, Barbara, don't ever talk to me like that again. I'm not jealous of Brandon or Suni, I don't want their sad constipated little lives. See, that's the thing you've never understood about me. I'm not at all like you say, you just make up the narrative of who I am in your head and then you do everything in your power to fit me into that mold. Well, guess what? You and your theories are crap and your precious son can get stuffed."

Brandon blusters on their end. "How dare you talk to Mom like that, Maverick? You are way out of line now. Mom and Dad have done everything for you, and this is how you repay them? By acting like a brat? Well, I for one am not going to stand for it. You owe Mom a big apology."

"Get a life Brandon, you're forty years old for goodness' sake, and you have no one to hang out with but your mommy. Get a wife, get some dignity, grow some balls." I hang up, and block their numbers so I don't have to get the repeat calls from them that I'm sure are already happening, there's nothing like narc rage. I'm sure they'll huddle in the living room tonight and smear my name till there's nothing left. I don't care, let them stew in their own juices, the jerks.

"Any luck?" Everest is in the same position on the couch as when I left.

I shrug my shoulders. "Not really. I picked the wrong people to call, that's all, I should have known they would backstab me."

"Coworkers?"

I shake my head. "My family."

"That's rough," Everest cringes. "Look, I've been thinking. Suni doesn't know what you have on her. You could just walk away now, let the whole thing go. You don't have to do this."

"That's where you're wrong. I can't just walk away, I love this country, sure I make fun of our Americanisms, hot dogs, soda pop, and weird linguistics. We think our cars are melded with our bodies and we can't even walk two feet. I don't agree with some people's opinions in this country, but I respect their right to have them. And who can be a person of color in America without experiencing casual racism? Not me. I mean we definitely have our flaws but fundamentally, we're good and I believe in our good and its power to always win."

"Of color," Everest repeats in a funny voice. "You wouldn't believe how many people assume because I'm Alaska Native I'm a drunk, or don't have a college degree."

"Shameful," I say, aware that's exactly how Mrs. Gustafson described Everest that afternoon, good thing I followed my gut and not her crappy advice. I finish my thoughts. "I know the political climate we've had these past few years has been cray, it's genuinely scared me. See, I'm not one of those people who says, 'Oh I'll move to Canada,' there's no way I'd let anything drive me away from here. I'm American, I don't think I could survive anywhere else. I can't imagine being a refugee, no drive thru coffee stands, no tanks on the road called SUVs, no pizza, French fries and ice cream as part of a nutritious meal. No big friendly American faces, smiles, and small talk that can stretch out into real conversations even if you don't see that person again. No, we're redeemable, we just have to bond together to find the way, that's all, and take care of us, all Americans. Even the ones who think grease is a food group and farts are funny, because when it comes down to it, we've all been molded and shaped by this country, and we have to protect our Democracy, our freedom at any cost. I mean, where else am I going to find people I can become friends with in an afternoon?" I look at Everest shyly.

Everest waves a hand. "Oh, definitely friends, trust me in a few months I'm packing my suitcase and coming to visit."

"Oh, you're so invited, we'll have so much fun, there's so much to see. So yeah, that's why I can't walk away from this, someone has to do it. I mean I don't have a death wish, I want to live, I just met this guy and well," I pause, "you know how that goes."

Everest nods her agreement, "It goes. You know what we need to do?" Hunter scratches at the door. She walks over and lets him in and grabs a remote on her way. "Dance," she cranks up "Love Me Olé"– Latin remix with MAJOR., Cierra Ramirez, and C-Kan. We crazy salsa around her living room, soul train it out, even Hunter gets in on it, and bounds at us off the couch. We collapse a few minutes later.

"That was fun," I manage to gasp.

"Well, I figure if we're going to die we might as well have fun."

"I like the logic, except I have no intention of letting Suni take me out," I say stubbornly.

"Do you know what's next?" Everest asks.

I shake my head, "Bed?" I offer.

"Bed," Everest agrees. We clean up all the food on the coffee table, give each other hugs, and go off to our rooms.

I'm glad I'm not in the hotel listening to every footfall in the corridor, waiting to hear my door knob turn, no this is better, but I'm still uneasy. Whoever was following me is in it to win. I need to come up with a plan, except I throw my hand behind my head, and am instantly asleep. Despite my worries, no one comes in the night and kills us and I wake up early in the morning, refreshed. Everest is already in the kitchen whipping up sourdough pancakes when I walk in.

She motions to the French Press coffee on the counter. "There's almond milk in the creamer jug and coconut sugar in the bowl. Hope you don't mind."

"Au contraire, you're a girl after my own heart." I pour a generous cup, splash in almond milk, and top it off with three teaspoons of sugar. "There's something I'm curious about so don't take this the wrong way."

"Go for it," Everest scoops up two perfect pancakes, pats them with vegan butter, and sets the bottle of real maple syrup in front of me.

I pour on the syrup and butter drips off the edge, I can tell the pancakes are super fluffy. "Why did Mrs. Gustafson say all those weird things about you when I went to see her yesterday?"

Everest freezes mid flip. "You went to see The Gus?"

I stop mid bite. "Yes, is that bad? I read about her in an old article of Suni's, I thought she might have valuable information and she did, that's how I found you."

"Now it makes sense." Everest says to herself. She flips the pancakes and leans across the counter from me. "The Gus hates me, she's a Suni fanatic. If you told her Suni was the woman version of Jesus, she would believe it. From the first day Suni came to school, The Gus watched out for her and gave her special privileges. She would argue down any teacher that dared to cross Suni. The Gus even got Principal Jarvis wrapped around her finger. That's how Suni's goons knew about you yesterday, The Gus. They must have picked you up when you started out towards the cabin in the woods. You must have lost them though cause otherwise they would have come here last night and destroyed the place. I always felt like The Gus knew Suni before she showed up at the high school. Like they'd known each other for a long time, there was something about the non-verbal cues that told you they were much more familiar with each other than they let on. The Gus…," Everest shakes her head, "she's one heck of an evil witch."

"Sounds like it." I've gotten deeper into this thing than I ever could have imagined I would. I finish off the pancakes, swallow down the rest of my coffee, and offer to clean up the kitchen, but Everest waves me away. I traipse to the bathroom, shower, and change into my flying home clothes. My plane leaves in a couple of hours, hopefully the rental car will be in the parking lot of the hotel waiting for me. Everest's already agreed to give me a ride to town.

Everest drops me off in the parking lot of the hotel near my rental car, which looks pretty good other than a slightly droopy front bumper. We say goodbye and I know with certainty that I'll see her again. I check out of the hotel, start up the car and head to the airport two hours early. They kick up a little fuss at the rental kiosk when I return the car, but I point out that I got the most insurance coverage I could and they back off.

I feel drained as I sit waiting for the plane. The flight is uneventful. I fall asleep shortly after take-off, shuffle through the switch at SeaTac, doze off again and am back at Regan the next time I open my eyes. It's good to be home. Ryan wanted to pick me up at the airport, but I told him not to bother. He has to be at work early in the morning, and I'm going to the CIA headquarters in Langley tomorrow. I'm driving out first thing. I'm not going to leave the building until someone listens to what I have to say, or I get arrested, either way.

I grab an Uber and get to my house in record time. Jay's out on the stoop, I'm tired but not too tired to chat. I drop my bag and pull up a stair. "Hey Jay, what's up?"

Jay's bursting with nervous energy. "A lady was here looking for you while you were gone. Suni from T.V. She wondered where you were. I told her you were at the drugstore getting your prescription from your doctor, and that you looked terrible. I figured you called in sick if she was here asking about you. I mean, she's your boss, right?" I nod my head yes, eager for her to continue.

"Well, she gave me her phone number and told me to call her as soon as you were back. She also told me she would pay me a hundred dollars for any information about you, like where you were going, things you were doing, people coming in and out. I just went into stealth mode and acted all sweet and dumb. I'm a kid, so people expect that more than the reality. Anyway, I think she bought it, but she was weird, like a deranged *Mary Poppins*."

"What day was she here?" Suni was supposed to be in Baltimore for the entire weekend.

"Saturday morning," Jay says with assurance.

"Are you sure?" I distinctly remember turning on the T.V. and watching Suni's statement about Brett and Maisy over breakfast in the hotel room. I let out a sigh. It all seems like so long ago, but it was only yesterday.

Jay checks her phone. "I'm a hundred percent." She flashes me her screen, on it is a sneaky picture of Suni with the date and time stamped.

"What the...?" Suni was in Baltimore at that time, making a live statement. How could she be here? It's more than I can contemplate. Cold is creeping up through the step and the sun's starting to set. "Want to come in? You can help me eat the vegan pizza I'm about to order?"

Jay nods her head. "Sure thing."

Even though it's Sunday night, a school night, I convince Jay to stay awhile and watch a movie. We watch *Space Camp*, an 80s classic, and she loves it. She laughs out loud, turns to me and says, "*Must send Max to space,*" in a robot voice. She stands and stretches when it ends.

"That was fun. Do they still have that?" she asks in a tentative voice, one I've never heard before.

"What? Space Camp? I'm pretty sure they do, but you should Google it and find out."

"It's probably expensive." Jay rubs the face of her phone against her jeans. "Dream never has money for stuff like that. It's why I want to earn my own, if I have money I can buy books, and the microscope I want. Plus, I could pay for a trip to Space Camp. I would love that. One day I want to go to a ranch in Montana and ride a horse. I've always felt like there's a cowgirl somewhere in me."

I look at Jay with regard. She's one woke kid. She has to be. She has no choice. At her age, I knew nothing. I didn't have to worry about how to get somewhere. I just had to learn to survive emotionally. "Well, it seems like you have some good plans, let me check around, there might be scholarships, money out there for kids like you to do things like Space Camp."

Jay takes my words bitterly. "Kids like me. You mean poor kids with hood rat moms that people think are going to end up in jail instead of president. Yeah, there probably is money out there for kids like me." She moves towards the door.

I intercede and step in front, I can't let her leave like this. I know why her dreams are so brittle. I know the pain of trying to show your humanity, of trying to get people to look beyond your brown skin, and Jay is still a child. It's so much harder to learn these lessons, to lose the innocence of 'we're all the same,' to the reality. Some of us are extremely privileged for no good reason.

"I didn't mean it like that. I just meant kids that don't have a lot of money, that was all. I don't think of you as some sad sack, I see you as Jay, and I totally believe that someday you will dominate the world. Trust me, I don't feel sorry for you, I fear you, but for right now you're just a kid, and even though you have lots of common sense and great things ahead, better things than I can hope for myself, you have to roll with the punches and that's not always easy. That was all I meant, Jay. I promise."

Jay nods her head and swipes at her eyes. "All right, I'm just going to go home now. I'm tired."

"Any tests tomorrow?"

She shakes her head. "Geography at the end of the week, but I know it already, how else can I..."

"Plan world domination," I finish. I pull her in for a hug and feel the pain of growing up course through her little body, I would give anything to change everything for her. "Okay," I pull back, and turn towards the window by the door. "Just let me check the street for weirdos."

"You're so old-fashioned," Jay scoffs.

I always go out on the stoop, and watch until Jay is inside her apartment with the door locked, but I like to check the street first and

96

avoid any shady characters that may be walking past. I twitch the current, and freeze in disbelief. Three men are coming up the sidewalk, they're dressed in black, I can see the glint of guns in the streetlight. It's time to make a quick exit.

"Quick come on." I slip on my shoes, grab Jay's arm, and my purse off the counter as we go.

"What are you doing? Have you gone crazy?" Jay squirms against my grip.

I shush Jay and push her out my back door. We go over the fence and down the stairs. I shuffle my feet in front of the back door of her apartment. "Do you have the key?" I ask. I can't believe how much my voice is shaking.

Jay doesn't say anything, she just opens the back door. I huddle with her in the bathroom. Dream isn't home, but that's for the best. We can hear thudding next door, things shattering in my apartment, the voices of men. I try not to let Jay see my fear, but it's impossible, I'm terrified.

We don't say anything we just stand together through the clomping and banging. The men talk amongst each other. At one point I think I hear muffled gunshots. Jay and I wrap our arms around each other, hold our breath and wait. After twenty minutes of silence, I figure they're gone, so we creep out of the bathroom. I don't even stop to think, Jay has to come with me, and the two of us are leaving now.

Jay's room is immaculate. I'm not surprised. Organization is the key to success, and she definitely has it down pat. She doesn't ask many questions, she just packs up her bag quick.

"Can you call your mom and tell her you're with me, so she won't worry?" I ask.

Jay sighs, "Well I would love to, but Dream left her phone here this morning when she stepped out with her new man. I have strict rules about guys in our house, and Dream isn't all bad. She listens to that part. Anyway, she forgot her phone and when she's off riding the wave of a new guy, she stays gone for days. I actually wasn't expecting her back until Wednesday."

I'm not sure what to do. I don't want to get arrested for kidnapping, but when guys with machine guns are knocking up my house next door, I know I can't take off and leave Jay alone, especially since Suni already pegged her. "Okay, well just write your mom a note and leave it on the kitchen table. Tell her you're staying with me, and to call when she gets back."

"Got ya," Jay tears out a sheet from a notebook on her desk, writes the note, sets it on the kitchen table, and finishes packing up some clothes and her books for school. "I'm ready."

"Good." I'm not even bothering with my stuff. There's no way I'm going back into that house, maybe ever. I always intended to sell it, anyway.

"Come on," I check the alley, we go out a side window and walk swiftly around the corner to the lot where I pay to store my car. It's a safe bet that they won't be able to find us where we're going, so I feel pretty good about it. We circle the lot twice before I figure it's okay. I'm a little paranoid, so I use my phone flashlight to sweep under the chassis of my car for bombs. Once I feel like it's all clear, we hop inside. I need to plant a false trail, and false clues, before we follow the real plan.

We pull into the long-term parking lot of Dulles. I don't even try to hide the car. I pick the most obvious spot I can. My car has Suni bumper stickers plastered across it thanks to Brandon. He thought it would be funny to deface my ride when I was over visiting one night. I tried, but couldn't peel them off so I'm a driving billboard for Suni's campaign.

"Grab all your stuff. We're not coming back here." I tell Jay.

Jay slings on her backpack. "Are we flying somewhere?"

"No, but I hope they think we flew somewhere, and expend energy on a dead end, that's why we're leaving the car here, but you and I have bigger plans."

We catch the bus leaving the airport. I plan to pay cash from here on out for most things, they can't trace cash. We get off at Tysons Corner and squeak into the UPS store just before it closes. I grab a padded

Manila envelope and ask Jay for a sheet of her notebook paper and a pen. I write a hurried explanation, and scroll through my contacts to Ryan. I make sure I really have his number memorized, then I drop my phone, and the letter, into the envelope.

I still have the flash drive, but I've made sure all the incriminating documentation is on my phone. It has the secret recording I made of everything I learned in that cabin in Alaska, plus the initial grainy video of Suni, and a few other nuggets. It's all evidence, and it's all damning. I address it to the head of the CIA. I might as well go straight to the top with what I have. I send it certified so that it requires a signature. So that's that.

Jay and I head to Best Buy to get a burner phone. I plug Ryan's number in immediately, I'll call him later. It's too late to grab a bus to where we're going so we'll Uber. I download the app onto my new phone and tap it; one minute, and we're out. The Uber drops us at a grocery store in Frederick, MD. Jay's unusually silent, and obedient, I don't know her moods well enough to know if I should be worried. "You hungry?"

She shakes her head. "Not really."

"Well, we should get some stuff just in case," I grab a cart, and beckon her to follow me through the aisles. I tell Jay to grab whatever stuff she wants. I still plan to go to Langley in the morning, to the CIA headquarters, but this is just in case things don't go as planned and we need to shelter in place, hunker down.

"Why are those people trying to kill you?"

I put the gluten-free vanilla sandwich cookies into the cart and turn to look at Jay. "Because I found something. I know something. It was in that package we sent off. You don't have to stay with me, if you have a friend, or a family member you want to call we can get you to them."

"No, there aren't any. I mean you're my only real friend, and that's probably just because you don't seem to have any friends your own age."

Her astuteness is startling. "I have friends," I bluster.

Jay sighs, "Look. This is a life and death situation; we really don't have time for this, let's just buy these groceries and go wherever you have planned for us to go, and then," she looks at me pointedly. "I want to know everything. I know I'm only ten but I'm not stupid, if I'm going to risk my life I want to know why."

I nod my head, "Sounds fair."

We grab a few more things, check out quick, and Uber out of town. I plugged in the neighbor's house, a few streets over from our actual destination…, 'cause well, you never know. We wait at the top of the fake driveway until the Uber speeds off and then we hoof it down the street, cut through the woods, and come to the house the back way. Jay let's out a low whistle when she sees it.

"Whose place is this?" she asks, her voice portraying her awe.

"Mine."

"You own this and you live in the city next to me? What is wrong with you? If this were mine, I would live here full time, I would never leave. Are we going inside?"

I lead the way and open the big rounded wood door with its fleur-de-lis wrought iron hinges. It's a castle. I mean literally a castle, a big stone castle, it was built in the early 1800s by a wealthy family as their summer home. They wanted to get away from the bustle of the city. Grandma Prue, and Grandpa Merv, found it mostly in ruins in nineteen seventy-six, bought it and brought it back to life, modernized it. Grandpa Merv was retiring from the CIA at that time and needed a project, Grandma Prue knew the house would be the perfect fit. It's grand, you could spend hours looking at the workmanship, the wood-paneled halls, crystal chandeliers, stained glass panels, but it's not overbearing. I've always loved the place, which is why when she passed away, Grandma Prue left it to me. She wanted it to stay in the family and she knew her daughter, my mom Barbara, would just sell it.

Barbara was angry, and bitter, when she found out I was the one who inherited the house. Even though she got the bulk of her parent's estate, most of it wasn't enough for her. She wanted it all. Her brother Henry died of a heart attack when he was young, so she's the last one standing from her immediate family. She tried to bully me into signing the house over to her, but when that wouldn't work she just came over before the funeral, and plundered the house, took everything she wanted and felt she should have. I didn't fight her. What would be the point? I'm not that petty. The thing is, she hated most of Grandma Prue's stuff. She always made fun of Grandma Prue's classic good taste, so in the grand scheme of things ninety-five percent of Prue's stuff is still here.

"Why didn't you ever tell me about this place?" Jay asks in awe.

I walk to the thermostat and bump up the heat. I keep it on just enough so the pipes won't freeze when nobodies here, it's a big place but not cavernous, still there's no use paying utility bills if you don't have to. Fifteen acres surround the castle, my dream is to make it even more modern, solar power, a wind turbine, totally off the grid, grow my own vegetables, raise chickens, be totally self-sufficient. Barbara says if I'm not willing to deed the place over to her I should just sell it, and get the money, but I'll never do that, the heart of Grandma Prue is in this home, and now that we're here I know we'll be okay.

"I guess cause I don't like to talk about it. I love this house, but coming here reminds me of my Grandma Prue and I really miss her. These past few months have been hard without her. Every time something good happens I want to tell her, and then I remember she's gone."

Jay brings me back to reality with a thump. "Hey, at least you had her, and she left you this house. Seems like she loved you a lot, and that kind of love. Well, it doesn't end just because someone dies. I talk to my dad all the time and he's dead."

"Your dad?" It shocks me. I mean, I figured she had a dad. I just thought he wasn't in the picture, not dead.

"Of course." Jay scoffs like I'm terminally silly. "It takes two to tango. How do you think I got so responsible and self-assured? It's not because of Dream, it's because of my dad. He spent a lot of time with me. He was a foster kid growing up, so family meant everything to him. He was way different from Dream. I mean, they both were young

101

when they got pregnant with me, but he grew up. Dream didn't, that's what ended up breaking them up. He got custody of me. The first seven years of my life I lived with him. I only moved in with Dream three years ago, when he died."

I had no idea. I feel bad for even bringing the topic of death up. I look at Jay with real concern. "Are you sure there's no one you want to call? Someplace safe you can go?"

"I'm sure."

She seems to want to keep talking about her dad, so I let her go on.

"My dad died of Hodgkin's lymphoma. You wouldn't believe how good you get at searching the internet when your dad is dying, even if you're only seven. He tried, we tried everything, and when we knew it was the end, we hatched this plan for world domination. He wrote it all out for me in a secret diary. So, every time I feel sad, or like I can't make it, I can read it, and know that he's still with me."

"That's beautiful. I'm sure he is still with you," I say, swiping away the tears I don't want Jay to see. She's so strong and I need to be too. "All right, let's go on the grand tour and I'll show you where you can sleep tonight."

Jay does a rare thing. She takes my hand, and we walk through the house. I show her the grand dining room with its elegant long table for twelve. The kitchen is a revelation. Grandma Prue insisted her kitchen keep up with modern times, and hers was fully renovated a few months before she died. It's full of the latest and greatest of everything. We put the groceries away and then head up the grand staircase, carpeted in a rich cheery plush red.

"I thought you could sleep in here," I say, pushing open the door to the blue room. It's a huge room, but it's not the master. The queen bed looks dwarfed in the space. A Persian rug warms up the center of the rooms perfectly square proportions. There's a fireplace with a carved pine surround, and beautiful cornflower blue patterned tiles. It's one of my favorite rooms, it has a study through panel sliding doors. In there is a pull-out couch, and that's where I plan to sleep. I figure it's best to stay near each other, in case something happens. I doubt they've tracked us here, but I realize I can't be too safe.

"Is this my room?" Jay looks around incredulously. The room definitely has fairy tale qualities. The canopy above the queen bed, the large spacious free-standing wardrobes that I used to think would transport me to *Narnia*. Grandma Prue always laughed at that, but she went out and bought me Turkish delight when I begged to try it.

"Yes, but don't worry. You won't be alone," I slide the panel doors into the walls, and reveal the connected study that's the same size as the bedroom. I point to the couch. "That folds out, so I thought I would sleep there. That way we can hear each other if one of us needs something. Okay?"

Jay throws her backpack on the bed and sits next to it. "Fine with me."

"The bathrooms in the hall, oh and just one more thing," I show her the beautiful calligraphic script on the wall. *Elizabeth 1811, aged ten*, it reads.

"Who's Elizabeth?" Jay asks with wonder in her eyes.

"I wanted to know the same thing too, when I was your age, so Grandma Prue did some digging and found really good information through the local historical society. She was the daughter of the family who built this place, apparently, she was strong willed, and brave, she never married and she became a doctor. She was on the battlefield during the Civil War, trying to save Union soldiers. She brought many of them here." Jay looks a little creeped out at this information. I laugh. "There aren't any ghosts, believe me I've spent enough time here that I would know. Do you want to go down to the kitchen and have a snack?"

"Why were you here all the time?" Jay asks as we walk through the stone-walled hallway to the back stairs that lead directly to the kitchen.

"Barbara, my mom, and Brandon, my brother traveled a lot when I was young. Brandon is a few years older than me, and he was something of a soccer prodigy. My dad felt like he was too busy at work to look after me when the two of them were gone traveling, so I came here a lot to Grandma Prue. I spent every summer here starting at the age of five while Barbara and Brandon were in Germany. They spared no expense trying to make Brandon the best soccer player he could be."

I open the big double door fridge, pull out the hummus and veggies, rustle in the cupboard for the potato chips. I figure we'll balance out something unhealthy with something healthy. *An eye for an eye,* or whatever they say. Jay takes a chip and crunches it down.

"So, what happened to Brandon? Is he a famous soccer player now?" she asks.

"Not quite." I dunk a cucumber in hummus and add my own crunch to the symphony. "He tore his ACL and had to retire at eighteen. He went to college and then law school and works for the DOJ."

"Oh." Jay seems disappointed.

"It just goes to show," I say, not wanting her to feel some vicarious discouragement through Brandon's story. Because the truth is, Brandon didn't really want any of it, Barbara did. A child that she could boast was a prodigy who needed special so and so made Barbara feel superior and that made her flourish. She lived and breathed through the idea that Brandon would be world famous. And when he wasn't, well then, she became intent on molding him into a super lawyer. Somewhere in my heart I have a lot of pity for Brandon, he'll never be his own man. I may get dumped on continuously, but I'm free because I know myself and my own desires.

I finish the thought I was telling Jay. "You can have everything behind you, every advantage, all the money in the world and it can mean nothing. But someone like you, well I can just look at you and know you'll succeed, because you've got it. That intangible quality, the quiet power that comes from within, and people can sense that stuff. Trust me."

Jay smiles. "I appreciate that, but you still haven't told me why we had to run away? And what we're doing here?"

"Right." I take another bite and chew for a really long time. How to put this? "Suni, the woman I work for, the one everyone says is going to be the first female president. Well, it turns out she's actually a Russian operative who is trying to get elected president so she can destroy our Democracy from within." I cringe a little after I blurt it all out. I wait for the judgement, but it doesn't come.

Jay takes it all in stride. "I thought there was something funny about her. Something not quite American. A Russian. Well Khrushchev said, *'We will take America without firing a shot.'* I guess they were trying to achieve that. So, is there more to your plan other than us running away and staying here?"

"Tomorrow I'll take you to school and go to the CIA headquarters. I'll tell them everything I know. That's the plan."

"So, tonight we just have to stay alive, and in this castle house no less. Talk about life imitating art, or is it the other way around?"

"How about we talk about bed?" It's almost ten and I want to call Ryan.

Jay jumps down from the bar stool she's been sitting on. "So, before I go to bed, can I make a quick video? I mean the room, the canopy, and all that fancy stuff. It's perfect for my brand."

So, this is modern day parenting. "Sure, I need to call a friend, anyway."

Jay pauses mid step. "The guy from the Uber?"

"Yes, him, he's very nice."

"Let's hope so, because that last one was a dud. Remember what I said."

"What did you say?"

"Try not to act too thirsty. You don't want him to know he's got you pressed."

"Pressed like a panini?" I say. "Oh, I won't." I chase her playfully up the stairs. "I'll just tell him he's my handsome prince, and we're getting married next weekend, that I already have the dress and the rings. Does that sound thirsty? What if I tell him that I already took the liberty of changing my name to Yamamoto? Does that sound pressed?"

Jay pauses. "Yamamoto, now that's impressive. You've gone international. You know people love mixed couples. You two could start a blog."

"Blog this," I say, as I hunch my shoulders crossways, hump my back, and stagger around on the upstairs landing all Quasimodo style.

"And this," Jay says, going into her room and standing in the doorway, "is why you have no friends." She shuts the panel doors to our rooms. In a few minutes, I hear music playing, and her talking to herself. I assume she's making her video. I resist the urge to burst through the sliding doors and make a crazy appearance on her film; instead I dial Ryan. It's a strange number, so he doesn't pick up. I leave a message. Thirty seconds later, my phone rings.

"What's going on? The last thing I heard you were back in town and now you're outside of Brunswick, with a burner phone?"

I can feel my defenses melt just from the sound of Ryan's voice. I really wish he was with me so he could put his arms around me and tell me everything will be okay. I guess I'll have to settle for comfort over the phone for now. "Two guys with some kind of big guns, maybe AR-15s, broke into my house. I managed to get out the back with Jay. The two of us had just finished watching a movie when they showed up. I didn't know where to go or what to do. So, I brought Jay here, to my Grandma Prue's house. I thought it would be a good place to hide out."

"You should have called me, you could have stayed at my place. Look give me the directions to where you are because I'm coming there right now."

"Don't, they probably know about you, and are tracking you. If you come here, it could lead them right to us. Suni already went by my house yesterday and talked to Jay."

Ryan sounds confused. "How could Suni have been at your house yesterday? She was in Baltimore. I watched her speech about Brett and Maisy on the news. I saw clips of her handing out potato salad dressed all in black at the barbeque."

I haven't figured this part out yet. How Suni can be two places at once, but I have my theories. "I know, it's all super weird, but after I

106

report everything to the CIA tomorrow, it'll be up to them to figure out. I've taken this concerned citizen bit as far as I'm willing to go, after tomorrow this whole thing is over, and then you and I can go out on our date."

"I still don't like it."

"What?"

"You being all alone with a child, and me not being there to protect you. I could take precautions, make sure I'm not followed."

"It's not that I don't want you to come, believe me I do. It's just that I think we're okay right now, we're both settled down ready to go to bed. The driveway is gated so no one can just drive in, all the doors and windows are locked, and I know it's silly, but I just have this strong sense that Grandma Prue wouldn't let anything happen to us here."

Ryan relents reluctantly. "All right, I trust you, and if the ghost of Grandma Prue is standing guard than who am I to interfere?"

I laugh. "I can't wait to see you again."

"I know, what about tomorrow night? After all this is finished? Where are you going? Even if the CIA believes you, you can't go back to your house in town."

"No, you're right. I hadn't thought of that." I mull it over for a minute.

"Then it's settled, you'll come to my place. I have a quiet guest room, clean sheets, my kitchen is mostly tidy. I have no food, but we can order takeout. What do you say?"

I don't hesitate. "I say yes."

"All right, then it's a plan. See you tomorrow at my place. I'll text you the address. And Maverick?"

"Yes?"

"I really like you so no sheroics. If something seems weird, or you hear a strange sound, call the police. Got me?"

"Yep, crystal clear. Goodnight Ryan. I'll call you in the morning."

"Goodnight Maverick, sweet dreams."

It seems like it's settled down next door when I get off the phone. I slide the panel door back a bit and look through the crack. Jay is in bed asleep. She left a bedside lamp on so she could see. I thought it would be smart if we both slept in our clothes with our shoes ready, just in case something happens. But like I told Ryan on the phone, this place is practically a fortress. It has secrets no one but Grandma Prue and I knew. If they do come for us here, they'll be on my turf, not theirs, and that would be a major win for me and a big disadvantage for them. I slide the door closed, pull out the couch bed, and make it up with sheets and blankets out of the linen closet.

I plod down the hall to the master bedroom, take my favorite photo of Grandma Prue off the dresser, go back to the study and put it on the side table where I can see it. I know she's watching over us and she won't let anything happen. I'm certain of it. I slide into bed. It's lumpy, but not bad. I'll have to buy a new mattress when Ryan and I get married and take over the place. I smile to myself in the dark, Maverick Yamamoto. Surely that's not thirsty? A wedding in June, the 20th, the longest day of the year, just like our marriage will be, long, and happy, and blessed. Okay, maybe I am getting a little ahead of myself, but I can't help it. It's only been a few days, but I'm already in love. I start thinking of children's names. I imagine us having twins, the names Hazel and Hedley are at the top of my list when I drift off.

Yellow WallPapered

I didn't think I'd sleep through the whole night, but I was wrong. I wake up in the morning and blink at the clear light that shines in through the windows. The house has good vibes, safe vibes. Jay is right, I should really think about moving here. I tiptoe across the study, slide back the panel doors, but Jay is already gone, her bed perfectly made. I find her in the conservatory, all the plants are gone, I gave them away to the many friends of Grandma Prue who came in and out of the house in the weeks after she passed. It seemed like the best way to give each of them a piece of her that would go on living.

"It's nice in here, huh?"

Jay stops mid spin and looks over her shoulder at me. "I could live here forever."

"Me too, hey, you want some breakfast? We need to get a move on if I'm going to drop you off in time."

"Can't we just stay here? Pretend like none of this is happening and we're princesses of our own magical land?"

"I wish. No, I have to go to Langley so I can give them the dirt on Suni."

Jay nods her head. "I understand, maybe some other time when you're done saving America."

"It's a date. Come on."

I toast up the healthy waffles we bought, heat real maple syrup, slather it all with a pat of vegan butter, and put some strawberries on the side.

"This is good," Jay says between bites. "I usually eat breakfast at school."

"Maybe I can take you grocery shopping once in a while. You can get some things you like and keep them at home. You're old enough to use a toaster, you could make waffles like these for yourself."

"I'd rather live with you," Jay mumbles into her almond milk.

"I would too, sweetie. I would, too."

There's nothing more to say. I'm not her mom and I'm not even morally sure she should be with me right now, except we have no idea where her mom is, no way of contacting her mom, and no relatives in the vicinity. So, I guess short of turning her over to Child Protective Services, which I don't plan to do, I've been unofficially elected as her current guardian.

"Hey, we're together now, and great things are going to happen. Suni is going to get busted. Who knows, they might even give me a reward." I drift, dreaming about a ceremony, a medal, one of those giant cardboard checks in my honor. I'm not a vain person, but hey, everyone needs a little fantasy in their life every once in a while.

Jay finishes eating and I clean up, then clamber back upstairs. I rummage around for something professional to put on. Since I didn't dare go back into my house after the gunmen shot it up, I don't have any of my clothes with me. I settle on an outfit I feel pretty okay with, and traipse down to the kitchen. Jay is at the kitchen table looking at her phone.

"You ready?"

Jay grabs her backpack in response and I get my purse and a set of keys off the rack in the office.

"This way." I lead the way through a series of corridors until we end up at the garage. The old castle didn't originally have a garage, but Grandma Prue had a gym, a mudroom, and the garage added and then connected them all. It blends seamlessly you would never know it's not original.

"Whose is that?"

Jay's jaw drops as I press the key fob and unlock the black Land Rover Defender 110, that used to be Grandma Prue's. It's a 2018 imported from Australia. Grandma Prue had it converted to left-hand drive. It goes beyond bad, it's El Diablo cool.

Jay whistles as she walks around the car. "This is what I call a ride. Is this yours?"

"No, it's my Grandma Prue's, but it comes with the house. So, yeah. I guess it's mine now," it feels weird to say.

"What did your Grandfather do?" Jay asks incredulously. "I mean a castle, a car like this, none of that comes cheap."

"Grandpa Merv worked for the CIA, but I have to say I'm a little shocked at your reasoning. The question you should be asking is what did Grandma Prue do? She's the one who bought the house, the car, everything."

"Wow, I'm impressed. Well, what did she do?"

"Well." I open the garage door back out and make sure it closes. I scan the property as we go down the drive. "She wrote books, mystery novels. See, she traveled the world with Grandpa Merv for his job and she went to all these far-off places, exotic locales, and met all kinds of people. Later in her life, after I was born, ideas just started coming to her, books with twists and turns, and characters she said were so real it was like she knew them. So, she wrote all the stories down, and then she managed to get them published. Ever heard of the *Fiona McTavish* mystery series?"

"I love those books." Jay claps with enthusiasm. "Your Grandmother was Lady Ethel Holmes?"

I laugh. "Obviously that was just her pen name, but yeah, that was her."

"Why haven't you ever told me any of this? Your cool points just tripled."

"I didn't know you were keeping score or I would have. Now that I have triple digit cool points, can I ask you a question?"

We're on the highway now, cruising along, half an hour and we'll be at Jay's school just in time for the bell.

"Sure, we have no secrets from each other."

"Are you happy, living with your mom?"

Jay lets out a sigh and looks intently out the passenger side window. "I knew what I was getting into," she says in a voice that is startlingly adult. "What choice did I really have? Become a foster kid? My dad already did that, and he didn't want that for me. Dream's not bad, I mean she loves me in her own way, she's not like your mother."

"You mean Barbara?"

"Precisely. I mean Dream may not be mother of the year material, but she always says nice things about me and to me. She thinks I'm

111

smart, she wants me to be more than what she is, she believes in me. I've seen your mom when she comes to visit, all she does is criticize everything about you and your choices. Plus, she's cold, she never gives you a hug when she leaves. She's more like a frenemy than a mom."

I can't argue with her; all her observations are very astute. *From the mouths of babes*, they say, and it couldn't be truer. I'm surprised she managed to ascertain that much just through watching us. Man, she's special. "No ordinary girl," Grandma Prue would have said, and she would have been right.

"Plus, your brother, that's she's always talking about, no offense," she shoots a look at me before she goes on, "he's not all that, personally he seems kind of khaki, inside and out."

"Khaki?"

"How to put this in terms you'll understand. He's beige through and through, no moxie."

"Oh, yeah, a dweeb, although I must admit, I like to tell people that racially I may be a mix of things but my DNA is one hundred percent dork."

Jay rolls her eyes. "Charming."

I clear my throat. I feel like I'm losing cool points fast. "Well, there's no doubt about his life in khaki, but Brandon's not all bad. I mean he's the one that got me into 80s movies and music, and every Christmas Eve we wear onesie pajama's and watch *Home Alone*. He can be a major pain, that's for sure, but he has some saving graces." I'm not sure why I'm feeling all nostalgic about Brandon, especially after the way he backstabed me.

Jay let's out a sigh. "Mark my words once a scapegoat, always a scapegoat, keep your guard up, and whatever you do, trust no one."

"Harsh words for this early in the morning."

Jay shrugs. "That's life, only the strong survive."

"On that note." I hit the radio. KT Tunstall's, "Suddenly I See," comes on, I turn it up. Jay and I sing, "Her face is a map of the world, is a map of the world," and it couldn't be truer.

"Drop me off here." Jay points to a faded curb.

We're still a block from the school, so I'm surprised she wants me to stop. "Are you sure? It's no problem. I can take you the whole way. I have time it's not like I have an appointment with anyone at the CIA. I'm just going to show up and hope for the best." I realize how dubious it all sounds as I say it and Jay gives me a weird look before she answers.

"No, I'm sure. You, this ride, it'll prompt too many questions. I fly under the radar here, no one needs to know my true identity."

"Got ya." I can understand her desire to just blend. "Do you want me to park here when I come back for you at three?"

Jay looks surprised. "You're coming back for me?"

"Well, we still haven't found your mom and under the circumstances I don't think it's safe for you to stay in your apartment alone. Like I said before, if you have a friend, or a relative?"

Jay cuts me off. "There's no one. I know that's hard to truly comprehend, but it's just me and Dream. Ok, sure, park here. I'll walk over. See you at three." She slides out of the car, and trudges off.

After this whole thing with Suni is over, I'm going to see what more I can do for Jay. She has great resolve, and great plans for her life, but she needs someone with a steady hand, someone like Grandma Prue was for me, and I'd be honored to be that person for Jay. I wave at her as I pass, she's turning into the school parking lot so I know she's safe. Here goes.

Morning traffic is heavier than I expected, it takes me a full two hours to navigate to Langley. The CIA headquarters building is impressive, and surrounded by miles of barbed wire and fencing, a guard booth is waving in a long queue of cars. Crap, this is the part I hadn't thought about and didn't plan for as I drove over here. You can't just waltz into CIA headquarters and say you've found a Russian operative that's running for president. The line of cars I'm in inches along, think fast, think fast, think fast. Oy, it's my turn. I show my ID. The prefect idea comes to me.

"I'm here to see Bob Perkins, he's expecting me. I'm Merv Robertson's granddaughter." The guard consults his list. He stalks into his hut to make a call.

Bob is an old friend of Grandpa Merv's, he's a few years younger than my dad so I doubt he's retired yet. Merv mentored him when he was just starting with the agency. I doubt he'll remember me, but it's worth a shot. To my chagrin the guard comes back, waves me through, and tells me where to park. I empty my purse of anything suspicious and walk towards the building. It's nothing special, just an ordinary office complex, but looks can be deceiving and I know I'm about to enter one of the most powerful places on the planet.

I get through the security check with most of my dignity. Bob is there waiting on the other side.

"Maverick." He throws his arms open like we're old friends. I'm a little surprised, but I give him a hug. "I'm so glad to see you. It's been what, ten years since I last saw you? You'd just graduated college. Your Grandpa was so proud."

"Right, yeah, I remember." This is going better than I thought. I follow him up to his office. He's obviously risen through the ranks since he was mentored by Grandpa Merv, a corner office, and a window. I look at the poor schlubs in their cubes as I pass and think with dread that after this I'm going to have to find a new job.

"So, I think I know what brings you today, Maverick." Bob is across from me at his desk, his fingers are folded over his hands except his index fingers which are steepled. I feel like he's about to play that game, here's the church, here's the steeple, open the doors and see all the people.

I'm filled with relief. He already knows. I relax and start to feel hopeful. Of course, the CIA would be on to Suni, and here I thought I was about to make some big revelation. "You already know about it? About Suni? About her crimes against America? Who she really is? I should have known you guys would have her number. I mean you're the best and brightest in the world, nothing gets past you. Did you get my phone? The evidence I sent? Is that how you know?"

Bob looks at me with pity. "Your mom called here Maverick. She and your brother Brandon are very worried about you. They understand that you've been under immense pressure and it's finally made you," he does some swirling motion near his head with his hand and I'm instantly offended. "A little off balance," he finally says, in a sympathetic tone of voice, all hushed and soft, as though I'm about to lose it at any minute.

"I have proof," I say a little too loud, as I lean a little too aggressively into Bob's desk. I'm trying to play it cool, but I'm a little annoyed that he seems to have already made up his mind before he's even given me a chance to explain anything.

"Whoa, whoa, there's no reason to get agitated." Bob waves a calming hand at me as though I'm a horse. "Look Maverick," he leans over his desk and I feel like it's story time. "Your Grandpa was a great guy."

I nod my head in agreement.

"One of the best, and his reputation still means something around here. That's why I agreed to talk to you. Your family loves you, they're just worried about you. And Suni is too, she's not even mad, what with the shootings at her offices, and everything else it's understandable that your mental state would be fragile."

"My mental state is not fragile," I say with vehemence, but even as I speak I know I'm not helping my case. My hair is puffed out all crazy, and the trouser suit I borrowed from Grandma Prue's closet makes me look like I'm playing dress up. Grandma Prue was tall, I'm a little above average height, but the pants are still several inches too long. I thought I could pull it off because I belted the whole thing, but now I feel like I'm teetering somewhere between bag lady and nut job.

"Would you like a drink of water?" Bob gets up from his desk and grabs a bottle out of a mini fridge in the corner.

"I don't use single use water bottles." I huff, not even trying to dial down the crazy. What's the point? Besides, single use plastic bottles are one of my biggest pet peeves. Want to save the world, kids? Stop using single use plastic bottles! Ugh, it makes me itch. I scratch a little and look at Bob who regards me curiously.

"Okay." Bob takes a sip of his water, sits back down at his desk, and thinks for a minute before speaking. "So, just for the sake of covering all our bases why don't you tell me why you think your boss Suni, is a Russian operative?"

Finally, now is my chance to tell it like it is, and Bob will understand what I've been trying to tell him all along. I start to talk. It spills out in a jumble. I talk too fast and have to go back and connect things I've already told to things I haven't told yet. It takes me twenty minutes, but in the end, I think I lay it out pretty good. From where I sit, Suni's goose is cooked.

"And you say you sent your cell phone to the head of our agency, and that it has all the proof to back up everything you're saying, right?"

"Right."

"Hold on a second." Bob picks up his phone to make a call. I let out a sigh, sit back in my chair, and work my tongue around my dry mouth. "Helen, hi, this is Bob. I was just wondering if you'd gotten any mail from a Maverick Malone? It's a Manila envelope with a cell phone inside. Yes, I'll wait." He makes a face at me like being on hold is such a pain, and shuffles through some papers on his desk.

My cell phone isn't the only copy of the proof I have. I made dozens of copies, they're stashed in different places. I could offer him more proof, but I'm starting to wonder how much I can share with Bob. It seems like his mind is already made up. Like Everest was right about trying to whistle blow on Suni. Everyone is only humoring you and whatever proof you offer, whatever case you make will just disappear and nothing will happen except Suni will grow more powerful. I wish Ryan could have come with me so I would have someone else to back me up and help me assess the situation. I study Bob while he talks on the phone.

"Okay, great, and you're sure it didn't come a few days ago, or anything like that? Right, okay. I know Helen. Give my regards to Joe and the kids. Yep, of course. Sure. You too, Helen. Thanks for doing

116

that for me, I owe you one. All right. Bye." Bob hangs up with an air of gravitas. "They don't have a package from you Maverick and there's no record that they've received anything like that in the past few days."

"It just hasn't arrived yet," I insist. "I mailed it yesterday. It'll probably get here tomorrow."

"Well, we'll be on the lookout for it." Bob's voice is condescending, like I'm a child.

"Look I'm not making any of this up. This is real. It's all really happening. Suni is a Russian plant. She's trying to destroy our country, she's dangerous, she's probably the one who killed Brett and Maisy, my coworkers."

"We already looked into that. Suni was in Baltimore at the time of the murders."

"No, you don't understand, she can be in two places at once. I've seen the proof. You have to believe me. You have to stop her before it's too late. She has people in high places, probably even here. This isn't some demented fantasy I'm having, this is real life, and you need to listen."

Bob looks at me with pity, starts to open his mouth to speak but the phone on his desk buzzes, he picks it up. "Yes? I see. Okay. Right away. Thank you for telling me."

"My phone, did they find my phone?"

"No, not quite. Do you want to come with me?"

I'm not sure what all this is about, but I grab my stuff and follow him anyway, back through the maze of soulless cubes, and into the hall. He pushes open the door to a room and I follow him inside.

"Mavie, my goodness, what's happened to you?"

The sight that greets me is beyond horrifying. I'm not getting arrested, questioned under hot lights, or tortured until I spill my guts. It's much, much worse, he's had someone call Barbara and Brandon. They rise from the conference table and stand awkwardly. Barbara clutches Brandon's arm for support. This is the last thing I need. Well, it's gonna be one heck of a scene, I can tell you that.

"I'm fine." I push a lock of hair back behind my ear. "You shouldn't be here. I'm trying to report all the information I have about Suni to the CIA. They need to investigate her. Stop her before she gets elected president and destroys our country. I know you don't believe me, but you're wrong. I have proof, lots of it, and I'm not going to stop until someone actually listens to me."

Brandon shakes his head. "This is just so hard to watch," he says to Barbara, before he turns to me and starts talking in a loud slow voice, like I've lost my ability to hear and comprehend at the same time. "Maverick, you're hallucinating, all these crackpot ideas you have about Suni are just not true. You made them up because you can't handle the fact that your life is going nowhere and you're probably destined to die alone."

I stiffen. How dare he? If anyone is going to die alone, it's going to be him.

"She's been a little off ever since our Grandma Prue died," Brandon says in an aside to Bob. "They were very close." He turns back to me. "Look we just want to help you. Mom and I found a nice place you can go for a couple of weeks to relax and help your mind get better." He holds out a brochure. Magic Meadows, it says, a mental health wellness retreat.

"You're trying to commit me?" I scream. "You honestly think I'm crazy? The only crazy ones here are you. I'm telling you Suni isn't who she says she is, I know it. I'm the only one that does, and I have to stop her. Don't you understand? Don't any of you understand?"

Barbara clicks her tongue. "She's never been very mentally strong, not the smartest either. When she was three, I found her eating glue, she's never been the same since. What can you do? We tried our best, thank goodness we have Brandon. We really appreciate you doing this for us Bob, you've been so kind. This is such an embarrassment. We're a good upstanding family, but Mavie's just so eaten up with jealousy. She just can't stand it that Suni is vibrant and successful and Mavie's..." her voice trails off. "Well, look at her. Need I say more? Oh, it's just shocking, shocking. I raised her better than this. Now Mavie," she also addresses me in an extra loud voice. "It's time for us to go. Your father is waiting downstairs in the car and we're going to drive you straight to Magic Meadows so you can get some help. Don't fight us, we're doing this for your own good. And don't worry about your job, we told Suni everything, and she already forgives you. She said you'd been acting erratic the past few days, even spouting nonsense at times. She said it was so bad that she had to get someone else to fill in for you at your job, Amy from Delaware. I've read some posts, they're great, Amy is a very talented writer."

I actually let out a low primal growl when I hear this. Not once has Barbara ever complimented any of my work and now she's talking up Amy from Delaware, and they're the ones who've told Suni everything? Who needs enemies when you've got a family like mine. I make a snap decision.

"Amy from Delaware can get stuffed and so can the two of you. I'm not going to stop telling people about Suni. I know people, you two aren't the only ones who have connections." I don't in fact know anyone, but these two numpties don't need to know that, especially after they've sold me out.

Barbara gives Brandon a head nod and they start advancing towards me. Bob is by the door. I move fast, bum rush Bob, push him aside, and run out into the hall. I semi remember the way back and out of the building. I don't waste any time. I book it.

I hear Bob, somewhere back there calling for people but I dust him quick, run through the lobby and out the doors, before they can stop me. Sometimes it pays to be a wiry little thing. I'm out of breath by the time I make it to the car, but I don't stop to rest. I turn the engine, blast out of the lot, right past the guard booth and out to freedom. I get to the highway as fast as possible. I keep checking my rearview mirror, but no one seems to be following me. "Those rats," I scream. I'm not surprised that Brandon and Barbara would go out of their way to undermine me. It's not the first and I'm sure it won't be the last. I have no idea what the plan is now, but I know one thing.

We meet at the Founding Farmers on Pennsylvania Avenue, not far from the DOJ. Ryan looks crisp in his navy-blue suit and red tie. He's already ordered me a salad by the time I get there. I pull out a chair and sit down warily. Ryan extends his hand across the white tablecloth, and I take it. I look up and into his eyes and see so much compassion, so much understanding, it makes me choke up a little. I'm not used to people looking at me like that.

"So, what happened?" he asks, pulling back as the waitress sets an appetizer platter in front of us. I order a lemonade and start the story.

"More like what didn't happen," I say taking a bite of fried green tomato.

"Are they going to investigate Suni?" Ryan eats a deviled egg with ham.

"More like they're going to investigate me. They think I'm crazy. Who knows, I may have just made myself a suspect in the murders of Brett and Maisy. It all went bad, really bad, worse than bad. I ran away. They were trying to lock me up at some place called Magic Meadows, a mental health retreat," I say mockingly.

"Wait, I'm confused. Who was trying to lock you up? The people you went to see at the CIA?"

"No, I went to see an old friend of Grandpa Merv's, but Barbara and Brandon were already one step ahead of me. They'd already called him, and warned him about me, they said I had a 'psychotic break' with reality." I use air quotes when I say 'psychotic break.' "Show me one person on this Earth who hasn't had a 'psychotic break' of some kind?" A fresh batch of outrage assails me as I think about how disloyal my family is. Who do Brandon and Barbara think they are, anyway? "I tried to tell Bob, everything I know about Suni, but since Barbara and Brandon had already warned him that I was mentally unwell, he treated me like I was some lunatic, psycho, and just disregarded everything I said. I have the videos I showed you on a flash drive, but I felt like he would just confiscate the evidence and that would be the end of that. I don't want to play that game, if they're not willing to listen to me, I'll keep going until I find someone who is."

Ryan nods his head. "That's the way," he says with a discrete fist pump.

Goodness, he's dishy! I take a sip of lemonade and go on with the story. "When I got finished telling Bob the facts, he led me to a conference room where Brandon and Barbara were waiting. They tried to take me by force, but I dodged them and ran out of the building."

Ryan looks impressed. "Wait, let me get this straight. You ran out of the CIA building with people who were trying to have you committed to an insane asylum chasing you? That's awesome. You're the coolest girlfriend I've ever had."

I pause mid bite at the declaration, girlfriend? I have to ask. "Girlfriend, as in a girl who is a friend, or girlfriend?"

"My crazy new girlfriend," Ryan jokes.

I smile, blush a little, it's good. I like him a lot too. It hits me. "Oh, I didn't tell you the worst part. Brandon and Barbara told Suni everything. Bob told me about it, and the two of them admitted it to my face, like they were doing me some big favor by selling me out to Suni. I would be gutted if it wasn't so typical. So, anyway, Suni knows we're on to her, and that we have proof."

The smile fades from Ryan's face. "I think it's time to play our ace in the hole."

"We have an ace in the hole?"

"You bet we do. You didn't think I'd let you run around, risk your life, and hatch all these plans without some kind of trick up my sleeve, did you? No, you're my woman now and I intend to watch out for you. I'll just step out in a minute and make a few phone calls. If that's all right with you? I tell you the plan when I get back and we can discuss everything."

I hear what he's saying, and it's registering, but I can't answer back because I'm swooning at the same time. I love how he's so take charge, masculine, and at the same time nurturing and understanding. It's all I can do to stop myself from declaring my undying love for him. And the fact that he called me his woman, it's so caveman—I can't even. I mean, I'm a liberated woman of the modern age, but hot is hot, and I'm definitely willing to be his woman. I take another sip of lemonade and try to cool myself down. I watch as he scrolls through his contacts.

Before he can leave the waitress whips away the empty appetizer plates, puts a crisp green salad with all the fixings in front of me, and butternut squash ravioli in front of Ryan. He waits till she's done, lifts his cell phone like it's a moment of triumph and winks at me.

"Go ahead and eat. Have some of my pasta if you want. I'll be right back." He walks through the restaurant and out the double doors with assurance, waves at me from the sidewalk, and starts to talk on his phone.

Grandma Prue was less than fond of Kyle. I suppose she could see him for who he was, while I was blinded by love and insecurity. I'm absolutely certain that she would love Ryan though, and that makes me feel a little emotional. His whole clear minded, protective man routine is just the kind of guy I've been looking for my whole life. I know without a doubt he will open car doors, just doors in general for me, treat me like a lady, and an equal, in my book that is what defines a real man, and I can tell Ryan is one.

I don't want to get ahead of myself or jinx anything, but I'm pretty sure we really are going to get married. I taste his pasta, it's delicious. I eat my salad while dreaming of our June wedding. I already know the dress style I want, and of course I'll wear my hair down, long and cascading, totally Pre-Raphaelite, that's my style. I'm so enmeshed in the dream I jump a little when Ryan comes back to the table and pulls out his chair.

"Sorry, I didn't mean to scare you." Ryan grabs his napkin and sits down.

"Oh, no, it's all right, I was just thinking," I say, pulling myself back from the dream realm to reality.

Ryan tries the ravioli. "Wow, this is good."

I nod my head in agreement. "So, what's the plan?"

Ryan puts down his fork. "The plan is for us to travel to Florida. I have a contact down there, Jack Snyder. I worked with him on a case. I've already told him the basics of what's going on and he thinks he can help. He was a Russian actor for the CIA for thirty years. He actually thinks he remembers coming across Suni years ago, she would have been young, about seventeen."

"Right before she showed up at the high school and burst onto the cross-country ski scene."

"Exactly. Anyway, if we can get down there in the next couple of days, he's willing to meet with us."

"Sounds good. I'm all in." There's just one thing. "What about Jay? I still don't know where her mom is. Should we really cross state lines with a minor? She has no other family, and I don't know anyone else she can stay with and we can't leave her alone in her apartment, not with Suni already knowing who she is."

"Well, it looks like the decision is already made then. Besides, what's one more crime in a long list."

"I like how you think." I joke.

"We just need to get some wheels. Should we hot wire a car after we blow this pop stand?"

"Oh, I think I have that covered. Eat up."

We finish our meals. Ryan pays the check and leaves a generous tip for the waitress. I tell him to follow me. He's as impressed with my ride as Jay was. I toss him the keys and tell him he can drive to his apartment. He's taken the rest of the week off. He told his boss it was a family emergency. We plan to pack and be ready to go when Jay is finished with school at three. We only have a few hours to make it all happen.

Ryan's apartment is nice, but nondescript. A condo tower block, glass balcony railings, a view of the city, two bedrooms, a perfect box. Ryan's style is mid-century mod, eclectic, and even though it's all cookie cutter, his flair makes it feel homey and unique. I sink down on the ink blue velvet couch while he packs.

"If anyone can help us, it's definitely Jack," Ryan calls from his bedroom. "He's got crazy stories about stuff he's seen, done, and those are just the things he can tell civilians. Imagine all the stuff he can't tell us."

123

"I'm just glad he's already clocked Suni and remembers seeing her. Who knows, maybe he can help us find some additional proof that ties her to Russia."

"I hope so." Ryan comes out of his room with a leather duffle all packed. "You want anything to drink or eat before we go?"

"I'm good. I guess we better just hit the road and pick up, Jay."

Jay's face is a picture when she comes out and see's Ryan at the wheel. I hop out of the passenger side and open the back door for her. We brought her a snack of hummus and veggies, and some juice. I offer it to her. She sets herself up in the back seat, gets comfortable, and eats her snack.

"There's been a change of plans," I start to say.

"Let me guess," Jay interrupts. "The people at the CIA thought you were crazy and now we're going to find some grizzled old cop or someone like that who believes you and is going to help us."

"How did you know?" I ask.

"Oh, please," Jay rolls her eyes. "This is playing out like every movie about this kind of situation ever, only it's full of multi-racial characters for a twist."

"Well, okay then." I lean back against the headrest, happy that we're in Ryan's capable hands. Traffic hasn't picked up yet, and we're already a few miles out of the city. "I'm glad you're holding up. I thought you'd be worried."

Jay looks out the window and shrugs. "Me, nah, I trust you. But one thing, where are we going?"

"Florida," I say. "Home of Disney World, except we're going to Cocoa Beach, but it's only like sixty miles from Orlando. We could try to go to Disney World, or if you don't want to do that, we can hit the beach or something while we're there."

"Cocoa Beach," Jay says with excitement. "It's only five miles away from Cape Canaveral, home of the Kennedy Space Center. Do you know what this means?" Jay is practically bouncing on the seat with excitement. She whips out her phone and starts to Google. "Can we go on a tour?"

124

"Sure, that sounds fun. When did you get this obsession for space?"

"Are you kidding, since you showed me that movie I've learned everything about Space Camp. The main camp is in Alabama. I plan to go there someday. You get to stay for a whole week." Jay claps her hands with excitement at the thought. "Did you know that even if you're an adult you can still go to Space Camp because they have one for adults?"

This is welcome news to me. I imagine myself in blue NASA coveralls whirling in the anti-gravity chair, or whatever that thing is that spins all your g-forces, adult Space Camp is a go with me. Wow, I can't believe I've inspired the younger generation with my penchant for 80s movies. I see *Say Anything* in Jay and I's future watching endeavors, after she gets a lot older of course. Who hasn't hoped they would meet a guy who would copy that boom box scene? Oh, là là, the height of romance.

"What movie did you watch?" Ryan asks Jay.

"Maverick showed me this old movie from the 80s, *Space Camp*. It was kind of corny, but kind of cool. It made me really want to go to the real Space Camp."

"I love that movie," Ryan says winning more points with me than he could ever lose. "*Must send Max to space,*" he says in a robot voice, and I'm even more determined that he and I are getting married in June.

Jay and I both fall asleep and when we wake up its dark.

"You two hungry?" Ryan asks.

We agree we could eat, and Ryan pulls off at an exit with a diner. We pile into a booth, Ryan orders coffee, Jay orders a club sandwich and a strawberry shake. Ryan says that sounds good, and orders the same. I get tomato soup with grilled cheese. I need serious comfort food right now. I can tell it makes Jay happy that Ryan copies her order, it's cool that they get along with each other so easily. Ryan is a natural with kids.

I munch my grilled cheese and tell Ryan my thoughts. "Should we get a hotel room somewhere in town, or do you want me to drive?"

Ryan shakes it off. "I'm fine. I've already got a hotel suite reserved for us when we get there. The hotel even has a pool," he says to Jay.

"I don't have my suit." She looks kinda sad for a minute. "I know how to swim though, my dad taught me when I was three. He always loved the water. He used to dream of going surfing. That's another thing I've always wanted to try, surfing. Maybe if there's time we can visit the space center and try surfing. Oh, and eat fish and chips. I know that's British, but I really want to try it."

The whole plan sounds great, the food, the activities are spot on. I don't need any convincing, I'm already in. Besides, we can't really drive this whole way and do nothing more than meet with Ryan's contact, Jack. We may as well have some fun and live it up while we can. This may be our last chance if Suni finds us and kills us all. The thought makes me swallow hard, but I push it back. I've always been a live for today, gal. Why change?

I look at Jay. "Well, we can check at the hotel and see if they give surf lessons, or if they know a company that does. It's on my bucket list too, so I'm all in."

"I've always wanted to try it myself." Ryan says, concaving his face as he tries to drink the thick shake through a straw.

Jay beams. "I like you," she says to Ryan. "I told Maverick the first time I saw you that you were promising and she shouldn't be too thirsty with you. So far she's doing a pretty good job."

Ryan laughs. "Well, thanks for putting in a good word. I like you too, in fact I have a sister only a few years older than you. She's a very talented ice skater."

Jay considers a moment. "That's cool. What's her name?"

"Pear," Ryan says around a bite of sandwich.

Jay makes a face.

"Don't ask," he says and they both giggle. It couldn't be going any better.

We get to the hotel late, but the receptionist is super nice, and checks us in without a fuss. The hotel is beachfront. It has a covered bar with a tiki theme, several pools, and is right on the beach.

"This looks expensive," I say as we walk into the suite Ryan's booked for us. There's a dining table for four, a family room with a couch and several comfortable chairs, a fireplace, and glass doors that lead out to the beach. I can hear the crash of ocean waves. It would be the perfect place for a vacation, if this was one.

"Don't worry about the money, I've got it covered. I've been working for the DOJ for years and I have yet to spend any of my salary, all I do is work." Ryan motions towards the bedroom. "I thought you girls could take the room, and I'll sleep on the pull-out sofa."

Part of me wants to tell him that Jay can take the sofa, and he and I can take the room, but I don't want to rush anything, or be a bad influence on Jay.

"Sounds great," I say.

I don't have any luggage, but I walk into the bedroom with Jay, anyway. It's nice, the bed looks soft and I can tell the sheets have a good thread count. Ryan is pure class; this place is amazing. Jay's so tired I don't even insist she brush her teeth. I just help her take off her tennis shoes and she lies down on the bed and falls into a deep sleep immediately. I go into the bathroom and survey my face in the mirror. I look stressed out, lines are etched around my mouth. I turn on the tap, splash some cold water on my neck, wash my hands, and then wander out to the family room with Ryan. He's pulled his bed out, but he's not in it. He's looking at the ocean through the long glass windows.

"Aren't you tired?" I stand behind him, reach up and rub his shoulders. He lets out a sigh and rolls his neck.

"That feels great. I'm tired, but all that coffee I drank is keeping me awake. Is Jay crashed out?"

"Yeah," I say giving Ryan one last rub, before I walk over and drop into an armchair. "She's zonked."

"I don't blame her, poor kid. What's the story with her? She's super cool. I can't imagine any parent not treasuring her. She's so smart and ambitious."

"I know." I'm happy he likes Jay, she's part of my life now, there's no way I'm ever not going to know if she's okay again. "Her mom had her when she was young, only thirteen."

Ryan lets out a low whistle. "Wow, just a baby herself."

"Yeah, her dad was fourteen, but he just stepped up to the plate. I guess he was a foster kid and when he had Jay he just made the decision to grow up. He had custody of her until three years ago when he passed away from cancer. He was only twenty-one. So, now she lives with her mom. I think Dream does the best she can, but like Jay says herself, 'Dream's not mother of the year material.'" I shrug.

"No wonder Jay's so wise beyond her years. That's a lot of heartbreak to navigate at such a young age, but at least now she has us."

I can't help the huge smile that comes. "She does."

We give each other a kiss on the lips that could go much, much deeper if we let it, but despite the beautiful surroundings the time just isn't right. We go to our own beds. I fall asleep as soon as I lie down.

Jay's up early in the morning, but she doesn't flip on cartoons, or jump up and down on the bed or anything you would expect a kid to do. So, Ryan and I don't even register that's she's awake. We snooze till a little after eleven. When I trudge out from the bedroom I find her on the patio, outside the sliding glass doors of our suite, she's staring at the horizon, watching the ocean meet the sky.

"You okay? You hungry?" I ask.

Jay raises a mug at me, the string from a bag of tea hangs over the side. "They had stuff for tea in the kitchen so I made some. We could order brunch."

I ask Ryan what he wants and place the order. I'm going to need to buy some clothes. Ryan comes out from the bathroom right as they wheel in brunch. We sit at the table and swap bites of Belgian waffles, French toast, and fluffy pancakes. The coffee is hot and strong. I drink my limit, two cups.

After we eat, Ryan and Jay play outside on the beach while I take a quick shower. We hit the Ron Jon Surf Shop on our way over to Jack's house. He's expecting us mid-afternoon, and we have an hour to kill, so I say we go shopping. We find everything we want, more than we need. Jay wears the swimsuit we buy her out of the store underneath a cute t-shirt dress, she's decked out in shades, and a hat.

I push the aviator sunglasses I bought up the bridge of my nose. I went for a boho beachy look and I'm feeling pretty good. Even Ryan, who brought clothes with him got a few surf shirts. We look like total tourists, but we're having fun so we don't care. Ryan lowers the windows, and pops the sun roof as we cruise along the road, sun, sand, and surf at our side. For an instant life feels perfect just the way it should be, and then I remember Suni, and my knees get kind of weak, and I can't believe that my own family betrayed me. But Jay is singing along to "What A Man Gotta Do," by the Jonas Brothers. The wind is blowing in my hair, Ryan's grinning from ear to ear, what more could I want? I give in and choose happy, start to sing too. Reality can wait just a bit.

We pull up to a bright yellow house, with pink doors and shutters, it's only a few blocks from the beach and our hotel.

"This is the place," Ryan says. He jumps out, hurries around to the passenger side, opens my door, and helps Jay out. I slide out of the car. I'm a bit uneasy. Palm trees are planted along the drive. Two white rockers sit empty on the porch. Ryan stands in front and rings the bell, I'm behind him, and Jay is behind me. I trust Ryan's judgement so I know this guy is going to be legit. I just have this creepy feeling like we're being watched. I'm not sure why.

The door swings in and there is who I assume is Jack, he's far from grizzled like Jay thought he would be. He's tall and handsome with distinguished grey hair and a fit physique. He's clean-shaven, with classic features, he has on loose white linen pants and a white linen shirt, his feet are bare. He throws out a "Hey man, long time no see," gives Ryan a one arm hug, smiles at me and Jay over Ryan's shoulder. "You guys come in."

We follow him through the sunny bungalow. I would call the décor *Golden Girl's* chic, wicker furniture with palm tree patterned cushions, tile floors, scatter rugs, and vases in shades of mauve. It's awesome. I half expect Blanche, Dorothy, Rose, and Sophia to come bursting out of the kitchen. The family room at the back of the house has a wall of sliding glass doors, out to the lanai and a pool. A shorter, dark-haired guy that reminds me a lot of Paul Simon is sunning himself on a lounge chair. He looks back and waves as we walk into the room. Iced tea and water are in pitchers on a sterling tray on the coffee table. Jack sits on the couch and motions for us to make ourselves comfortable.

"Do you want a drink, sweetheart?" he asks Jay.

"Sweet tea please," she says with her prettiest manners.

"That's my kind of girl," Jack says. He pours her a glass and raises his eyebrows at me.

"Just water," I say. I'm not a fan of iced tea. Ryan requests water too. Once everyone has drinks, we settle back in our chairs, there's a pause then Jack turns to Jay again.

"I think it would be okay with your parents if you went outside and hung out with Saul for a few minutes so we can talk."

Saul, I almost snicker, the resemblance, rhyming names, it's just too much, "Obvious Child" starts blasting through my head, and I can't get it out.

"I have my suit on." Jay looks down shyly.

I take note, seems she is human after all. I rush into the gap. I feel so protective of her. "It's fine with us if you want to swim as long as Mr. Jack says yes?"

Jay looks at Jack with hope.

"Of course, have Saul show you where we keep the fun stuff. I think we have a unicorn float that you would look great on. Just put some sunscreen on, and there're towels in the cabana. Don't be scared of Saul, he looks meaner than he is."

Jay smiles, stands, places her glass on a coaster, opens the sliding glass door and walks out, and I see her. I mean really see her. The Jay behind the dreams of world domination. The one who's just a little girl with such a long road ahead, and a wave of love hits me. Suddenly I'm kind of grateful to Suni, because she really brought this little impromptu family together for me, and I'm starting to see just how great the future can be, provided we live through this of course. I focus back on what Jack and Ryan are saying. Saul is up out of his lounge chair, showing a delighted Jay the unicorn float and spreading a towel over a lounge chair for her.

Jack has his laptop open. Ryan gave him one of the flash drives and he's watching all the videos. He grunts a little at the one from Alaska, and then looks through everything I've written down on hotel stationary to outline the case, and help organize my thoughts, not like my rambling rant at the CIA.

"Who did you say you saw at the CIA again?" Jack asks me.

"Bob Perkins."

Jack thinks for a minute. "I'm not familiar with him, he must push paperwork. Saul's retired FBI, I'll ask him if he's ever heard of him. As for me, I think Suni is Dasha Pavlova, a Russian operative who was in St. Petersburg in the early two-thousands. Dasha was good, a shapeshifter, you could never quite pin her down. She killed one of our best men. We tried to catch her again and again, but poof she'd just slip away each time. I always wondered what happened to her. I must be losing my edge. I watched Suni Wainwright on T.V. during the debates and I didn't recognize her at all, but seeing these videos. I have no doubt it's her, Dasha. She's infiltrated further than I ever thought she could. She definitely needs to be stopped, but damn she's good. You have to admire that." Jack claps his hands and stands up. "All right folks, I'm just going to step into my study and make a few phone calls. There are some people we're going to need to go see."

Ryan and I nod our heads. I'm just relieved that someone else is finally taking this thing on. Ryan and I step outside with Jay and Saul and introduce ourselves. Saul compliments our new threads. Ryan and I take over loungers and watch Jay splash happily in the pool, while we sip our water.

"Jack making a few phone calls for you folks?" Saul asks over his iced tea.

"Yeah," Ryan confirms. "He said you're retired FBI, and that you might be able to help us too?"

Saul gives Ryan a wink. "Don't worry, Jack and I have been partners on and off the field for over thirty years. He'll tell me everything later. We'll see what we can do for you."

I lean back in my lounger and let the sun warm my skin.

"Oh honey, you need some sunscreen," Saul fusses at me. "Even with skin like a bronze goddess you're still a redhead and prone to freckling and what's cute now isn't at sixty or eighty. No, no, sister, come here and get applied."

I rise like an obedient child and let him spray me with sunscreen. When he's done, he grabs a big floppy hat from the cabana. "Trust one who knows," he says with a wink, as he plops it on my head.

Jack comes out of the house, flashes us a double thumbs up, and I know we're on. He sits on the edge of Saul's lounger and we all talk amiably for an hour. The sun starts to shift so we call Jay out of the pool and get ready to go. This afternoon we're going to try surfing and tomorrow we'll tour the Kennedy Space Center. Then tomorrow night, we'll meet Jack here, and head back to D.C. I'm not sure why but Jack wants to travel at night, he says it's more discreet. We agree to whatever he says cause we figure he knows what he's talking about.

Jack would rather take off right away, but he relents when he sees how much going to the space center means to Jay. Plus, he says since the only person I've actually tried to report anything to at the CIA is a paper pusher who thought I was psychotic anyway, chances are we can buy ourselves a little time. Suni's goons are probably after us, but he doubts they followed us here.

I'm relieved to hear it. I don't know how far this thing is going to go when we get back. If my life will implode? If I'll be fodder for a tabloid press? Headlines like *Maverick goes Rogue: The amazing journey of a woman who single-handedly fought the destruction of our Democracy and won.* It's a little dramatic, and very wordy, and of course I couldn't have done it without Ryan and Jay, but still a girl has a right to dream.

We head back to the hotel. Ryan and I change into our suits. We meet our surf instructor on the beach at three. The water is calm and glassy. It's hot, so it feels good when we wade in after doing practice positions on the shore. I rise and fall, rise and fall, but both Jay and Ryan kind of naturally get it. Before I know it I'm alone in the waves, as Camden our surf instructor cheers Jay and Ryan on and tells them that their naturals. Finally, when I'm water logged, crusted with salt, and the sun is starting to slip behind the horizon, my luck changes. I catch a pretty big wave and ride it all the way into shore. Camden just stands there with his mouth open, his dreaded blond hair full of surprise, but Jay and Ryan, who are worn out and waiting on the beach, revive, jump up and down, hoot and holler like you wouldn't believe. I feel like a champion, and I know no matter what happens with Suni, for them I'm already a shero.

1, 2, 3... Blast Off!

We get to the Kennedy Space Center right as they open, there's a bit of a line but not much. People gape and grin when we roll up because the night before, after Jay fell asleep, after over an hour of Googling I found a local store that sells replica NASA blue coveralls. They're awesome. Ryan volunteered to run out and get them so we could surprise Jay. I swear I saw tears in her eyes when we showed them to her over breakfast.

I have a red tank top on under my coveralls, red canvas sneakers, my sleeves rolled up, and a couple of hemp and bead bracelets I bought from a stand on the beach on my wrist. With my aviator shades on, I feel legit cool. I want to dress like this every day. Ryan and Jay styled their coveralls too and we make quite the picture as we stroll up, shades on, all rocking really big hair. It's something we all have in common. Jay pointed it out while we ate pizza on the patio of our suite last night. We were still wet from surfing, all of our hair was wild, crazy, and very big. We dubbed ourselves The Poof Hair Family. Personally, I like to refer to my hair in princess or Pre-Raphaelite terms, but I can do poof. I do poof very well.

We go through the self-serve ticket line, get right in, head to the Rocket Garden as our first order of business, and take the tour. A worker with a headset, white NASA emblazoned shirt, and navy pants, takes us around, explains the different rockets, their histories, like which rockets first launched satellites, or Ham the chimpanzee. Poor Ham, he must have been terrified leaving gravity against his will. I mean if you think about it that's one serious abducted by alien's mind warp we put him through. I wonder what the rest of his chimp friends said when he told them that tale? I resist the urge to make any commentary to Jay, she's hanging on every word our tour guide says, so I just smile at Ryan, and follow along.

We spend the morning wandering through everything. I get a little crazy in the astronaut training center. As soon as I slide into the seat, I feel a heady sense of power. There are all kinds of screens, buttons, lots of buttons, and controls, so much to press and command. I can't help it.

134

I lose it. I know it's not real and that I'm over thirty, and again it's not real, but as we go through the imaginary scenario, I shout out commands to Jay my copilot, and get all micro-managey. When our turn is over and I slip off the headset, Jay snarks, "a little power goes straight to your head," and I have to admit she's right.

A family is standing behind us when we slide out of the seats. The mom of the group a mid-western, shorts and t-shirts, tater tot casserole, football and dip type, stops me before I can leave.

"That was so cute. If I did that my kids would go ballistic on me. We're the Morrisons, we're from Oshkosh, Wisconsin. I'm Tammy."

Nailed it, I think. "Oh, Oshkosh, like the clothes," I say.

"The one and only. We're just here for a week. We've been at Disney World the past few days, but Davie, my youngest, say hi to the nice woman, Davie." A slim brown-haired boy of about ten who slipped into the seat after me gives us a distracted wave. "Insisted we come here, he's obsessed with all things space."

"We'll this is the place to come." It's time to make my exit. "It was really nice to meet you." Ryan and Jay have already wandered off, leaving me trapped.

"What did you say your name was again?" Tammy asks.

I didn't, I think. I can tell Tammy wants to chat, her husband is on a bench in the distance looking at his phone. Her kids other than Davie are running wild. She seems not to notice any of the chaos.

She goes on without waiting for my answer. "Where's your family visiting America from? Let me guess? I'm really good at this." She gives me a hard look, scans Jay and Ryan, who are looking at another display. "You guys are Polynesian from Tahiti?"

I stop myself from rolling my eyes. Why does every looky loo need to know who you are, and what you are to satiate the boredom of their cheese puff lives? I think fast, make up our fake name and story. I'm not trying to be mean, but Tammy deserves to be played for all her prying questions. And this weird nationality game she thinks it's okay to play, give me a break.

"We're the Poofay family," I say. "It's Mysophobic, we're originally from Mysophobia. We've only been in this country for a year, but we've learned so much. We love your American custom of fist fights at the mall on Black Friday, and your holy AR-15s for church. And of course, we love the big food, big grease, big fat, big fun. Who needs Universal health care, actual vacation days, and good education, when you can be broke, unhealthy, and gullible, like real Americans. God bless America," I say with my hand on my heart, inching away as I wind up my rant.

Tammy gives me a dubious look. "Well that's, well that's exciting. Welcome to our country. Your English is very good. Is that what you speak in Mysophobia? Such a funny name for a country," she laughs. It's pure cheese curd.

I'm a little shocked she's buying any of this. Has she been so duped by the history of race in this country she can't see we're just an ordinary trio of race shifting Biracial's? I give it to her full blast.

"We actually call our language Mysotopian." I wish I could be a fly on the wall when she repeats these alternative facts to someone. "And of course, in our culture the woman is the goddess, the essential force of the home to be worshipped. So, the man does all the work and when I say all the work, I mean all the work. We're a very advanced culture. That man over there is completely under my thumb." As if on cue, Ryan waves at me. "See. It's a glorious, blissful life. I shop. I lunch." I laugh. "You know."

Tammy's face starts to crumble. I decide I better leave before she has a total melt down and starts screaming, "I hate my life." She and I are around the same age, but she looks at least ten years older. Baked into her existence like a pan of brownies, the needle of excitement destined to stay on empty. Suddenly I'm glad my path is unusual, out of the norm, there's something freeing in it. I decide to give Tammy a break. Like I said before, I'm not trying to be mean. It's just over the years I've honed the skill of toying with people who just can't let me and other shape shifters live our best lives. We didn't ask to look unusual, we're just "Born This Way," by Lady Gaga rages through my head, it's time to cut Tammy loose.

"Well, I better go. My husband doesn't make a move unless I say so. Nice to meet you, Tammy."

Tammy nods her head, her bug eyes glued to Ryan. "Likewise."

I don't blame her for drooling over Ryan, he's hot. And with the thought that he's from some made up country with a culture where men do everything. Well, it's like the start of some womanistic fantasy novel with lots of tawdry bits. I smile over my shoulder at Tammy as I rejoin Ryan and Jay. I slip my hand into his and our little trio makes our way out.

We're heading to the shuttle launch simulator. The Morrisons trail behind us. I can tell Tammy is watching me the whole time, it's hilarious. The shuttle launch simulator is so realistic my stomach drops and I wonder if I really could hack it in space. Plus, with the space suit, and the bathroom conditions, and the food, the list could go on and on. I mean, I definitely still love space exploration, but I think I was more meant to be a Space Camp goer than an actual astronaut.

We don't have time for the bus tour through the complex. We squeeze in as many more attractions as we can handle before we all agree we're ready to go. We haven't even gotten close to seeing everything, but we promise ourselves we'll come back when we have more time, when we're just on vacation, when we're not running for our lives from people who are trying to kill us.

"That was the GOAT," Jay says as we load into the car, tired, hot, and thirsty.

"I have to agree," I say.

"Who was that strange woman?" Ryan asks.

"What woman?"

"The one who kept calling us the Poofays and talking about our home country of Mysophobia. Which is fear of bacteria, by the way. Didn't you talk to her for a few minutes?"

"We had a pleasant exchange," I say. "Nothing big. You know how nutters are these days. They read something on Facebook and believe it.

Now we have just enough time to eat before we get Jack. What does everyone feel like?"

"Seafood," Jay calls from the back.

"I second that," Ryan agrees.

"Well, I guess the motion carries," I say hoping they have something I can eat on the menu.

Jay and Ryan are insatiable. They order coconut shrimp, bacon wrapped scallops, sweet potato fries, tuna rolls, and a shrimp Cuban, and of course Jay's fish and chips. They ask for two plates and split everything. Luckily the place has vegetarian options and I settle for a black bean burger with fries that turns out to be pretty good. Ryan orders coffee after he and Jay finish their feast, and I sip some too. It's going to be a long night. Jack wants to leave right after dark, travel until sunrise, and be in D.C. by early morning, to surprise people.

There's a jukebox in the corner, and people are dancing on a small dance floor. I'm swaying to the strains of "Neon Moon," by Brooks & Dunn, when Ryan winks at Jay, stands, pushes in his chair, and offers me his hand. I take it and we saunter onto the dance floor, and fall together in perfect rhythm.

"Someone knows how to dance," I say impressed.

"Square dancing, middle school P.E., I tried to get out of it, but my mom wouldn't hear of it, she made me practice at home. There's nothing worse than being a middle school boy and being forced to dance with your mom after dinner."

"Horrifying."

"Right," Ryan says easing me into a turn, "but oh so useful now."

"Definitely." We two step around the floor, pretzel, promenade, do a series of turns, and end it all with a dip to end all dips. Jay claps from the table when we're through.

"Don't think you're getting off easy," Ryan says to Jay when we go back to our seats. "The next dance is all yours."

"Oh great, more dad dancing," Jay teases, but I can tell she's thrilled.

Ryan walks over, picks something off the jukebox, holds out his hand to Jay, and they start to dance as "Easy Love," by Sigala comes on. "This is one of my favorite songs." I hear Jay squeal.

I'm impressed, Jay's got some serious moves, but Ryan keeps up. They look cool together, like they fit, like we all fit. I feel tears prick my eyes a bit. I swallow them down with a hot sip of coffee. No need to get emotional now, it's time to be tough. We're about to head back into the lion's den.

We pull up to Jack's house right at eight like he asked. Cars line the drive, and the house is lit from the inside out. It's not discreet at all.

"This is strange," Ryan says, his forehead creased into a thousand furrows. He parks our ride down the block and turns the engine off but leaves the keys. "You guys stay here, lock the doors, and drive off if anything weird happens. I'll be right back."

I hit the door locks as soon as Ryan's out of the car. I watch him walk down the street and disappear up the drive.

"Maybe they're having a party," Jay says from her blissful state in the back. It's been the ultimate day for her, she's happier than I've ever seen. "I liked Mr. Jack, but Saul was my favorite. Maybe he's having his friends over, he said he likes to entertain."

"Maybe," I say, my heart suddenly beating wildly, a feeling of dread pressing down on me like a ton of bricks. It's twenty minutes before Ryan comes out of the house, his face looks grim from the side mirror where I watch him. "I'll be right back," I say to Jay. I slip out of the car to intercept Ryan, there's no use in frightening Jay if it's bad news. "What's up?"

"Jack's dead."

"What?" It's like my feet are encased in concrete. I stand motionless. It seems unbelievable. Yesterday Jack was full of vivacity, fight, and hope, and today… "Dead?"

Ryan runs a hand through his hair. "He was hit by a car on his way to buy croissants for Saul this morning. He was crossing the road and apparently didn't see the car coming. Hit and run. The driver didn't stop, they just kept on going. They have a description of the vehicle, and the police are on the lookout. Saul's in a bad way, but that place is filled to the brim with family and friends so I think he'll be okay."

"It's terrible, and also very coincidental."

"I know." Ryan and I lock eyes.

"I'd say it's time to go."

Ryan walks towards the car and opens my door. Jay is listening to music with her earbuds on. She waves at me as I slide in. I dread having to tell her. Ryan hops into the driver's seat and starts the car.

"Where's Mr. Jack?" One of Jay's ear buds is out. She regards us curiously. "I mean you guys are cool and I love being with you, but if anyone is going to get us out of this mess and beat Suni, it's Mr. Jack. Is he meeting us in D.C.?"

I clear my throat, terrified. "Mr. Jack—" I can't finish. I don't know how to say it. Ryan swoops in.

"Sometimes things happen in life that don't make any sense. What I'm about to tell you is sad and shocking. You're probably going to feel really bad. You might even want to cry, and that's okay. I just don't want you to feel scared, because Maverick and I are here to protect you. But life is unpredictable, that's just the reality, knowing that will give you the peace and the fortitude you need to survive. So, on that note, here goes. There was an accident this morning and Mr. Jack was hit by a car. Unfortunately, he passed away."

Jay sits in stunned silence for a moment before nodding her head, her lips wobble and a big fat tear slides out. "I understand," she manages to whisper from strangled depths.

My maternal instinct goes into overdrive. I throw myself over the center console, and hug Jay up as best I can. "We don't want you to worry, sweetheart. Everything's going to be okay. Ryan and I are going to make sure that we get help, and no matter what, we would never let anything happen to you." Jay hugs me back. I hug hard, make sure she's okay and then let go. I slide into my seat and hook up my seatbelt.

"You can count on that," Ryan assures, doing a three-point turn and heading us back down and out towards the main road. We slow down as we pass Jack's house, the yellow paint, pink accents, white rockers. I imagine him and Saul planning how they'd decorate their cozy home, and now Saul is all alone. I look at Ryan and admire his profile in the dark. I've only known him a short time, but already I can't imagine life without him. I let out a world-weary sigh, and glance back at Jack and Saul's house. The door bursts open just as Ryan starts to accelerate. Saul comes rushing out, frantically waving at us to stop.

"Stop," I scream. Ryan automatically follows my command, and presses on the brake. We jolt forward, and jerk back, as we come to a dead stop. My seatbelt seizes up and crushes my chest. Saul walks fast to the driver's side back passenger door, flings it open, and jumps in.

"Let's roll," he says shutting the door, and strapping on his seat belt, before he pats a sad and shocked Jay on the shoulder.

Ryan's flummoxed. "Don't you have to stay here? Don't you need to make arrangements? What about everyone at your house?"

"It's all taken care of. Jack wanted to be cremated and have a memorial service on the beach in October during Dias de los Muertos. His grandmother was from Mexico, and he always loved that holiday. In Mexico it's a time to celebrate those who have passed, aid them on their journey, memorialize and revel in their spirit. A time when the lines between the living and the dead are blurred, and we are no longer separated, as solid and vapor. It's a beautiful holiday. Jack and I always had a big party every year. It was a fusion of old and new. We kept his grandmother's traditions but added our own. We would tell everyone to bring pictures of their dead. And then we would tack them up on a board, light candles, tell stories, share our hopes for them, and revel in the memories. It was amazing. We really got into it."

"That's beautiful." I can't keep my voice from cracking, but I'm trying to be brave. If Saul can hold up in the face of his loss, so can I. Plus, I don't want to cause him any unnecessary pain through my own grief. We only met Jack yesterday, Saul's known him a lifetime.

"So, you want to come with us?" Ryan's still puzzled.

Saul taps the driver's seat headrest. "I do. Jack told me everything and I know I can help. Plus, that was no ordinary hit and run. It was an assassination. All the signs are there, a dark unmarked car, fake dealer plates, not reported stolen, it's too convenient. I know a setup when I see it. Dasha Pavlova killed my man, and now I'm going to take her out."

Jay suddenly bursts to life, and fist pumps the air. Tears stream down her face. "Yeah," she summons.

"Yeah," I summon it too, and pound the dash.

"Yeah," Ryan says as he hits the gas and we cruise out of town. We eat up the miles, lost in our own thoughts. We pull into a gas station three hours later. Jay and I jump out to stretch our legs. Saul grabs his cell and stalks into the darkness to make a call.

"Want to buy some junk food and pig out?" I ask Jay. "I could use a little lift right now."

Jay eyeballs me. "I thought you didn't eat junk food. All we ever have at your house is spicy green smoothies, avocado toast, and broccoli. Now that I think of it, you eat a lot of green stuff."

"Hey, I know how to have fun, and eating junk when you feel sad is fun. Come on, let's go."

Jay nods her head. "Okay, I'm down."

We grab chips, candy bars, cakey things, gummy bears, and popcorn, we draw the line at pop though we have water in our reusable bottles back in the car. We walk out with our arms loaded with bounty.

"You guys practically bought the whole store." Ryan says, tearing open a candy bar I offer him and finishing it in a couple of bites.

"None for me." Saul waves away our toxic sugar and salt. "I haven't eaten stuff like that in twenty years, my body would probably go into shock if I had a chip, but thank you, it was sweet."

Jay grabs a cakey thing and a small bag of chips. I decide on the gummy bears, my favorite, biting their heads off never gets boring no matter how old I get. I slip my shoes off, fold my feet underneath myself, and get comfortable, there's still a long ride ahead. Twenty minutes later we're cruising along, slicing through the dark, I'm just about to ask if anyone would mind if I turned on the radio, when out of nowhere a truck comes up fast behind us. Saul is immediately on alert.

"Steady on," Saul says to Ryan. "Maybe pick up the pace a little. You ever done any defensive driving?"

Ryan's grip on the wheel is white knuckle, his eyes scan the road ahead. "No, but I have a feeling I'm about to learn on the fly."

"I think you are too," Saul concurs. "You're doing just fine, but we're at a disadvantage in this rig, that truck's got some power, and this thing is great," he pats the center console, "but it's gonna drive like a brick. So, we're going to have to think on our feet and use this tank for what it was intended. Just listen to what I tell you to do and everything will be okay."

Ryan nods his head. "I'm all in."

His foot presses the accelerator, and the wagon responds, charging us momentarily ahead. The truck flips on its high beams, it's got a light bar across the roof that sends blinding shafts into the cabin between us. I wince as light reflects off the mirrors. Ryan keeps his head low, peers into the darkness, and concentrates on the shapes ahead.

Saul breaks the silence. "Now I don't want you to slow down, but when I tell you to turn, turn whichever direction I say, okay?"

Ryan nods again, his focus unbroken. Jay and I each reach up, curl our fingers around the grab handles with all our might, and get ready to take a ride.

"Turn, hard right, no brakes just turn that wheel baby." Saul coaches from the back. His voice is a smooth steady stream despite the imminent danger that we're in.

Ryan takes a hard right, and screeches onto a gravel road. We drift for a second, and rocks fly. I can hear them ding the car like bursts of popping corn. Ryan wrestles the wheel, manages to straighten us out, and hits the gas. We bump over ruts and holes into a black deeper than I've ever seen. We're on a remote road being chased by thugs in Georgia. This is my ultimate nightmare. I pray we've eluded them, but sharp lights behind us let us know they're right on our tail.

"See that meadow on the left?"

Moonlight shines across an open field, grasses stretch blue in the dark, camouflaging a multitude of sins.

"Got it," Ryan calls.

"Jump the ditch and start heading straight through, it's time to go off-road."

We jump the ditch, land with a thud, my jaw snaps shut, then open, it feels like I crack half my teeth and break my tailbone from the impact. The ground is pockmarked with holes, we jolt, and thud through, never losing speed, a small pond comes up on us out of nowhere, it's the only way through, the meadow has come to an end and thick forest is on either side of the pond.

"Don't stop," the truck is still behind us. Saul turns, gauges how much time we have before they overtake us. "Floor it."

Ryan presses the gas, and we churn into the water. I look over as it gets deeper and deeper, Ryan just keeps plowing through, keeping it steady, trying not to stall us out, there's no current, but the water's higher than expected, it rises above the hood, and comes through the door seals, puddling around our feet.

"Keep pushing it."

Ryan doesn't hesitate, he bites his lip a little, but he soldiers on, we pop up on the shore, out of the water, and into the woods.

"Now it's time to play tag," Saul says, the truck hasn't hesitated either, it's already plunged into the pond and is coming towards us, like a shark after prey. Ryan keeps it rolling, he weaves in and out of tree groves, we finally bump onto a gravel road, the truck is two minutes behind.

"We don't have much power, but you've got to put the pedal to the metal son," Saul screams. "Give us everything she's got."

Ryan floors it, we buck ahead, take the left at a Y in the road, turn sharp right, fly past a few houses lit from within, cozy little Thomas Kinkade's in their own fairy land, dust flies through the air. I grit my teeth and try to remain calm. Falling apart now won't do anybody any good, least of all me.

It seems silly, but I meditate a little. I imagine us all in the castle on a Saturday morning eating fresh fruit and pancakes. My dream cracks open, the truck's right behind us, we don't have nearly the power we need to outrun it. They ram us hard, our spare tire is on the back and it absorbs most of the impact, but the windows rattle, and it jerks us. We brace for the next impact, when it comes it's a doozy, it feels like the truck hits us with everything it's got, but we're flying in a bucket of steel baby! and I don't hear the sound of jarring metal, so I know there's minimal damage. We're coming to another junction, the road is wide, Ryan manages to put a little distance between us and the truck.

Saul leans in between Ryan and I and looks at Ryan hard. "I know this is a little out of the norm for a lawyer from the DOJ, but you're about to learn the basics of tactical maneuvering. Do you know what a J-turn is?"

Ryan shakes his head. "Like you said I'm a lawyer from the DOJ not James Bond, but I've watched most of the *Fast and Furious* movies. I like to think I'm not a total stuffed shirt. What do I need to do?"

"Just listen, we have a few minutes before they catch up, when I say go, grind that gear into reverse baby and hit the gas. Get going as fast as you can, once you've got some speed take your foot off the gas and I want you to crank that wheel as hard as you can, once we're at about 90 degrees hit the gas again, straighten us out, and get ready to play the ultimate game of chicken, this is going to be like ripping off a band aid. Now take a deep breath, and," Saul screams, "Go!" so loud it reverberates through my head.

Ryan cranks the wheel with violence, like our lives depend on it, cause they do. The car spins, gravel flies, for a minute I can't catch my breath. It feels like we're flying out of control, about to crash, it all plays out in slow motion, and not in a good way, not in a *Matrix* way, but in a stomach churning about to be sick kind of way.

"Straighten, straighten," Saul barks.

Ryan executes the move flawlessly. We kick up gravel as we straighten out and come head to head with the truck blaring towards us. Jay and I both hunker down, I steel myself for impact, the crunch of metal, breaking glass. I feel us whir faster and faster, the trucks lights loom ominously into the cabin. Ryan holds the line and doesn't flinch once. I peep up and his face is a mask of steely concentration. The truck veers into the ditch at the last minute, and we fly past.

Ryan speeds down the road. I feel the drum of our hearts pounding in unison, I'm sweaty and cold at the same time, a car chase in real life is no joke. We crane forward, and scan the dark. We're almost back to the highway when the truck comes up on us in stealth mode, no lights, no warning.

"Steady on, old man," Saul urges, "hold your line, give it gas. Maverick, Jay, get down, huddle as best you can in your seats but keep your belts on, they may have guns."

We hunker down. I reach my hand back through the gap next to the door, and Jay takes it.

"Keep on towards the highway, we'll lose them yet."

We fly onto the highway, fishtail a little, but Ryan's steady hand evens us back out.

"Get in the left-hand lane."

Ryan crosses over. He doesn't slow down, traffic is light so at least that's good, the truck's lights are on again and it's close, really close. We've already crossed over the Savannah river and entered into South Carolina. Where we're driving now, there's no guardrail blocking the median, just pavement and then grass. I know what Saul's going to tell Ryan to do before he does it. I squeeze Jay's hand then pull back. We both hunker down, ready for the action.

"Turn hard left now."

We fly into the median. The hood bucks up as the wagon jars down, but keeps going like the tank it is. We crash up over the side of a slight embankment and careen onto the road, all tire screech and black rubber skids. Ryan holds the wheel as we drift for a minute, and then he punches it when we straighten.

"You're a natural kid," Saul slaps him on the shoulder. "But this is the easy stuff, we're going to have to do our most fancy dancing now if we want to get away."

I un-scrunch a little and glance back, I can see the truck midair flying across the median in hot pursuit. The air is still and remorseless.

146

Somehow in the deep Southern night we're the only two cars on the road.

"Ready to do it again?" Saul chuckles.

My stomach lurches at the thought of all that spinning, the forces of gravity skewed, your body thrown around like a rag doll. I look back, and flash Jay a 'you okay?' look, she gives me a weak smile, I turn around and hunker again.

"Now," Saul screams and we're flying, twisting, turning, I brace one hand against the glove box, and keep my head pointed down, my body taut, as we thud to Earth. "Right lane now, up the off ramp, left onto the overpass, it's time to lose these losers."

Ryan's execution of the directions is absolutely perfect. We pick up a road that runs north, parallel to the highway. The full moon casts her rainbow aura on the depths of puffy night clouds.

"Do you think we've lost them?" Ryan loosens his grip on the wheel and runs his hand across the back of his neck. We've been on the road for a while and no head lights shine behind us.

"Not, for a second, we just slowed 'em down a bit. You can bet they're still back there, but we bought ourselves some time."

"Not enough time," Jay says looking back into the night. "I see their headlights coming I recognize the shape."

Saul pats Jay's shoulder. "Good girl, you'll make an excellent agent in a few years. Ryan, it's time to show these suckers our tail lights permanently. They're going to catch us, they have more power and speed, so just hold tight, they haven't shot at us so far, so all we need is a little luck and some demolition derby driving."

The truck catches us easily, I can hear the whir of its menacing tires on the road before they arrive, it's dark grill is the epitome of evil.

"Now I want you to lure them in and get them right on our tail." Saul scans the woods to either side, I'm not sure what he's looking for but whatever it is I hope it's our key out of this mess.

Saul spots his target. "See that stand of trees with a path between them about two hundred yards to your left across that patch of grass."

Ryan nods. "Got it."

"I want you to give it gas, and I want you to head right towards those trees."

Ryan looks at the path Saul wants us to follow, and for the first time expresses doubt. "Are you sure we can squeeze through there? The woods are pretty dense and that looks like a path for bikes or walking."

"Exactly," Saul says, "that's the point friend, now hit it."

Ryan turns the wheel, and sends us careening across the soft grass, leaving clumps of torn up turf in our wake.

"Atta boy," Saul coaches.

It feels like there are centimeters between us and the inky trees. We fly through the mouth of the opening. The truck is right behind us. They shoot the gap. We hear a loud crunch, look back, and see them wedged, their body too big to make it through. Ryan laughs, I breathe a sigh of relief, Jay and Saul high five. We hurry through the velvet night.

"Looks like you did it," Ryan congratulates Saul.

"Looks like we did it," Saul says, "but don't get too comfortable, if there was one there will be others, we've just got to keep on moving."

Ryan grins. "Who says a lifetime of video game playing will lead you nowhere? Oh yeah, my mother, well it turns out she was wrong."

We all laugh, and it breaks the tension. We cut through the dark, take a couple different routes, go across a different overpass, and end up paralleling the highway on the north-bound side again. It's ten in the morning when we find ourselves on the outskirts of D.C. We've stopped for gas, laid low, and been discreet. We haven't seen the truck again. Saul says the odds are they're still out there somewhere shadowing us, and we know he's probably right. Saul taps me lightly on the shoulder as I half snooze in my seat. Morning sunshine is paralyzing my best efforts to stay alert by making me woozy in its tranquil depths.

"Maverick, is there somewhere we can drop you and Jay off? Ryan, I need you to stay on as my driver, if you feel comfortable of course, but I think we should leave Maverick and Jay somewhere. Split up so you and I become the decoy, throw the people looking for us off the scent of the girls, get them to safety. Maverick I know you started this whole

148

thing and I'm not trying to exclude you, but…" his eyes stray to the sleeping Jay, despite all the drama of the night before her face is that of a sleeping child, all peaceful calm and innocence.

I get where Saul's going with this. "No, I agree." I rub my eyes, and wish for a coffee, double espresso, fresh ground beans, steam, my mouth waters. Later, I tell myself. I scan my brain for anywhere Jay and I can go in D.C. besides my house. Definitely not my parent's house, they'd be on the phone with Magic Meadows as soon as I stepped through the front door. There has to be somewhere else, somewhere no one would really know, or think of. Then it comes to me, Sister Agnes.

I call the main line of Trinity Washington University where Sister Agnes lives. She and Grandma Prue both graduated from the college in the late fifties, a few years before Nancy Pelosi went there. Grandma Prue went on to get married and have a family. Her best friend Agnes stayed and became a nun in the Sisters of Notre Dame who have lived and worked there since the college's inception. Heck, the nuns were the ones who founded the University in the first place so women would have a chance to go to college. Apparently Sister Agnes got really close to a few of the nuns in the order when she attended school there and that's why she joined their ranks, it's pure *The Trouble with Angels*.

The school operator connects me through to Sister Agnes. I don't have to give Sister Agnes too many details, she's delighted at the thought of visitors. She's moved out of the convent in the main hall where all the sisters used to live, "There aren't many of us left these days," she says, "only eight." She lives in a small stone cottage in the northwest corner of the campus. She gives me directions. I tell her we'll be there in half an hour.

Sister Agnes is delighted to see us. She walks nimbly out of the cottage, beams at Jay, and says hello to Ryan and Saul. Saul quickly moves from the back to the front passenger seat. I walk around to the driver side and look intently at Ryan.

"Are you sure you want to do this?" I ask.

"Wouldn't have it any other way." Ryan returns confidently, but I know inside he's a heap of nerves and it makes me love him even more.

"Don't take any chances. I need you, Jay likes you, and I can't imagine living the rest of my life never seeing you again."

"That won't happen," Ryan says definitively.

"Hey, *Romeo, and Juliet*," Saul calls impatiently. "I hate to break this thing up but right now we're trying to outrun a vicious gang of people trying to kill us. Cause you know, we're trying to stop Suni Wainwright aka Dasha Pavlova, a Russian agent from becoming the first female President of the United States. Plus, I have a death to avenge so excuse me if I'm not Mr. Romance right now but Ryan we need to hit it."

I stretch up and give Ryan a crushing kiss. I wave as he pulls the wagon out and away. Jay and Sister Agnes have already gone up the front walk. Sister Agnes turns back and motions for me to come. I cross into the cool depths of her stone cottage, where there's coffee and donuts waiting. Jay and I each refuse the donuts, we're still sugared out from the night before. I accept a coffee though. I sip it nervously as I look out the kitchen window, towards grassy knolls, and big evergreen trees, squirrels scampering, just another normal day on campus, except it isn't, not for us.

Jay's so tired she's crashed on the sofa where Sister Agnes set her up so she could watch the news. I think she's scanning for any information on us, if the police are looking for us, or if American's are even aware of the enormous escapades taking place right under their noses while we scramble to save our Democracy, but no, there's nothing, and she falls asleep patiently waiting.

Sister Agnes crosses over to the family room, switches off the television, and drapes a homemade afghan across Jay's sleeping form. She comes back and pulls the kitchen door closed just enough so that we'll be able to hear Jay if she gets up, but so that our voices will only drift out of the room as murmurers, nothing that will disturb her.

"What's this all about?" Sister Agnes places her hands, palms down on the table. She spreads her fingers, and looks into the spaces between them for a minute before looking me directly in the eyes. Her pupils are pools of liquid calm, friendly, and wise. I know it's all right to tell her, there's no way a kindly old nun that was friends with my Grandma

150

Prue for over sixty years could be in on a nefarious plot to overthrow our government, right?

I've gotten much better at explaining the chain of events that criminalizes Suni, or Dasha, whatever her name is, and I lay it all out there. When I get done Sister Agnes sits back and lets out a low whistle.

"Your Grandma would be proud of you. She always said you had common sense, a good brain, and lots of spunk, and that combination was like rocket fuel, she thought you'd go far." Sister Agnes points a gnarled finger at me. "This calls for a nip of sherry."

I glance at the clock, it's just crested one, but what the heck. Why not? It's all mums the word from Ryan and Saul so I guess I'm not needed. I may as well relax and take a nip of sherry. Sister Agnes and I segue into memories and funny stories about Grandma Prue, she shares a bunch of tales from their college days I've never heard before and I laugh at their antics. I'm not surprised Grandma Prue was saucy in her youth. She was a rebel until her last breath. It makes me happy that Sister Agnes remembers so much about Grandma Prue, it feels like it keeps her spark alive. I just wonder who will tell the stories once Sister Agnes is gone? But I guess that will be me. I vow when this is over to have Sister Agnes up to the castle to record her memories.

Sometime later Jay wakes up, and we all agree it'd be nice to stretch our legs. We take an afternoon walk around campus with Sister Agnes. She's retired from her duties due to her mobility, but she still likes to get out. We go back to the cottage and watch a little television. Dusk sets in and Sister Agnes talks about running down to the dining hall to pick up some stuff for us to eat. She doesn't cook much herself, and she likes the food the dining hall serves.

I volunteer to go. I pull on an old coat of Sister Agnes's and head out into the waning dusk. Trinity is mainly a women's college, though men attend too, but the students I see milling about are young women. Laughing while they hike back to their dorms after their classes, or head to the dining hall to eat, talking about the antics of the party they went to the night before. It all seems so simple, so safe. It takes me back to my own college years, when my whole life stretched before me.

151

It's not like I'm ancient or anything, no matter what Jay says, I'm still young, but I've come to realize how quickly time churns. How you can be carried downriver by decisions you don't even remember making and struggle to swim up-stream again. I let out a sigh, climb the dining hall steps, and go inside. It's all floor to ceiling, rounded windows and hallowed wood. It's a beautiful building. I grab a few salads, and some hot dishes for us to share. Dark is settling as I start the walk back. I resist the urge to text or call Ryan. I figure he'll contact me as soon as he can. Whatever he and Saul are up to, I just hope they're safe.

The table is set when I get back. We take our seats, hold hands, and bow our heads, while Sister Agnes offers a prayer of protection for us. We each give each other's hands a little squeeze before we let go. The gravity of everything that's happening doesn't escape us just because right now we're cozy and safe.

We stay up a little while, and play a game of Scrabble that I think we both let Jay win, before Sister Agnes says it's time for her to turn in. She gives me a hug, Jay a kiss on the forehead, and says another prayer with us. When she's done she seems content, sure about whatever is worrying her. She offers us cake and milk, which we decline, before she shuffles off to her room. Jay takes a shower and changes into her pajamas. I make her cozy on the couch, and squeeze myself onto the end by her feet, while she snuggles in.

"Doing okay?" I feel like all I do is ask Jay the same set of phrases over and over again, but it's hard to think of new things to say in this situation.

"Do you think Ryan's okay?" Jay looks at me with luminous eyes, young eyes, full of light, and hope for the road ahead.

"Ryan," I scoff. "That man is made of steel, you've seen him dance, and he didn't even wince or turn green during the launch simulator ride. I was practically curled up in my seat just trying to survive, but Ryan, nah he'll be okay, and if there's one thing I know it's that he'll call us as soon as he can."

Jay crinkles her nose. "You need to work on your nonchalant technique, it's a little too corny, but other than that, pretty good. I give you an A for effort. I like what you said about Ryan. I think he'll be okay too." She rolls on her side, presses her hand to her cheek, gets comfortable, and starts to drowse. "You'll make a good mom one day Maverick," she says, just before she drifts off.

I choke up, god I hope she's right. I sit in the glow of her compliment for a minute before I hit the lights. I do a security check of all the doors and windows, and position myself behind a curtain where I have an excellent view of the drive. It's time to settle in for the long wait.

Fury of the Gemini

It's a little after two in the morning when headlights bump down the drive. I twitch back the curtain and recognize my Defender. "Thank goodness," I whisper. I'm so excited I don't even think. I'm in thin pajamas, but I don't grab a coat, I just slip on my shoes, and take off. The headlights and engine of the Defender are off when I walk out the door and shut it quietly behind me. I can't help it, I run to the driver side, and peer anxiously in the window… it's Suni.

"What the—"

Suni gives me a wicked smile, I back away from the car. I think about running into the house, but that would lead her straight to Jay and Sister Agnes. I don't want to do that. I have to be the decoy and keep them safe by leading her away. So, I do what comes naturally. I run.

I don't know the campus intricately, but I know it well enough to have a vague idea of where I'm going. A shroud of silence lies over the whole place. Most of the lights in the dorms are out when I skitter through. I take the stairs down to the road two at a time. I can hear footfall behind me and I know it's Suni. From what I could see she was alone in my car, but how did she get it in the first place? And where are Ryan and Saul?

I'm not used to this much activity, my lungs feel like they're about to burst, and I'm seriously winded, but I know I can't stop and somehow the adrenaline from that keeps me moving. I take a risk, and glance over my shoulder, I can't see or hear Suni anymore, but I know she's back there. My eyes light on the grotto with its candles and statue of the Virgin Mary. I duck inside, squat behind the figure, and wish I could light a candle for myself. I try to still my ragged breathing, the savage beat of my heart.

I hear Suni run past, but I stay crouched, hidden from view. It feels all *Sound of Music* flight scene, but it's Suni chasing me, and I know if she finds me she'll kill me. There aren't any buildings or dorms on this side of campus, just the empty dining hall, the science building and an empty parking lot. It won't take Suni long to suss out where I am. All

154

the buildings are locked there's no way to get in or out of them. And like I expected, Suni figures it out quick. She's not running anymore when I hear her coming, her steps are slow, deliberate, and measured. I freeze. The grotto is up a flight of steps, built into a little hill all by itself, her tread on the stairs is heavy, this is about to get ugly.

"Maverick," she calls, her words echo off the stones. "Come out, come out wherever you are." She's on the landing now, there are only a few feet between us.

I breathe deep, and summon my Chi. There's something Suni doesn't know about me. Barbara's right, I was horrible at ballet, it just wasn't for me. It was only by coincidence, a documentary I watched on the Shaolin monk soldiers that I found something that clicked, and decided to learn Shaolin Kung Fu. I've been practicing since I was ten. I was a black belt by eighteen. I don't like to brag, but I have a few trophies to my name. The thing I like about Kung Fu is that it has a little more oomph than ballet, but you still have to employ form, strength and grace. It's like dance, but with an element of danger, and plus you learn how to kick some serious butt. Also, I like the philosophy behind the practice. The goal is about controlling yourself, finding the power from within. It's been a few years since I've done any Kung Fu, well fourteen to be exact, but I figure if I move my body will respond. Well, at least I hope...

I go all *Crouching Tiger, Hidden Dragon,* I know some Wing Chun method too. It's all about staying flexible and being strong, it was created by a woman so it all seems fitting. Suni's on the top step, she walks into the shadow. I pop up behind the statue like a gargoyle and start throwing the heavy candles encased in glass that line the grotto at her. One hit's her squarely in the face, she flinches for a moment, and I don't wait, I burst. I'm up and out, most of my strength is in my legs so I know the key is going to be controlling the distance between Suni and I; never let her get close. I must guard my inner sanctum.

I give her a good side heel kick as I pass. She's still reeling from the blow to the face she took, blood is pouring from her nose. She staggers under my kick, lurches back, loses her balance and starts to slide down the little hill. I use every ounce of my flexibility to leap from crouch stance onto the handrail of the stairs. I cross my arms like a genie, and use my balance to slide down. I come off the end with a whirlwind kick, it's a little show boaty considering Suni is just getting to her knees, shaking off the dirt and dust, not to mention the leaves that have gotten stuck in her hair from her tumble down the hill.

I head towards the parking lot; the campus is surrounded by fencing. I'm looking for a way out, but the gates are closed. Suni recovers fast, I don't even hear her catch me. She goes for my weakest link. I'm mid run when I feel my hair whip back, it's long enough that I can turn with my head down and to the side and see her.

"That was good." Her eyes are all ragey, she's wiped away most of the blood, but there's still a smear on her cheek. "I didn't know you could fight Maverick. I underestimated you."

"And I overestimated you."

"Well, it looks like we both made mistakes, but that's over now. Time to go, horsey." She pulls my hair hard.

I go to that place inside myself, a place of calm, the place I find my Kung Fu. I move quick, and go into formation, the yank to my hair brings tears to my eyes, but Suni let's go when I try to take her in a leg sweep. She surprises me, she twists and doesn't lose her balance, she gets in horse stance and thrusts her fists. I block her with a double palm guard. I can see this is about to get ugly. Like I said before, I knew someday Suni and I were going to go *millennial a millennial*, and this is it.

"I guess we both know how to play this game." Suni sneers, she comes at my eye with a crane's beak. I block her and counter with a cross over knee kick. I go into a forward stance, and punch, she blocks me with a back fist. I do a roundhouse kick, and drop into a crouch. Suni tries to get me with a snap kick, but I back step, and spring forward into eagle seize the gullet. I get her by the throat. I do another side sweep, and this time it takes her to the ground, and I know I have her. I use my knees to pin her arms to the pavement. I keep my weight steady on her chest. The veins in her neck bulge. I'm just going to choke

156

her out, not kill her or anything. She's trying to struggle, but lack of oxygen is fuzzing her brain. I'm almost there, about to let go, when it hits me. I mean literally hits me. A branch from behind swung directly at my head. I see it right before impact in my peripheral vision. I slump over, and it all goes dark.

I wake up with my right ankle zip tied to the right leg of a chair, my left is in the same position, my biceps are zip tied to the wooden side slats, and my hands are zip tied together in front of me. I'm not blindfolded or gagged, and when I look around, I see we're in some kind of basement. I blink a little and realize it's my basement. I'm in my rowhouse. I start to move, so I can see what my range of motion is, and weigh my options for escape. Suni must be just at the top of the steps in the kitchen because she hears the chair scrape across the concrete, flips on the light and comes down.

"Oh, Maverick, so nice of you to join us."

I can't help myself, I launch right into a tirade. She needs to know the jig is up. "The FBI already knows about you Suni, about who you are, about what you are, if you kill me they'll know it was you."

Suni laughs. "Silly Maverick, your own family doesn't believe you about me. What makes you think the FBI will?"

"Because we have an inside person who is informing his contacts about you right now. That's why."

"You mean these two?" Suni whips out her phone, flips the screen towards me, and hits play on a video. It's Ryan and Saul, they're bound together on the floor in some kind of storage shed, neither moves, nor opens their eyes, they're either drugged, or…

"That's how you got my car."

"And your man, he's very nice though, he really believes in you. You should have heard the threats he leveled at me before I put him to sleep. Seems like he really likes you, poor Maverick." She slips her phone back into her pocket and pushes a lock of hair out of my face. "Just when you finally meet a nice guy this had to go and happen, but you were causing too much trouble for me." Her face twists and I see the ugly behind the beauty for a second.

"You can't win this Suni. I already raised too many suspicions. Things are in motion now whether you like it or not. There's an eyewitness who can identify you as Dasha Pavlova, it's a reputable source, they remember you from the early two-thousands."

"Poor Jack," Suni purrs. "He's pretty much cat food now, isn't he?"

I'm on a roll so I just babble on. "You killed Brett and Maisy too. Why? What did they ever do to you? They had families, all these people had families, you took them from their lives. You had no right."

"You want to talk about families, you want to talk about rights?" Suni whirls on me, her eyes are hard, bitter marbles. "What about my family? What about what happened to me? My story, that's been silenced by the shout of all these Western voices."

"I know what happened to you, it wasn't fair, but—"

She doesn't let me speak, she's so mad she's spitting. "What do you know of what happened to me? What do you know of being born in a country like Afghanistan, a place where war, suffering, and terror are a constant presence? What do your Western eyes know of the beauty of our countryside, of our culture, of our people? All you see are the stereotypes, the soundbites on the news. What do you know of losing everything? You've lived a sheltered life Maverick, and you lived it in part thanks to your government, to your soldiers, to what they've done to defend people like you. People who go around complaining about the small things, while people like me, people born in a country that's in turmoil, we recognize how lucky you are, how blessed. You think a tragedy is when Starbucks is out of almond milk and you can't get your grande peppermint latte."

"That was only one time," I hiss, before I stop. Why am I even arguing with her? "You've lived a hard life, no one can deny that. I'm not excusing what happened to you, it was wrong, but I'm not condoning what you're doing now because of it. There are other avenues, other choices you could have made. I know—"

Suni cuts me off. "It wasn't wrong, it was murder. I was sixteen that year, 2001, the year the Americans came to Afghanistan." The way she pronounces Afghanistan doesn't have the American twang, it's the accent of her people, of her language, it's haunting. "You came to defeat the Taliban, to make sure girls like me would be safe, and could go to school. But I was in school, my father and brother homeschooled me. They took great pleasure in my education. My father firmly believed that woman were the equals of men in thought and philosophy. He said, 'A smart woman is the equivalent of any smart man.' He loved me, and I loved my life. I was intelligent, learning came easy, everyone was so proud of me, and I was so very happy. My older brother, Aarash, was never too busy to play football with me, or as you Americans say soccer. We were close. He was a good person. He used to say that he was the sun and I was the moon, that we never needed to compete because we moved in different realms, and when we aligned, it was an eclipse. I've never known another human being like him. He was so good, so pure. The reason I worked so hard at school was because it made him so proud. Our family was at peace, life was good, and I looked forward to a future where I would do something for my country. My parents had scraped and saved, my extended family, my village, they all believed in me. I was going to be different, go to college, come back and change things, do something. I was special, powerful, my voice was going to be heard, until you, until your troops came that night. Someone reported my father and brother as insurgents, there were so many soldiers when they swept our house, it was so loud, the lights were so bright."

Her eyes look into the nothing and I know she's lost to memory, reliving the terror of it all over again, and despite the fact that she's trying to destroy our country, and that she currently has me at her mercy. I feel so much empathy for the why's of her actions.

Suni's face is anguished. She sees my look of pity and morphs. She displays the depth of her scorn, and swallows down her pain. "You talked to my grandparents, you know the rest of the story. How the soldiers took my brother and father outside and shouted commands at them in a language they didn't know. How they treated them like terrorists without any proof, and then when the goats and sheep became afraid, began to rustle, and stamp their hoofs, they shot my father and brother. It was a burst, a flash of light, a moment that seemed to stretch into eternity but was over in a blip. Have you ever felt anything like that? Have you?" She wipes her eyes. "There they were slumped against the wall, their blood smeared, their eyes open, but unseeing. My mother screaming, me holding her back, the look of surprise on the soldiers' faces. American faces, and one scared, trigger-happy soldier who they bundled away. And when they left, there was nothing but emptiness. Everything we were, everything we had, had been destroyed. For what? For you to liberate us? My mom got ill a few months later, she wouldn't eat, couldn't sleep, she got pneumonia, and succumbed. She wanted to let go, she loved me but her body couldn't survive the shock of it all. Every time she slept, she dreamed of the moment they killed my father and brother. It played in an endless loop in her head, anguish is a crushing emotion." Suni pauses, she's tormented, she breathes deep and continues. "Then she died, and we were powerless, and voiceless in our despair." Her voice rises an octave and I can tell she's crying. "We tried so hard, to get them to listen to us, to hear our story, but nothing, no one cared, and there we were, left to eat dust, to live broken, because of you." Suni lunges, all her anger and rage explodes as she swipes everything off the table I use for detergents, bleach, and a place to fold laundry. The cap comes off the bleach when it hits the floor. Its stringent scent burns my nostrils as it empties and forms a pool.

"What happened to you is a tragedy—" I say

"Casualties of war," Suni cuts in. "My brother and my father were casualties of war, but they were so much more. They were men who were good, progressive, and fair, who loved me, and they didn't deserve to die like that. They were not the enemy. If you can't separate the people of the place, the people who live there, whose legacy stretches back for centuries as who they are, everyday people trying to survive, to care for their families. If you come to liberate us, but you can't see our humanity and you kill us, then what is the point? Because we lose too many good people this way. Now it's drone strikes doing the killing, it's a cycle that's never ending, and you watch it repeat, until you ask yourself, what you're going to do about it? And that's how you create people like me, people who used to revere your country but come to hate it. I don't represent my people by doing this. Those everyday men and women, those good people, they would shun me for the actions I've taken, the things I've done. They don't want revenge, they want peace, the chance to live, to look forward to a bright future. I do this as an individual, as me, as someone who's a casualty of war, only I'm still living. And now I'm a monster, an outlier, an American made anomaly."

"Do you think we want anyone in the world to hurt because of actions taken by our country? We have humanity too, good hearts, and care for people. It's not what we want either. Do you think the average American likes being at war? Do you think we want you to suffer or for stories like yours to be a reality? Do you think we want to lose our loved ones either? Our brave men, women, fathers, mothers, daughters, brothers, sons, sisters, do you think we want to let them go any more than you do? We're a Republic that doesn't know it's controlled by the people and so much of what we live through is not what we choose. Our voices drown in a sea of corruption, gerrymandering, games played with the truth to twist and turn it to fit an agenda that benefits the supreme few. Do you think we want that? Don't you think if people knew your story, if you'd written a book instead of plotting to destroy our government, don't you think that would have been a better solution?"

Suni pauses. "Your Western arrogance, your sense of entitlement never ceases to amaze me. You want me to what? Write a best seller, get picked for the Oprah Book club, give gushing interviews, cry about my country, my family, become tragedy porn for your consumption? And what will that change? What will that change about what happened in the past to my family or what happens in the future to another brother, father, or mother? You tell me?"

"I don't know. I can't tell you. I don't have the answers. I just know that this isn't it. Life is hard, I can't deny that, but we all make choices, and yes, some people's lives are full of hardships that they must overcome again and again. But those people, those people who life has dealt more than their fair share, they gain wisdom, they gain perspective, and mental strength through their suffering."

Suni shakes her head. "You're such an American snowflake, with your little *Pollyana* hopes and sugar plum dreams. Too bad real life isn't a fairy tale, and even though you can't see it from your isolation bubble, there's a whole world out there. A world of people that would scratch and claw just to get a little piece of what you Americans piss and moan away every day." Her voices changes it's high pitched and nasal. "I have to go to work. I can't afford a big truck like my neighbor Bill. Oh, cable's more expensive. The grocery store was out of nacho chips. The powers out. My school has a dress code. I missed the latest hit T.V. show. I lost my phone. These are your worries, these are your American tragedies. And yes, it's real life, real things happen but overall, when compared to the world, you have no idea the extent of your privilege. The geographical luck of your births, freedom is a right from your first breath, and all you do is complain. We on the outside know, we see how endowed with opportunity you are and the means to do great things you have at your disposal, but all you Americans do is spend your time infighting. Refusing to see the truth of things, running down the climate clock for everyone with your pollution and your insolence. It's time for it to end."

A lot of what she says makes sense, and we are working on it as a country. I mean, we're a little behind the rest of the developed nations, okay a lot behind, but we can catch up. That's us, America, sometimes we're the underdog, and who doesn't love an underdog comeback story? It's our pattern, we challenge and battle ourselves from within morally, so we can evolve ethically, and in the end, we choose the side of good, the side of right. That's the essence of America, that's what it all stands for, what it means, right?

I believe in us, in our country, so I get defensive. I know the depth of my privilege. I don't turn a blind eye to the suffering of the world, but life is filled with all kinds of obstacles and just because I started with the serious advantage of being born in this country doesn't mean my life has been easy. I know what it is to hurt, to feel doubt, to struggle to survive. I've made terrible, horrible decisions, and have had to pay the price. I've had to dig myself up from unimaginable depths, so no, just because I live this life doesn't mean it's automatically good. There is no Utopia, it hasn't been invented yet. I've had enough of this game, I want to know what's about to happen next. "What do you plan to do to me?"

Suni comes back from the place she's occupied in her head and gives me a crooked smile. "I'm surprised you don't know already Maverick, you've been so busy playing *Murder, She Wrote*, I thought you had it all figured out. You're going to take the fall for me. Your family already thinks you're unstable, you made a fool of yourself ranting to Bob Perkins at the CIA headquarters." She nods her head. "Oh yeah, he called me right after you left, and told me all about it. He said he hoped you would get the help you needed. Such a nice man, so easy to manipulate. The only ones that were hard were Brett and Maisy, but they caught me. They saw something they shouldn't have, and I had no choice. I'm not proud of it, but sometimes—"

"There are casualties of war," I finish the sentence.

Suni's the one who's had the mental break, the one who went around some bend in her mind the night her father and brother were killed. I figure if I can keep her talking I might have a chance. I slowly start to move my legs. I position the zip ties, so that the fastener is against the sharp corner of the chair leg. I flex my ankles, move them, and start to let friction very subtly do its work. I'll keep Suni busy talking for as long as I can.

"Why did you become an operative for Russia?"

"Because there was motive, opportunity, and a pathway to meddle. The groundwork had already been laid. Someone like me was perfect. I thought up the cover story. Being Alaska Native was perfect. You Americans can never tell anyone's nationality. If they have a slight tan, round features, and curly hair, you stamp them Black. If they have straight hair, a tan, and soft features, you call them Hispanic. Original features, and a tan, they're Native, which for some reason Americans also love to claim. You wipe out an indigenous people and then assume their identity? Bizarre. And don't even get me started on what you do to Asian people, with your stereotypes. Half of the offensive things you say about minorities in your country are ingrained into your society. Time to get woke America, time to see yourselves for who you really are. The alarm is set, and I get to press the button. You people really are amusing though, good for laughs. And you have the gall to hold yourselves up as the standard the world should live by. Talk about twisted." She scrutinizes me. "You're different though Maverick. You've had to think deeper, push beyond the boundaries, define who you are outside of their rules because you blur the lines and deep down you know you have to decide for yourself or be eaten alive in a system that decides for you. You're a race shifter, you confuse people, they can't place you. You would make a good asset, you can blend, you become what people want to see, themselves. That's what I did. I rode in on the wave of your country's racial fragility. It's your biggest weakness and will probably lead to your eventual downfall, the undoing of America," she laughs.

"That won't happen."

"You think so." She cocks her head and really looks at me. "Of course, you do. Big buns, big guns, big delusions, that's America. Trust me Maverick things are already in the works, where one plan fails another pops up. The only way for your country to win is for your people to come together and that will never happen."

I don't argue with that one. I could get all *Hands Across America, Buy the World a Coke* on her, but I'm a Biracial American, she doesn't have to tell me how far we have to go on race in this country I already know. I live it. It's my reality.

Her eyes narrow, she's good, she pegs me. "But you already know that Maverick, don't you? Another tragic mixed kid story?"

"Nothing tragic here, Suni, except your choices. Now either kill me or let me go." I know it's dumb to call her bluff, but I might as well try it. "I feel sorry for you Suni, you're smart, you're capable, life happened, and it was crap, it was unfair, and it was wrong, and it took a major dump on you, but you had a choice and you made the wrong one. You can kill me, and incriminate me for all your psycho actions, but somehow, some way, you're going to get caught."

"I haven't been caught so far." She moves a stool over from the corner, sits on it and starts cleaning her nails. "Those people who burned up in the cabin in Alaska, not my parents obviously, bums. I lured them up from their homeless encampment by the railroad tracks. They never caught me for that. Fake name, social security number, piece of cake. Infiltrating that high school was easy, they were so hungry for their cross-country skiing victory they didn't really check out my background too much. I mean, after all, I was a sensation. It's really hilarious if you know how I did it, how I won. Time after time, they were easy to fool. Until the Olympic trials, but that only cemented my place as the states tragic fallen shero. I was a shoe in for the next step, politics. All I have to say about that is if you're a woman running for office it's better to be easy on the eyes and short on the skirts, rather than heavy on the brains," she snorts. "Sometimes you people make it too easy, like taking candy from an extremely ill-informed baby. All those years, I waited and plotted and worked, and I was almost there. Heck Maverick, you were helping me on the path to victory, and then you betrayed me, and that's why you have to die." She starts to get up, and move towards the stairs.

Crap! I can't let her go up there. I didn't think she'd really do it! I can't let her leave. "Wait, how did you do it?"

She turns. "Do what?"

"Win all those cross-country ski meets?"

"Oh, those." She edges closer. She can't resist the urge to brag, hubris is one of her major weaknesses. She perches back on her stool. "You haven't figured that part out yet? Oh, you're not as clever as you like to think. Duh sweetie, I have a twin. It wasn't just me holding mama back that night, it was my sister Arezo. Armineh and Arezo, we do everything together, always have, always will. We took a vow that night to do something, be something, and here we are. But back to your original question, Arezo used to hide in the woods ahead of me on the track. I would gain a lead, be out of sight of the pack and everyone else, and then I would duck into the forest, text her, and she would come out and take off. We were masters of it by the end, but you can't play that game at the Olympics, that's why I had to take a dive."

"Where is she?" I crane my neck, there's silence upstairs, so I know she's not in the house.

"Haven't you heard? It's a special meeting of the Senate, she's addressing them as me right now. It's the final act of your crazy scheme, the one where you planted a bomb in the Capital building. Unfortunately, there are casualties, but one heroine emerges from the fray, shows her courage, her valor, and then goes on to win the election. In case you haven't guessed it, *Nancy Drew*, I'm the heroine who saves everyone and goes on to certain victory."

She turns back and her face is changed, twisted, almost like she's a different person. "Now time for you to go bye, bye. They'll find your note and your cold limp body in the tub, wrists slashed, so horrific, so messy, poor, poor Maverick. Your mom will just eat it up. Do you know she tried to fix me up with your brother when they came to tell me about your," she does air quotes, "'psychotic break.' I can't thank them enough for informing me. That's how I found out you were in Alaska. I called The Gus, and she said she'd take care of you. That road has some hairpin turns, too bad you didn't slide off on a steeper part of the mountain." She sweeps her arms around. "We could have avoided all this."

"What about Everest?" I hate to throw her name out there, but I have to stall for time. I'm sawing through the zip ties as fast as I can.

"So that's where you went after you rode off on some Alaska bush dude's dog sled. The Gus went crazy when she couldn't find you. You're lucky, she's one of my best assassins, no conscience, she's homegrown American style crazy. I should have known you would find Everest. I should have taken her out years ago."

I think quick on my feet, something that will tie her up in knots. "What about your grandparents?"

Suni looks sharp. "What about them?"

166

"Well, once you're president, you'll have Secret Service following your every move. You won't be able to just nip off and see them anymore. They told me you come every two months. You love them."

"You think I don't have that planned, Arezo and I will pull the old *Parent Trap*, and wham. I see them, they see me, America sees me too. You can't rattle me Maverick, there are powerful players on my side, and I've thought of everything, it's unfortunate that it has to end this way. I actually like you, a different time, a different place," she shrugs. "Who knows, we probably would have been friends."

"We still can be."

Suni looks at me sideways. "What do you want to switch sides now? Come play our game?"

"No, but you can still turn yourself in, and do the right thing. What would your brother want you to do? What would your father want you to do? You said they were good people, they wouldn't want you to do this."

Suni whirls on me. "Shut up, don't you talk about them. You know nothing of what they would want, they were good people, they didn't deserve what happened to them. Don't you understand that? I told you before this isn't even about them anymore. I'm not representing anyone but myself, and this is what I want, what I need, this is my revenge."

"What about the kids?" I can tell Suni is losing patience for this topic and I better switch it up pretty quick.

"What kids?"

"The ones who just lost someone they loved, the ones who are going through exactly what you went through. Who's going to help them?"

"They'll have to help themselves, and the sooner they learn that life lesson the better off they'll be. Now enough stalling. I'm going to get the pills, take them without a fight. Your boyfriend bit my sister, but we made him pay for that." She turns and clomps up the stairs. I hear water running in the kitchen.

It's time. I flex my feet, and point them down. I work the zip ties as hard as I can and finally they snap. I've been discreetly doing the same thing with my wrists, expanding and contracting against the ties. I use all my force against the fastening point and I get lucky. It caves. I'm not the Incredible Hulk, so I know I can't just flex my biceps to break the ties. Instead, I tip forward onto my feet. I make sure to use my bum to lift the chair legs above the floor so they won't scrape. There's a utility knife in the drawer of my toolbox, I grab it. I slice through the ties, lower the chair to the floor, and get ready for Suni to come back down.

"You eat some weird stuff Maverick." Suni doesn't immediately notice I'm not in the chair anymore, she's carrying a glass of water in one hand, and a pill bottle in the other.

I'm under the stairs. Once her feet touch the basement floor, I pounce. I use Wing Chun style Kung Fu this time, it's better for tight spaces like the one I'm currently in. I step out of the shadows and roll punch Suni hard in the kidneys. The best thing I can do now is throw her off balance, and end this fight quick, she drops everything she's carrying. I sidekick her right calf muscle, and then snap kick the back of her left knee. I dig my elbow into the crux of her neck and force her down. I pin her arm behind her and pull her up and onto the waiting chair before she can even react. I have the duct tape waiting. I use the whole the roll and tape her to the chair like a mummy. I zip tie her feet to the chair legs just in case.

"You're off your game," I say when I'm done.

"What can I say," Suni says nonchalantly. "You seemed like such an easy target. Had I known you were going to turn into Bruce Lee, I would have pinned it all on Beth."

"After all she's done for you?"

Suni laughs. "Beth doesn't do those things for me, she does them for herself, you're the only one among us who doesn't have ruthless ambitions Maverick. Why do you think I hired you in the first place? You actually care, you're all sad sack sappy about your beautiful country and the good of your people. It's gag worthy, but I knew I needed a dose of that to win. You people eat that crap for breakfast."

I've had enough. "It's over Suni, you're going to jail. Now tell me where Ryan and Saul are?"

168

"What so you can play the shero? Maverick rides in to the rescue. How cute, just like that movie you're named after. You fancy yourself as an intelligent being, you figure it out. Let's make it fun for me though, here I'll give you a clue. This quote fits the agenda, hopefully you'll get the crux of it. '*If you look the right way, you can see that the whole world is a garden.*'"

"You're quoting *The Secret Garden* to me?" There are no words, I'm incredulous, she's starting to really tick me off, my sympathy like mozzarella cheese is only so elastic.

Suni is in a far-off dream place, she talks from depths I've never known of her. "That was my favorite book when I was about ten. I had a neighbor who'd lived in America for many years, she had an old worn copy she treasured, and she gave it to me. It helped me learn English, along with the dictionary of course. I always dreamed of having my own secret garden one day." Suni drifts off.

I can't help myself. I'm a straight up bibliophile. Suni knows how to bait me. I recite my favorite line. "'*She made herself stronger by fighting with the wind.*' It was my favorite book too. I can't tell you how many secret gardens I've hoped to find over the years, that book planted a seed in a girl like me."

I pause for a moment. I can't believe Suni has sidetracked me into bonding over a childhood memory when the Capitol is about to blow up, and Ryan and Saul are trapped in a shed. But when she and I are each ourselves, and it us, and we are real, we fall into this place where I can see her and she can see me, and the if only's overtake me, and I wonder. "That's all well and good Suni but this is right here, right now and it's real life, these are real people, someone I love." I stop myself and take a moment to breathe.

"Remember that passage the one that says: '*At first people refuse to believe that a strange new thing can be done, then they begin to hope it can be done, then they see it can be done--then it is done and all the world wonders why it was not done centuries ago.*'" Suni shivers despite the duct tape. "Ugh. That part always gives me goosebumps. I committed it to memory. She wrote that part for me. I was that person. I was the strange new thing. A woman with so much power and purpose in a world still ruled by men. You don't recognize it in yourself Maverick, but you're a womanist. You eschew labels and stereotypes, and that's good, that's how you should be, that's the way you were raised. The lines you straddle as a person living in the in-between have made you a virtuous person. The kind of person who sees the spirit inside the being, all beings, but you were longing for the victory of women. For the time that will come when we assert ourselves and our voices are heard. For a time when women will speak truth to our experiences and be valued as highly as men. That's why you fell so hard for me. When you looked at me you saw what you wanted for yourself, to be a voice for the under-represented, the marginalized. To reach a pinnacle, to make history for womankind. That's what you craved, Maverick, and you were just as hungry for it as I was."

She sucks me back in, her pull is a sticky web. "Yes, I wanted that. I wanted a time when the boundaries of being a woman are erased. When America has a woman president, there will be progress in it, just like when a Black man became president there was progress in that. I wanted that for me, for us, for every girl child born into this world who will have to live and die within the yoke of being a woman, a task that only a woman can understand. I wanted that because I love who Americans are, what we stand for, who we can become, and who I hope we will be. At this point in our history, I want to hear another perspective, to see a woman lead us towards evolution. At this juncture, as women fight for equal pay, as the stories of women who have suffered sexual assault, harassment, and abuse, have come to light and started a movement. When war and sickness is just beyond every horizon, and one false move could send us over the edge. After a hundred- and fifty-year history of having male presidents, and a hundred years since women gained the right to vote, yes, I want a woman. If believing the time of women has come makes me a womanist, then I guess I'm a womanist."

"We're bound by this Maverick, by the commonality of who we are in this world. I know that you empathize with me. I saw it in your eyes when I told you my story. I am that woman Maverick. I can be that woman, and I can lead you to Ryan and make everything else go away. There are powerful players in this. I can take you to the top with me and give you the power to evoke change. Real change Maverick, the woke kind of social justice warrioress stuff you love. Green juice in glass bottles kind of projects Maverick, helping communities of color, women, children with special needs, the elderly and impoverished, you could make a difference. We can bring back the White House greenhouse. It used to be a huge complex. Zero carbon emissions for organic produce. We can plant avocado trees. Think about it, murder free avocados. Remember how upset you were when you found out about the mafioso type cartel infiltration of avocado farming and how it was hurting the farmers who had been there all along and criminalizing avocados. You waxed about that one for an entire day. To eat or not to eat the avocado," she says mockingly. "We can go all Jimmy Carter and put more solar panels on the roof, a wind turbine in the rose garden. I will be the most progressive American president the world has ever seen. It's what people want, it's the way we're heading whether the status quos like it or not. There will be a shift, and you can join me, Maverick, be part of all of it. It's just you and me in this space, all you have to do is let me go, and I can take care of the rest."

"You right. I want those things, but I want them the right way. I want them because the people have spoken and chosen them, and I want them with integrity. We are alike Suni, and like you said, another time, another place, we'd have been powerful allies. The skies the limit for what we could have accomplished, but in this place, in my home, I don't want to win so badly I would do anything to undermine the Democracy of my country. You see, I may be full of greeting card platitudes about America on one hand, and scathing criticism on the other, but that's because I can, because I'm invested and not just in people who are like me and think like me, in everyone. From the farmers in Iowa, to the coal miners in Pennsylvania, to those living in the smoky mountains in the land of Dolly Parton—god I love her—to the Oregon coast, to California cool, to all the inner cities, every reservation, my heart is theirs. And yes, some Americans are racist, some are misogynists, some and I would so disagree because I am liberal and they are right leaning, but I understand what made them. I understand what drives them, and that's why I include them, because I know they can change, they're American. Everyone in this country, from the immigrants I see walking with their babies, to the homeless, the wealthy, and all those in-between are a part of me, a part of my American experience. And I know that underneath it all if push came to shove, and there were no more America and we were cast out to wander other countries, whether it was a deep twang, or nasal elite, should another American voice break through our exile in that sound we would be home. And we wouldn't care if they were White, Black, Brown, or somewhere in-between, we would be kindred immediately. Through America I know comfort, love, ideals, and dreams. Plus, who else can I speak the language of Starbucks with?"

Suni shakes her head like I'm crazy, but it's a real thing for me. I came of age on their coffee, when the deep rich smell of their blends hits me and I hear the jazz its pure solace. Just like when I hear my neighbors talking to Alexa, I feel a part of something. It's us, it's uniquely American, it's what I know, a culture I'm indoctrinated in, the good and the bad. I focus back on Suni.

"The difference between you and me, Suni, is you want to force a revolution and I know a revolution will naturally evolve, because the idea of America is not who you are, but what you are. Free of spirit, rebellious of soul, inventive, creative, humane, and caring, that's America. And you and no one else like you can ever defeat or collapse us—we're doing just fine making that happen all by ourselves, thank you. But as I believe in the Universe, and in all things under a canopy of stars, in life in trees, and breath of air, I believe in America. This is my home, my love, my country. So, no Suni, you're not tempting me. We can stop this game right now, and you can tell me where Ryan and Saul are?"

"Too bad, we could've really been something Maverick, it could've been beautiful, prophetic." Suni presses her heel down hard on the

172

basement floor. "That's my bat signal Maverick, they're coming for me and if you want to live, you have thirty seconds to leave. As to Ryan and Saul, like I said, you'll find them in your American garden. Now go, before you force my people to do something I don't want to see."

I jump onto the washing machine, crack open the window above it, and turn back before I slither out. What do I say to her? What do I say to this person I've had this odd, deeply personal conversation with while in the process of all this other drama evolving? What do I say to the human connection, to us as women of this world and our struggle, all the commonalities? To the potential that was lost when the world lost the good in Suni, what do I say? I have no idea.

"I'll never stop hoping for you, Suni. Someday you'll harness all the power inside you for good, for the betterment of humanity. I know it."

"Thanks *Anne of Green Gables*," Suni shoots back at me, but she grins.

I'm down the block cutting through the alley when I hear tires screech in front of my house and I know Suni's people are there. I dislodge my cell from the depths of my bra where it was hidden and hit the app. There's only one way to make it to the Capitol building in time.

"You are from my country!" he cries as soon as I open the door and slide in.

There's no time to explain. "Yep, and you and me and Uber and our country are about to save America, so step on it. Get me to the Capitol as quick as you can."

"Oh, I love America, we will save it no problem, hold on."

And we race through the streets in his little tan sedan. Security at the Capital is tight, but I've been there many times. I've attended meetings, and sat behind Suni, and been glimpsed on T.V. by Barbara and Brandon who critiqued me on the state of my hair afterwards. I know a back-way in. The one the vapers use. As soon as the car pulls up to the curb, I jump out.

"Make our country proud," the driver calls before racing off to another fare.

"I intend to," I call. I dart down the sidewalk, and around the perimeter. There's a plume of vape, a disappearing figure, the door is just closing. I run. I glimpse the vaper's coat and then they're down the passageway, but I'm in. Granted, I'm still wearing pajamas, but I'm in. I don't waste any time, I scurry to the north wing. I take the back stairs two at a time, no use calling unnecessary attention to myself before I have too. I burst into the visitor's gallery, scream "STOP!" and am immediately tackled.

"Terrorist," a woman screams, and immediately clutches her pearls. For real I think, before they yank me to my feet.

"There's a bomb," I scream. "Suni Wainwright planted a bomb."

Arezo posing as Suni looks up at me with scorn from the Senate Chamber floor, "Right," she mocks from her little desk. "I planted a bomb and then I came here to address everyone."

"Arezo, I know it's you. I know about you, about Armineh, about your family. I know everything, it's all over."

Arezo shakes her head. "Clearly delusional."

"Hey isn't that the cyber chick who works for you?" One of the intern's chimes in.

Arezo feigns surprise. "Maverick? Oh, my god, she's crazy, and delusional, she probably has planted a bomb. We need to go and we need to go now. Everyone get up, we need to move quickly. Don't get excited form an orderly line."

The crowd starts to panic, the two men holding me let go, but Arezo is ready. "People in the gallery go easy, don't push, there's enough time for everyone to get out. This is my arena, the one in which I hold power, and the power I have now is my voice. Listen to it, let it guide you." Arezo stands alone, and radiant. I can see the tale she's planting in history, it's a good performance, she comes off as strong and brave. People don't scream, or panic, they just file out to the sound of her voice, she shines. "Good, let there be no hysteria, just keep moving, peacefully, steady, everyone will get out. I'll be here until the last person is out of this room. We won't have one fallen American on my watch. I would rather sacrifice my life for yours than live and see you die."

174

"Nice try, Arezo," I shout down to her. I know the Capitol police are probably running through the building right now to come and overpower me, but I'm going to use this time while I can. "Do the right thing, turn yourself in, Armineh is already captured. You played the game to win, and you lost. It's over, they'll be able to trace all the murders and the bomb back to both of you."

Arezo's eyes narrow and for a split second I can see I've thrown her off her game, she's not quite sure, but then she adjusts, and slips back on the mask. "You need help Maverick, you're having delusions."

The Capitol police are at the door. I don't try to run, I just turn and wait for them to come for me.

"We have to go now," Arezo urges.

"What are you worried about?" I call as they turn me, pull my hands behind my back and cuff me. "I thought you said I was crazy, and delusional. Are you worried because you planted the bomb and you know exactly how much time is left and you know it's going off soon?"

Arezo, starts to walk towards the door, she doesn't look up or respond to what I'm saying.

"Your grandparents say '*Dostat daaram*'," I say as one last parting shot, she doesn't turn back but I see the falter in her step.

The police whisk me away, we move quickly through the corridors, the bomb squad is already there looking for the location of the bomb. I'm taken out a back way. Most of the people from the Senate chamber have spilled out of the Capitol and a crowd has gathered out front. Arezo posing as Suni is standing on the steps of the building addressing the crowd, more police, and firefighters arrive every second. I can't tell what Arezo's saying, but there's a cheer from the crowd before she's escorted off the steps and they're all ushered away. A photographer from a newspaper is mercilessly taking snaps of everything, and he points his lens in my direction when he sees me. My hair is wild and crazy. I'm still dressed in pajamas. I'm protesting my innocence as I'm being stuffed into a squad car. Needless to say, nothing so far has gone as I envisioned, but that's not unusual for me.

Now I just have to figure out how to make them listen, see beyond Suni's smoke screen, and that isn't going to be easy.

Errands for Fools

It seems like forever that I'm in a small cell I have all to myself. They booked me as soon as I got here, but they're waiting for the FBI and goodness knows who else. The bomb was found in time, so the Capitol didn't blow up. I know because the two policemen who stuffed me in this place were discretely trying to discuss it between themselves, but I overhead everything they said.

I don't know what to do so I go between pacing and sitting forlornly on one of the hard metal benches. There are no windows, and no clock, so I have no idea what time it is. Apparently, I'm a high-level security risk/threat, which doesn't sound like it bodes well for me. If I wasn't so cold, and scared, and worried about Ryan and Saul, I would snort laugh at the irony. Me as the evil villain with a plot to bring down America? Please.

The only problem is Suni said all the evidence pointed to me so I'm really going to have to pull out all the stops to make them listen. It seems like ages before a guard appears. He leads me to another room with one of those two-way mirrors and a table with two chairs on either side. An FBI agent is already there dressed in khaki cargo pants and a button-down shirt. Before he even opens his mouth, I clock his type. This is going to be trouble. I take a seat.

He starts the interview. "Is your name Maverick Johnson Malone?"

"Yes." I don't want to waste any time so I just dive right in. "You have to listen to me, my boyfriend Ryan Yamamoto, a lawyer who works for the DOJ and Saul Listman, a former FBI agent are being held captive somewhere. Suni Wainwright captured them. Except Suni isn't really her name, her real name is Armineh, she's from Afghanistan, she's a Russian operative who goes by the name Dasha Pavlova, she's dangerous. She's the one who planted the bomb and killed my coworkers, Brett and Maisy. Plus, she has a twin sister, Arezo. It was Arezo who was at the Capitol today. I know this all sounds crazy, but you have to believe me. I have proof, videos on flash drives. I don't have one with me, but I did send my cell phone to the CIA. Check with them and see if they've got it yet, it has all the evidence you need. I can

177

also tell you where Suni's grandparents are, they live in a cabin in Alaska. I know everything, all of it, please you have to believe me. You have to send your people out to search for Ryan and Saul. They could need medical attention. Please," my voice cracks. I get all shaky and sob a little. After a few minutes I manage to pull myself back together. I'm a little surprised and mad at myself for crumbling under the pressure. I've always prided myself on being able to deal with adversity, but I've never been in a situation like this before, and nothing in my life has prepared me for it.

"All right, Ms. Malone."

"Maverick," I say. I hate being called Ms. Malone it makes me feel like Barbara.

"Maverick, I'm Jim Sheridan, let's focus on Ryan and Saul first. You said you think they're in danger and could need medical attention, but you have no idea where they are?"

"That's right, Suni gave me a clue when I had her tied up in my basement." I cringe a little after the words fly out of my mouth, they don't sound good, but I plow on. "She quoted a line from *The Secret Garden* about them being in a garden, she called it an American garden, and then I left to warn everyone in the Senate Chamber about the bomb. I saw a video of Ryan and Saul, they were all tied up and it looked like they were in some kind of shed." I know I'm all over the place with my story, but I can't help it, everything just seems to be spilling out at once.

Jim looks at me skeptically. "You say Suni Wainwright was tied up in your basement? When did this occur?"

"This morning, like I said before the woman at the Capitol wasn't Suni it was her twin Arezo. Those are their real names Armineh is Suni and Arezo is her twin sister. You have to find them, that's how Suni was two places at once. Don't you see, don't you get it?" I'm starting to get agitated, and bumble. I know it's not good, but I want them out there searching for Ryan and Saul, not spending their time questioning me.

"Okay, so if Saul and Ryan are in danger where do you think they are?" Jim jots something down on the legal pad in front of him as he speaks.

"I don't know, a garden, there are thousands of gardens they could be anywhere."

"Well, I would just like to let you know we've already spoken to Suni Wainwright. As you know she was the one who coached everyone into remaining calm and orderly in the Senate Chamber after you burst in screaming about a bomb. She's being hailed as a hero."

"A shero." I interrupt with my correction.

"Excuse me?"

I know I should just let it go, this is neither the right time nor place, but that never seems to dissuade me. "She's a woman so she should be referred to as a shero, heroes are men. I believe in making the distinction, the world can always use more good sheroes."

"Okay, well on that note Suni is being hailed as a..." he pauses and looks to me for confirmation, "shero." I nod, and he continues. "And everyone in that room feels they owe their life to her. You on the other hand are being painted as a terrorist who was radicalized by your association with the fringe group the Guardians of Earthly Sanctity the Black and Brown Coalition."

"The what, who?" I ask.

"The GES believe that the Earth is a living spiritual being that is endowed with the inalienable right of preservation of her Earthly body. They think all human infrastructure should be demolished and rebuilt with only natural materials. They also think the combustible engine should be outlawed. They believe that all people of color, this includes, Blacks, Asians, Hispanics, Natives, Self-identified minorities, whatever that means, known as BAHNS are the chosen ones who will unite together and preserve all Earths specious and natural resources while at the same time uniting humanity in world peace. They're suspected of doing a few bombings on big oil operations, fisheries, and zoos. They also have a sophisticated cyber scam to con big corporations out of large sums of money and redistribute it back into under-served areas.

They call it 'Friar Tucking,' which I don't get cause technically it was Robin Hood who did that, but maybe you can explain that to me."

"I can't explain anything to you. I've never heard of this group before in my life, though their intentions sound noble, virtuous even and I like the idea of people of color saving the world." I muse for a minute on that part. I imagine all the stereotypes about people of color being flipped on their heads, us BAHNS being pegged as heroes and sheroes. It makes me feel really good about myself for a minute before I snap back to reality. "But it's obvious that their actions are misguided and I'm not a part of it."

Jim's writing furiously on his pad now, and I know I've blundered.

"You have to believe me. I've never done any bombings. I'm not a spy. I've never done anything besides go to work and lead a pretty average to boring life. It's Suni you should be going after, not me. She planted all this information to keep you busy while she makes her getaway. Trust me she's visible now but in a few days poof she'll disappear and by then it will be too late."

Jim shakes his head. "She's running a presidential campaign. She's the most visible woman on the planet right now. She literally drives the media news feed. Suni isn't going anywhere except for straight to the White House."

"Well, someone's not very impartial for a government employee," I say.

Jim reels it in. "Suni has given us a lot of interesting information concerning you. Like how you were jealous of your coworker Brett's success as a speechwriter and were angling to get his job at the time of the attack on him and Maisy. Also, there's some talk that you may have had romantic feelings for him and been upset when he rebuffed your repeated advances."

I choke a little on my own spit and start to cough. "Are you kidding?" I manage to wheeze out. "Brett was not my type, may he rest in peace, he was good people." I pause a moment, and conjure a good memory of Brett, he deserves that much. "Besides, he was married and despite all his big talk he was devoted to his wife. He and I were

180

friends, there was nothing between us. This is all a smoke screen to throw you off track. I can't believe you're falling for all the false information Suni's feeding you."

Jim ignores my declaration. "It's not just Suni who has provided us with information about you, and your recent travels, and activities, things you think are happening. Your mother and brother have corroborated Suni's statements and expressed deep concern about the state of your mental well-being. They spoke of trying to get you to go to a place called Magic Meadows, where they feel your mental health issues can be properly addressed. Bob Perkins from the CIA has also given us a detailed account of his meeting with you. He stated that when he and your family tried to speak to you rationally and present you with the facts, you fled from the building."

I shift in my chair. It is true. I did flee from the CIA building, but the rest of it is false. The fact that Brandon and Barbara are out there bad-mouthing me to anyone that will listen doesn't carry any weight with me either, they can't see beyond the bubble of being total twits, anyway. I give it one more shot, take a deep breath, sit up straight, and stare Jim straight in the eye. He has to know I'm telling the truth.

"Look I know that I seem highly suspicious, that's because Suni planted the evidence all along, she was just setting me up, she knew I was going to take the fall from the very beginning. You need to listen to me. Ryan and Saul are out there, and they need help. Whether you believe me about Suni or not, the important thing is, Ryan and Saul and they need you to believe me right now."

Jim looks hard at his notepad. "We have a flash drive of yours recently found at the bombing scene. If you're not involved with planting that bomb then how do you explain the load of forensic evidence we've found so far?"

I lose it completely here, I can't help it, I fling myself forward at the waist and say in a loud voice. "Why would I be stupid enough to leave a trail of incriminating evidence behind if I was masterminding all these crimes? Don't you think I'd try to cover my tracks? Not blatantly announce that I'd been there? Check with the CIA to see if they found my phone, rip my house apart looking for incriminating evidence. I don't care anymore, just listen to me about Ryan and Saul."

Jim gives me an indecipherable look, and stands. "I'll be right back."

I lay my head against the cool wood of the table and close my eyes. I can't believe this is happening. Not only does it seem like Suni may get away with everything, but I'm the number one suspect. Boy, they weren't kidding when they said *no good deed goes unpunished*, the thing I'm most worried about is not myself; although a life spent in prison scrubs, eating cafeteria jail food (I wonder if there are vegetarian options?) sounds horrific. Most of all, I just want Ryan and Saul to be found. No matter what the outcome of this whole thing is for me, I don't want anything to happen to Ryan.

Jim's gone for a long time, and I kind of doze off in the meantime, so it's a surprise when the door opens and Genesis and Bashir walk in.

"You guys are here?" I rub my eyes, a little unsure of what I'm seeing. "Did they arrest you both too?"

Bashir and Genesis each pull out a chair. Bashir clears his throat and speaks first.

"Nothing like that, we're agents."

I'm thoroughly floored. "But you're Man Bun, you work the front desk, and give tours. You're getting your Masters in Humanitarian Action so you can help save the world. And Genesis, you're from New Mexico, your parents immigrated illegally and then went on to become citizens. They rose from struggle, from nothing, to send you to Georgetown, and now you're working on becoming a lawyer."

Genesis shrugs her shoulders. "Back stories, with some hints of truth."

A flash of clarity hits me. These are my allies. "Were you in our office investigating Suni? Do you know about her being a Russian operative? There's a safe in the floor of her office where I found the clue that led me to the evidence. She's trying to destroy America from within."

Bashir shakes his head. "No, that's not why we were there."

182

Genesis sighs. "I guess we can tell you, we just wrapped the case up anyway, you'll see it in the newspaper sooner or later. Beth was the head of a drug ring operating in all sectors of our government."

You could knock me over with a feather. "Beth, sweater set wearing, perfectly poised, cookie baking Beth? Are you sure you have the right person?"

Genesis nods. "It's shocking, but yeah. Beth baked her stash into the muffins, that's how she got it into the building and distributed them to various sources."

I'm astonished. "Beth? Drugs?" It's all I can muster.

"People are never quite who they seem," Bashir says. "But now let's talk about you, about the accusations you're making against Suni. She refutes everything you're saying very strongly, and there's evidence against you Maverick, lots of it. That's why we're here, we know you, we've heard you singing along to "My Favorite Things" in your cube."

"I told you, Julie Andrews makes me feel happy on rainy days."

Bashir cracks a smile. "Me too. Now look, we had to battle with senior agents to get permission to question you, and I'm not going to lie, we're here because they think you'll trust us and confess. So, tell us the truth, and we'll listen, don't leave any details out, no matter how small they seem."

I take a deep breath and start at the beginning. I go through the whole saga again, leave nothing out, add every detail, and they listen, jot notes, and bring me a cup of water when I get thirsty. When I get to the part about Suni and I's conversation in the basement, about her quoting *The Secret Garden* to me, I mull over the clues again while I watch them scribbling, and then it hits me and I know where Ryan and Saul are.

"The National Arboretum."

"What?" Genesis scrunches her face at me.

"That's where Ryan and Saul are, that's what Suni's clue meant. You have to go search for them. They're in a shed, please listen to me, send people immediately, they need help."

Genesis and Bashir give each other a long look, before finally turning to me. "We believe you." Genesis says, and I'm so relieved.

I get transferred back to a cell after Bashir and Genesis leave. I can't have any visitors besides a lawyer, so that's good. At least I don't have to deal with Barbara and Brandon descending on me, attributing every word I say to their invented psychotic break. I know Jay is okay with Sister Agnes so that's one less thing I have to worry about, but I can't help but rail against the injustice of a system where I end up in jail and Suni is out there walking around free. I just hope Bashir and Genesis can help me. There isn't a bed, just the hard metal bench, but I lie down on it anyway, and drift off to sleep. I wake up with the certainty that everything will be okay, that justice will prevail, and truth will succeed, they're just platitudes that I tell myself. Plenty of people have believed the very same things and been jailed despite their innocence, but I feel like for me it will be different, and I hold on to that.

It's right before lunch the next day, when they bring me out of my cell, and take me back to the same room as before. I sit in the same chair, and wait until someone comes into the room, it isn't Jim, Bashir, or Genesis, who finally enters it's someone I've never seen before.

"Corey Branigan." He extends a hand. I take it and give it a firm shake. He takes a seat and looks at me hard. "We found Ryan and Saul."

My relief is so immense I can't contain it. I laugh and cry all at the same time. "Are they okay?"

"They're dehydrated and weak, but nothing they won't recover from. They're in the hospital now."

I start to rise from my chair. "Can I go to Ryan? Can I see him? I'm sure they told you everything, backed up my story. Am I free now?"

Corey looks pained. "You will get to leave, but I want you to remember that we're not done putting all the pieces of this puzzle together, we're still gathering evidence, so we're going to keep an eye on you. However, the charges against you have been dropped, for now." He says it like an imminent warning but it doesn't faze me, I know I'm not guilty. "Since no new pressing evidence has come to

184

light, and since you have an airtight alibi that places you nowhere near the scene when your coworkers were killed or the bomb was planted, we're releasing you to your family."

Oh, dear pudding pie, it's worse than I expected. "My family?"

"Your mother is here."

It's the words I dread most in this world, and suddenly the barren cell with its metal bench sounds pretty good.

"For goodness sakes, Mavie, what have you got on?" Barbara is in the lobby of the police station when they escort me out from the back.

"You really got yourself in deep this time Maverick," Brandon scolds.

"We got your old room ready. I mean it's still the home gym, but we put a cot in there for you, so you'd have someplace to sleep." Barbara's eyes are cold as she surveys me and I know this is just one more irritation she'll add to the long list against me. Just once I wish she would be more worried about my welfare than her own.

"It'll be kinda like prison, huh Maverick. You can sleep on your cot, eat, and get ripped, maybe you can even give yourself some cool ink." Brandon laughs at his own joke.

I shake my head. "No thanks, there's only one place I'm going."

Brandon is instantly irritated. "Where are you going to go? Do you realize how serious this whole freaking thing is? How embarrassing for me, not to mention Mom and Dad, you getting dragged out of the Capitol building in your pajamas because you planted a bomb there is for our family? You never realize how it impacts us when you pull crazy stunts like this."

I can't even, I snap and glower at Brandon. "Make it make sense Brandon, when have I ever pulled a crazy stunt, huh? Never that's when, and for your information I didn't plant that bomb, that's why I'm free right now. I haven't done anything wrong. I put my life on the line for this country and if my own family can't appreciate that, then that's your problem. Now I'm leaving, I have a million things to do."

"Your rowhome is still being searched by the police, Brandon and I drove past it on our way here." Barbara throws out.

"I don't care, that's not my home, it never was. Now if you'll lend me twenty dollars, I'll just be on my way."

Barbara rolls her eyes, she's never been one to help me monetarily, even when I was young she resented fulfilling my needs, but she hands me the money, and I start to walk out of the police station. I don't even care what I look like, I'm going to find the nearest Metro, find the line that gets me closest to Trinity, and take it there.

"You're a huge disappointment, you know that Maverick." Brandon calls to my retreating back. I don't even bother to turn around.

Jay bursts out of Sister Agnes's stone cottage when she sees me walking up the drive. "We saw everything on the news. It was incredible, unbelievable. They thought you did it. I wanted to call the police and tell them my side of the story, but Sister Agnes wouldn't let me, she was worried about my safety. They found Ryan in a shed in the National Arboretum, he's in the hospital. Sister Agnes and I are going to see him this afternoon. There're all kinds of crazy theories and things being said about you. Oh, and the best part, Suni's gone. She disappeared, no one knows where she is."

I grab Jay and give her a hug. I'm glad she's safe. "Has your mom called yet?"

Jay shrugs. "No, but she will."

Sister Agnes is at the door of the cottage. "Come child, give Maverick room to breathe. I'm sure she's tired and hungry."

It feels nice to have someone fuss over me. Before I know it, I've showered and changed, and am sitting at the kitchen table while Sister Agnes plies me with banana bread she and Jay baked that morning. Jay is still in full go mode, she's got every piece of technology she has alerting her to what's going on in real time. Once I've eaten and feel human again I suggest we go visit Ryan and Saul. We stop at a drugstore along the way and get silly things to amuse them. Jay bursts into Ryan's room without even waiting and runs straight to his bed, throws her arms around him and gives him a big hug.

"Well that was epic," Ryan says when she's done.

I walk over and we do more than hug. We meld into each other, replace two hearts with one, hold on like we'll never let go, and in that moment, I know he was just as afraid of losing me as I was of losing him. I sit on the edge of the bed, Sister Agnes calls to Jay, and suggests they go visit Saul. Jay cheers at the idea, Sister Agnes gives me a knowing look before she shuts the door behind them.

"Are you okay?"

Ryan gives me a wan smile. "Pretty good. Luckily for me, Saul's a regurgitator, so he was able to bring the pills Suni and her sister forced on us back up. He used his finger to make me sick and after that it was just a waiting game until we were found. They trussed us up pretty good, we tried to get out, but we couldn't."

"How'd Suni and her goons get a hold of you, anyway?"

"The oldest trick in the book, they blocked a road we were traveling on. They had an old woman out there with a broken-down car and a baby. It seemed real enough, I guess. I mean Saul was super suspicious, but they had a guy in a car behind us so there was no way in or out. Saul got out of the car to see what was up, and that's when they pounced. I went willingly once they had Saul. I knew it was no use."

"I was so worried." Tears prick my eyes.

"I'm still worried." Ryan pulls himself up in bed and looks at me intently.

"What do you mean?"

"Suni. The news is reporting that she's suddenly disappeared, they have no record of her anywhere, a huge search is under way. I don't think they totally believe our story, but I think they're on to Suni and she knows it. What if she comes back and tries to kill you?"

I sit silent for a minute, and then I say what I think I know. "She won't."

"How do you know? How can you say that? You blew her cover Maverick, if it wasn't for you she would have been elected America's first female president. I think you should consider witness protection and you won't have to go alone."

"It's not like that." I know it sounds weird, I can see that Ryan is confused by what I'm saying. "Suni and I came to some sort of truce, some sort of agreement the last time I saw her. She won't ever come back for me. She won't ever come back, period. Trust me."

Ryan looks skeptical. "It's just that I want you to be safe. I want our future kids to be safe. I don't want to have to constantly look over our shoulders because you had the courage and integrity to do what most people wouldn't. I just want to live the rest of my life with you and know that you're taken care of, comfortable, and happy."

"As long as I'm with you, I will be." A thought occurs to me. "Is your family on the way?"

Ryan shakes his head. "No, Pear had this figure skating thing that was super important, and my mom needed to be with her for that, and my dad, well, who knows what he's up to. He's not the type to travel alone or be overly involved with what his kids are doing. I guess he figures that's my mom's domain."

"Sounds familiar," I say. "When are you getting out of here?"

"Tomorrow morning, they just want to hold me for observation. I feel fine. I mean, I never want to spend another night being trussed up with Saul again, but I'll recover."

"Maybe this will help in the healing process." I lean in and we kiss with all the weight of our beings.

"A couple of those a day, and I'll definitely be healed," Ryan jokes.

I stay a little longer, but then Ryan looks tired, and I am too. I tell him I'll be back in the morning to collect him and then I go find Sister Agnes and Jay. We have a super chill night. We eat and watch movies. Jim Sheridan from the FBI calls at around eight and I take it in the kitchen.

"You're lucky you have two young savvy agents with a lot of energy on your side," he says when I answer my phone.

"What's happening?" I ask.

"We found more evidence, it doesn't look good for Suni. In light of all the recent information we've uncovered, we want to offer you protection."

"What have you found out?"

"I'm not at liberty to divulge that to you, only to inform you that we firmly believe your life may be in danger, and we want to assign an officer to you at all times, as well as have you think about moving into a safe-house."

I know everyone thinks that Suni, or one of her goons is coming back for me, after all I'm the whistle blower. The one who just couldn't let go when faced with something that struck me as odd. The one who risked everything because the Democracy of our country is precious to me, and the one who knows that despite it all I'm safe from Suni and she won't ever let anyone else do anything to me either, but I'm not stupid.

"I'll take an officer stationed outside my home," I say. "But I don't need witness protection."

Jim grunts. "We'll assign an officer and send them out to you right away, but don't count out witness protection Maverick. The more this thing unravels the uglier it's going to get, and once the media gets hold of it… it's going to blow up into a scandal the likes of which this country has never seen. Trust me."

I know he's right, but I'm stubborn, and somewhere deep inside me, I believe in Suni. In her integrity which might displaced, but is not lost for good. I know she wants me to live so I can succeed and go on and try to do the things we've both dreamed of doing, to make a difference in this world.

"Thanks for the offer Jim, and if anything changes, you'll be the first to know. We'll be on the look-out for your officer."

We both hang up, and Jay bursts into the kitchen, she's obviously been listening.

"You turned down witness protection? This is just like in the movies, you could start a new life, a new identity, you could go anywhere, be anyone." Jay throws out her arms and whirls with the excitement of the thought.

I shake my head. "Everything I want, everything I am, is right here, and I have no intention of leaving, no matter what."

Jay pauses. "That's powerful. Looks like there's more to you than just another avocado toast eating millennial after all, Maverick. You're braver than I gave you credit for."

"Oh, I'm braver than that. How about if I tell you how I kicked Suni's 'beep' with Kung Fu?"

Jay perks up even more. "You know Kung Fu?"

"Black belt, baby. Come on, I'll tell you everything."

We settle on the couch, Sister Agnes is in her chair knitting, and for once Jay puts down her phone, turns off the T.V. and just listens to me. I fill in the gaps of what happened the night Suni came to find me, and when I finish the story Jay lets out a low whistle.

"That was lit, truly amazing. I can't believe you can fight and escape like that, Maverick. I relinquish my crown to you a little bit, maybe there is some wisdom in age."

I wince a little, but I take the compliment. "Thanks Jay." I give her a hug and then say in a grandma voice. "Well, if these old creaky bones can make it I suggest we all go to bed."

Jay laughs, Sister Agnes kisses us both on the cheek and tells us to have sweet dreams. I check on the officer out front, before I lock up the house, and we all fall into our own tranquil slumber. I invite Sister Agnes to the castle in the morning, but she refuses, and says she'll come another time. Jay and I thank her for everything, and we head off to collect Ryan. Once we're all loaded into the Defender I point us towards the castle and drive us home. Ryan's jaw drops when he sees the house.

"This is yours?" he stammers.

"Her grandma was Lady Ethel Holmes." Jay chimes in from the back.

"Lady Ethel Holmes?" Ryan seems even more impressed with that than the house. "I loved those books; *The Last Lost Treasure* mystery was my favorite book as a kid. I swear she wrote the Jose Takahashi character just for me. It was the first time I remember really feeling like there was someone I could relate to in a kid's book."

I figure I might as well tell them. "I inspired that book. I inspired the whole *Fiona McTavish* series. When I was born Grandma Prue wanted me to be able to see myself reflected in the world so I would grow up knowing I could do anything. But when she looked she couldn't find enough books with characters like us, characters of different races, religions, and worldviews, so she wrote her own books and she based them off me." Both Jay and Ryan look shocked.

"Why have you never told us this?" Jay demands in scandalous tones as we empty out of the car.

The gates close behind us. The officer is already pulled into the drive. He gets out and starts to scout the grounds. I shut the garage door. We grab our things, and I beckon them into the house.

"I don't know, none of it ever seemed like that big of a deal. Like I told you Jay, I spent a lot of time here when I was a kid, and Barbara was trying to establish Brandon as a soccer prodigy."

"Sounds familiar," Ryan chimes.

"Right," I acquiesce. "Grandma Prue would just notice things I was doing, or ask me about the imaginary games I played and then she would get book ideas from them. The summer she wrote *The Last Lost Treasure*, I was obsessed with finding an old root cellar that the historical society said had been here during the Civil War. They thought that it had been used to hide the families treasured possessions from Confederate Soldiers. I can't tell you how hard I searched for that place. I was sure it was filled with riches."

"Did you ever find it?" Jay asks, squeezing close. Her face lit with the fires of curiosity and intrigue.

"Never," I say.

"Wow."

I can tell Jay is going to spend some long Saturdays looking for that treasure, just like I did. "You can have the same room you had before," I say to her.

"Great," she says, and bounds up the stairs to unpack.

"So, you own a rowhouse in the city, and this estate?" Ryan asks.

It sounds weird to hear him call it an estate. When Grandma Prue was alive, it was just her house. Her spirit filled the place from top to bottom. If I stop and think about it for a minute it still does, and somewhere in there is my spirit too, the fondest memories of my youth, of my life are all here.

"Yes, I do." I say it with pride for all Grandma Prue's accomplishments. I don't tell many people about her books. I know she's beloved the world over, but it was always Grandpa Merv who seemed to shine. Grandpa Merv, who told wild stories of his times with the CIA and whose life seemed so important. For the first time the paradigm has shifted and I realize the enormity of who Grandma Prue was, of what she did in a time that was pretty restrictive for women and I make a decision.

"I'm going to sell my rowhouse once this thing blows over, and move in here permanently. This is where I belong. Hey, want the grand tour?"

"Yes," Ryan says, with no hesitation. "Is her office here? The place where she wrote the books? Do you have first editions?"

"Yes, yes, and yes," I say, and I feel really great, like maybe in all this madness there's a glimmer of future sanity.

We spend two nice, really calm days before Dream calls Jay. Instead of taking Jay back to the city, Ryan drives the Defender to Dream, picks her up, and brings her back to the castle. Her new boyfriend is history, and she seems downtrodden and depressed. She doesn't even realize the gravity of everything Jay's been through until Ryan and I explain it to her that night after Jay goes to bed. She's shocked, and then appalled by what we tell her, and then a curious thing happens, she opens up, breaks down, and her story comes out.

She was born to a drug-addicted mom. She's one of nine kids. She's never known who her father was, the best thing she ever had was Jay's father, but when she got pregnant so young, and had Jay, she just couldn't cope. It nearly killed her when Jay's dad died. He was the only man she's ever loved, and that just pushed her even further over the edge because somewhere in the back of her mind she'd always imagined them all reuniting, and being a family. Her story tears me up, and I talk it over with Ryan that night after we go to our room, and we both agree.

In the morning we offer Jay and Dream the caretaker's cottage. The schools in the area are pretty good, and since I plan on living in the castle full time I could use some help keeping up with the cleaning and caretaking the place. Dream's face lights up when Ryan and I lay the plan out there. Jay's already bundled into her coat and out the door. She had breakfast early, and is searching for the root cellar, dreaming of treasure, it's a good occupation, I know it well. Dream starts to cry when we finish talking, she's never had anyone offer her an opportunity like this before so it's overwhelming, but she accepts.

We all throw on our coats and walk out to the caretaker's cottage. It's not exactly a cottage, more like a nice-sized family home, four bedrooms, two baths, plenty of room for Jay and Dream, and the pièce de résistance, is that they get their own sunroom with an atrium ceiling. Dream is lost for words when she sees it.

"I never dreamed I'd live in a place like this," she says. "I mean, I hoped. I read this book once when I was a kid. *The Glass Ceiling Masquerade*, there was a room like this in it, and I could just imagine what it was like to sit in that room and look up and see the sky. Plus, the main character was a Biracial girl. I'd never read a book with a character like that before. That was the last book I read. I've always wondered what would have happened if I'd been more like Jay, studied, read, and worked hard at school."

"You still can," I say. "You're young. You're only twenty-three, it's not too late. There's a community college not far from here where you could take classes. The woman who wrote the last book you read was my Grandma Prue, she left this place to me when she died. You're exactly the kind of kid she was trying to reach with that book. I think she'd be so proud and honored to know you were living here, and I think she'd want you to keep on striving. I know Jay does."

Dream looks shy all of the sudden. "Yeah, I'll think about it."

Ryan looks at me. "What a legacy, you're immortalized by a woman who loved you so completely that she created an entire series of books based on you. You have to preserve this place Maverick and the memory of your Grandma Prue, it's really important."

I'm touched to the core, so I blink, blink, a few times before I answer. "I think we'll all do that, this new little family of ours." I link my arms through Dream's on one side, and Ryan's on the other. We walk out into the grounds to search for Jay, amidst the hope of finding treasure.

It's a few months later when they call. After I've gotten used to having a protection officer always skulking around and Jay has settled into her new school and Ryan has moved in and uses the train and buses to commute to his job at the DOJ. I sit down when I hear the news. I can tell everyone else around me is relieved, but there's an emptiness that overtakes me. They've captured Suni.

It's not that I wanted her to get away with what she's done ethically, it's just that emotionally I think she's suffered enough. The news makes me introspective and I get a little depressed despite the fact that Ryan asked me to marry him two weeks ago. The proposal was more than I ever hoped it could be. He lured me away by having Dream ask me to go out shopping for clothes for the classes she's taking at the community college. She'd said she wanted something that made her feel like she fit in. I had no idea it was all a ruse to get me out of the house.

While I was gone Jay and Ryan turned the conservatory into a fairyland. I got home to Jay dressed as a butler telling me that my gown was already laid out on my bed, and when I went up to my room, the most beautiful shimmering metallic dress was waiting for me. Dream was in the kitchen cooking and soft music was playing when Jay lead me to the conservatory, and there under twinkling lights, with champagne and hundreds of flowers blooming, (Jay and Ryan ordered potted flowering house plants from a florist in advance so they would live beyond just that night) was Ryan in a tux. I walked in and he turned and looked at me with a passion and love I'll never forget.

We danced, drank champagne, and ate a divine meal, and after it was all done, we wandered onto the stone terrace, and under the light of a full moon, and a galaxy full of stars Ryan asked me to marry him. I said, "Yes," of course, and somewhere in the Universe Grandma Prue cheered. The wedding is June 20, the summer solstice, just like I said it would be.

It's not really rushing it because we already have the venue, the castle of course, I can't imagine getting married anywhere else. Jay says she's turning the whole thing into a novel, and she spends long hours typing in her room like she's playing a symphony. The wedding's just family and friends, a small affair, but I've invited Everest from Alaska, and a few other people. Bashir and Genesis, Brett's wife and kids, Maisy's parents, friends from college, and of course Brandon and Barbara will be there.

Those two are kind of busy these days. Brandon got a new girlfriend named Lily, she's forty-two, demure, and sweet natured. She's a librarian who's never been married before. Both Brandon and Barbara bully her relentlessly. Every time I see her at family gatherings I try to help her grow more of a backbone, but she's infatuated with Brandon for the time being.

"Well, now that Suni's captured, at least we know you're safe." Ryan says later when we're getting ready for bed.

I just nod my head, slip under the covers, and curl up tight next to him. How could anyone else but Suni or I understand what passed between us? The sadness I feel that she's mortal after all, and the rest of her life will be spent in captivity is too much.

The public outcry against Suni is fierce. Everyone still calls her Suni instead of her real name, because well, we're used to it and that's just what the media does, once you're branded as something they stick to it. As much as she was once loved, now she's hated, and demonized. No one talks about her history, about what made her.

The trial is a sensation, and of course I'm called as a witness. How could I not be? I'm as embroiled in this whole thing as anyone can get. I'm not nervous when I take the stand. Everyone is there watching me, Brandon and Lily, Barbara and my dad, Ryan, Jay, and Dream. I've only seen Suni in pictures since that time in the basement of my old rowhouse, so as soon as I take the witness box, as soon as I swear in and look at the table where Suni is sitting, I know.

It's not Suni on trial, it's Arezo. Now that I've seen both of them, I could never mistake one for the other. Everything about them physically is identical, but it's the demeanor, the flashes in their eyes that gives them away. I'm pretty much ready for all the questions the prosecutor throws at me. I state the facts, tell things like they were, it's when the defense starts to question me that things turn on their head.

"What did the defendant tell you during the time in which you were held prisoner by her about what happened to her family as a child?"

"She told me that American troops shot her father and brother in a horrific accident, a mistaken identity tragedy, the kind that happens during war."

"And she told you that it was the culmination of these events which radicalized her?"

"Yes, when she witnessed the deaths of her father and her brother she had a break with reality, and she became the person she is today because of it. If that hadn't happened we would have seen an entirely different side of her, the good side, the powerful side, because either way the world was destined to know her name. She was special, she was chosen, and if we're completely honest with ourselves, we all take the blame for this broken life in some way."

Of course, the prosecutor objects, and the judge bangs her gavel, everyone in the courtroom just kind of looks googly eyed at me for a second, except for my posse, they get it. I've told them everything in detail, repeated my conversation with Suni in the basement verbatim. We've wrestled with the ethics of how we feel about it around the dinner table more than once. It's hard to feel hatred for someone who was thrust into a tragedy they didn't create. What would any of us do outside of our own safe bubble? Who would any of us be if we were born into a world where we had to scrape and sacrifice to survive and our life was devoid of opportunity?

I can't answer that question. I'll never see the world beyond the horizon of my Americanness. Sure, I can empathize, be a force for good, try to evoke change, but I'll never know that gnawing hunger, or the reality of being devoid of free will, captive in my own country like so

196

many of the world's people. I live in a cushioned box, a padded cell, it has its drawbacks, but it's comfortable, and it's lucky, and I know I'm blessed, we all are. So, at the trial I speak the truth as I know it, as I see it, and since the facts are known about Suni's background but the moral dilemma of America's part in it has never been raised, it starts a real whirlwind with the media. I mean there was interest in my story before, but now, well now my big head looms out from all kinds of front covers. It's awful. I cringe every time I see the awkwardly shot pictures of me.

I give my first T.V. interview to Gayle King, Oprah's best friend. I chuckle at the irony and flashback to what Suni said about getting picked for Oprah's book club, because here I am about to tell both our stories. I haven't alerted the authorities that Suni isn't Suni but Arezo. I'm kind of sick of doing their job for them, plus despite everything I said, they never could dig up any conclusive evidence that there were an Armineh and Arezo. No one seems to have seen Arezo when Suni was growing up, so it throws the whole theory into doubt, and now that they have their woman the FBI is just busy congratulating themselves on a job well done. Is it right, is it wrong not to raise the alarm again? I don't know, that could be debated until the end of time. I just figure, they've never really counted my story as that credible anyway, and how could they ever prove any of it? How could I?

The interview with Gayle is good. It goes smoothly. She asks probing questions that are smart and savvy. It's the last one she asks that hits me and makes me really think hard about how to answer. "You sound like you have a lot of empathy for Suni and her backstory about her family being killed. Do you think your empathy for her overrides your loyalty to our country?"

"My loyalty to this country is unbroken and has never been in doubt. But I think we have to remember it's not just about us, and who we are on this land that we call America. Or what it means to be part of this country, full of people who create this culture. I think we have to see the bigger picture, the humanity of humans as a species. We came from one, when the world was one, and we will end as one. How could

I not see Suni? She's a woman who's different from me by degrees, by chance and circumstance, and the randomness of who we are in this life. She's a spirit, a soul that is powerful and could have been a force for good like the world has never known. So yes, I love my country, but I consider it a tragedy on the most essential human level that we lose people like Suni. And we don't just lose them on the world stage either, we lose them right here at home. Because they're trapped in inner cities, or on reservations, or they were brought here as babies, but they're considered illegal in the only home they've ever known. I guess what it boils down to for me is what this life is all really about. Is it about honoring all these laws, rules, territories, places, languages, that we've made up and consecrated for ourselves? Or is it about overcoming barriers and boundaries for humankind, and the betterment of our Earth, you tell me?"

Gayle looks straight into the camera. "And on that note America, we say goodnight."

The credits roll to Tracy Chapman's, "Talkin' Bout a Revolution." I requested it that way when I agreed to the interview. Gayle's people run up and unhook her mic. "Great job," she says to me, before heading off. And the spark has been lit.

That night when I get home I start writing *World of a Billion Sisters*. When Jay finds out what I'm doing, she calls it my femifesto, and that makes me feel pretty proud. The book intersects my life with Suni's, how at one stage our lives mirrored each other, elementary aged girls who liked to read and looked forward to futures where their only limits would be those of their own imaginations, but how the reality of what we lived as we grew separated our experiences and shaped who we each turned out to be.

I think you can apply this logic to a lot of things. I mean racial ambiguity is what separates my experience from a lot of other peoples, and provides me with hilarious fodder for stories, but also helps me step into another's shoes. I've been mistaken for being Native, Hispanic, Middle Eastern, a non-American, as in a foreigner despite my straight up American accent—this one genuinely amuses me—like have to hold in the pee funny. I mean, what are people even thinking? I guess all foreigners over sprinkle their conversations with 'super' and 'like' in a semi-valley-girl accent, um, okay.

I have to say a lot of these mistakes have come from the people who are part of these ethnicities and cultures themselves, and I never mind that. I like that they feel a spark from me and want to include me in their international community group, or when the Black community says I can come to the barbecue, that's cool, that's nice. It's the times, where someone has stereotyped me as a Native American, who is poor and living on a reservation, and said as much to my face. Or screamed at me in Spanish because they mistook me for Hispanic and said that I don't belong here and started to chase me—this really happened it was terrifying with a capitol T—that I see just how deep the ugliness of race goes in this country.

It's amazing to me that people can see a projection of my brown self that they want to see, which isn't the reality. The reality is that I'm sauntering around with my reusable Starbucks cup like, 'What…? Are you really talking to me?' And it all seems to happen when I'm just being myself, a multi-layered complicated individual in a one-dimensional world.

I won't even get in to anti-Blackness, we can all see how it's destroying our country, but that's a rant for another day. Still there's a fair amount of people who don't realize my heritage and casually share their prejudicial views against Black people with me. I always give them a good tongue lashing, but their attitudes are dangerous and disheartening. Anti-Blackness is a problem that plagues the entire world and the time has come for it to be addressed and stopped.

I take most things with a grain of salt though because it's allowed me to see the other side of ugly. The prejudice myself and my people of color allies face when we take our place in society, and it's helped me be more aware, fairer, more willing to educate and talk about how we can end these disparagements. And when I take everything I know, everything I've learned through these years, in this body and apply it to what happened with me and Suni, an enlightenment happens and I look at the world with new eyes, and an indelible shift in my consciousness.

No matter what happens I want America to succeed, because like I've said the whole time, I love us, and our country. But I see it more clearly now. We have to be ready on a global level to work in alignment with our worldly allies. We face so many more challenges than what happens inside our own country, and sure we have a lot that needs to be addressed here first, but we can't forget that we're part of the world, and the power and influence that comes with how we live and what we do. It challenges me to be a better person, and not just recycling, and growing my own vegetables, starting programs for under-served Americans, but more than that. Being open to people whose struggles may be thousands of miles away, immersed in another culture, knowing they are not the enemy, they could be someone just like me, someone like Suni.

Fairy Tales for Fireweeds

What can I say about our wedding? It was spectacular, more than I hoped it could be. Ryan spent the night before our wedding in a yurt we put up on one of the castle meadows. I found my dress right away. It had a flowy, goddess quality to it that I loved. It made me feel like I'd sprung from a Pre-Raphaelite painting, exactly what I had wished for. I wore my hair down with flowers woven in.

It was all pretty low key and casual, just how Ryan and I wanted it. His parents and Pear came two days before the wedding, and of course there was the usual whirlwind of last-minute preparations. Luckily our dads clicked right away, they fell into a friendly conversation and wandered off. We found them later in the castle den, watching a western and talking about politics. I think they still stay in touch through email, goodness knows what they discuss, but it's pretty cool.

Barbara and Beverly didn't jell quite as easily, they spent the whole first day of their meeting trying to establish who was queen bee and I don't think the logistics have been figured out yet. Every time they see each other they try to outshine the other's golden child, needless to say I know everything Pear has done since birth, and Ryan has learned the same things about Brandon. Ryan and I just kind of laugh about it. We've promised each other we won't be like that with our kids. There'll be no favorites, no winners, and no losers, just kids. They'll be part of me and part of Ryan and we'll love them all equally, no matter who they turn out to be, cause that's what makes life interesting.

Jay and Pear were my two bridesmaids, and Ryan had Brandon, and his best friend from grade school, Dylan, as his groomsmen. I could have asked Dream and Everest, and some of my friends from college to be bridesmaids, but I knew there was no way around asking Pear, and I didn't want to make it a whole big thing, so we kept it small and simple.

Jay said she wanted to look like she was dressed for a fairy wedding, she has a reproduction of *Midsummer Eve* in her room that she's obsessed with, so we made crowns of flowers for them to wear, and picked out ethereal dresses. Pear loved the whole theme, and when Jay told her it was her idea, the two became fast friends. They spent a lot of time giggling in the treehouse we built Jay, about their plans for world domination. As long as they don't outlaw coffee and avocados when they take over the world, I'm fine with it.

I think for the most part Ryan's parents liked me right away. Well, maybe not immediately, immediately. I mean their first introduction to me was a piece they saw on the news so that's a bit of a different way to meet your son's fiancé, but once they met me in person, they liked me. Brandon is over the moon that Ryan, and I are married. He lets everyone know that he was the matchmaker behind our union. He also calls us the Yams, which I find slightly annoying, but whatever, that's to be expected from Brandon.

Everything I went through feels surreal. I mean everything with Suni, and then the media frenzy that followed. It was crazy. I'm still sifting through the experience of it all. The stuff Suni and I said to each other in the basement of my old rowhome has stayed with me. I sold the rowhouse as soon as the FBI cleared me. I used the money to clear all my debts and plus there was a little extra so that was nice. With all the hype surrounding me, Kyle tried to get in contact with me and it was immensely satisfying to tell him that I was married and never to call me again.

The experience that I went through is a strange thing to carry around, it's hard to explain to people. I mean Ryan, Jay, and Dream understand everything, but they weren't in that basement with me. They didn't hear the things Suni said and watch her face as she recounted her story. Sometimes, in the middle of it all, in the chaos of the day to day, I stop and reflect on what it all means.

I mean, I really just stop. I watch people fly around in their cars in a hurry. I watch people more in tune with their phones than their fellow humans and what's happening right in front of them, and it hits me. What's the purpose? We're part of the world elite, a select few who have the luxury of a system that works for them, well most of the time, and it's certainly something we need to protect. Most Americans have gadgets, access to the internet, not everyone, and I'm not overlooking

202

American poverty, but many of us have more materially than people in third world countries. It's amazing, and yet what does it all mean? It doesn't ensure we're happy, or even healthy?

I've had to look hard to find the answers, and trust me, I've been searching. You see, I want to do more with the time I have here on this Earth. I used to think I wanted to make a difference with politics, or something systemic, but now I see I can do more of what I want on the outside and that's what I focus on. It's not like I think I'm going to end world hunger, or establish world peace, although being able to accomplish those things would be nice. It's more like I want to see people happy, flourishing, and living life with substance. That's another one of my slogans I'm trying to make fly—*Bring Back Substance*—Jay bit her lip and narrowed her eyes when I told her this one, so I know it's good.

I finished writing my second book, *Tribe of the Noble Spirits*, and it's getting pretty okay reviews. My viewpoints have kicked up some discussion, but that's what I intended to do, that's why I wrote it in the first place. I've been asked to do a few talks, and there's even talk of a lecture tour, but I'm not so sure about that. Rather than me traveling around like some big-headed supreme woke guru, I'd rather see money funneled into spaces where people could discuss these things amongst themselves.

Like instead of book signings, having open forums where people talk about the themes of the book or which things struck them. Even the criticisms, the things that didn't get considered because they're beyond my horizon, but once I know them I'm open to them. And of course, I want to do it all in diverse places, places people are normally too afraid to visit.

My agent and the publisher are still getting used to the idea, and I'm sure there will have to be some kind of comprise, but I want to do things differently, to be different. Because I'm aware enough to know that none of this is about me. It never was. It's about life, and circumstance, and all the things we've come to believe. It's time to sort through the old ideologies and decide what we take with us into the new thought millennium. I call it *Boomillexzalpha,* it's as many generations as I can squeeze into one word. Jay say's "It sounds like a laxative," but I'm trying to make it a thing, even though it's slow to catch on.

Having a new name is great. I love being Maverick Johnson Yamamoto. It adds a whole new layer of confusion about who I am, and I get quite the startled 'oh' of surprise when they call my name at an appointment and then I show up. I can tell it's not quite what they're expecting, but that's okay. Ryan and I have endless jokes between us about it, and I can tell we're going to have an interesting race shifting kind of life and I'm so excited.

It's amazing when you can manifest a dream to reality and that was something really cool about our wedding. We got married in the backyard. I walked down an aisle we set up in the open space of the rose garden. We had a beautiful pergola built to be married in front of and we carved a totem of sorts with things that had meaning to us.

When it came to my wedding accoutrements, I found a dragonfly pendant of Grandma Prue's in her things and wore it as my something old. Ryan gave me a pair of antique earrings that I loved and so those were my something new. Well, technically they were still old, but they were new to me. In an unusual move, Ryan insisted I let him pick the music I was going to walk down the aisle to, and I readily agreed. I hadn't wanted to make all the plans without him, anyway. So, it was nice for it to be a joint effort.

He didn't tell me what he was planning to do, he just said it was a thing he'd thought about doing and thought he could pull off. Even though I wanted to marry Ryan all along, I wasn't sure how I'd react to getting married. I mean all the *till death do us part,* and stuff like that did give me a bit of cold feet. I think Ryan is the greatest guy I could ever find, and our lives just naturally meld, but still there was a bit of commitment phobia I never knew I had.

I told Ryan how I was feeling and he said; he wasn't surprised. When I asked him, "Why?" He said, "It's always like that when you're *Taming the Shrew.*" I chased him around the house, and eventually brought him down with a side sweep, before I kissed him relentlessly. He loves that I know Kung Fu, he says, "It's sexy."

I definitely liked having a wedding but I would never want to repeat the process so I tell Ryan he's stuck with me for life. I mean everyone has an opinion when you're getting married, and it's nice and fun, but I couldn't help feeling relieved when it was finally over.

The décor was eclectic elegance, and of course Jay's theme of the fairy wedding. I was glad that we used our natural setting with the castle grounds, the rose garden and all that, but I was also happy to get to use all the great china, glassware, and tablecloths, in the castle too. It made it have the perfect ambiance. It was also nice to see a lifetime of Grandma Prue's things on display. I could tell that Barbara got a little green with envy every time someone asked me about Grandma Prue leaving the place to me and not her daughter, but once I explained that Grandma Prue was Lady Ethel Holmes and that her mysteries were based on me they got all excited. Barbara still thinks I should sell the place, but I just tell her "Never."

I know you're not supposed to see the groom before the wedding, but I watched all the guests find spots on either side of the aisle through my window. I saw Ryan, laughing with Brandon and Dylan where they were waiting over by the greenhouse. I could tell by the way Ryan kept running his hands through his hair and looking at the index card he was taking in and out of his pocket that he was nervous.

We wrote our own vows to each other and I think we both took it pretty seriously. As Jay enjoyed pointing out, when Barbara had a hissy fit at the engagement party, and insisted Ryan and I were rushing things with our June wedding, it's not like we're spring chickens. We have enough life under our belts to know what's what, and we didn't want to wait, and observe some tired old tradition, we wanted to start our life together.

Our life, well, it's everything I hoped it would be since the first time Ryan and I met. I never feel the need to pump him up or make more of what he does than I need too, because who Ryan is just as himself is perfect, and there's nothing I would change. Well scratch that, maybe a few things, but they're minor. I know that in life and marriage there will be disagreements, even squabbles, but through it all there will be love, and that's all anyone can really hope or ask for.

I'd asked to be alone the morning of the wedding. I'd wanted to take all the time I needed to be really in the moment. To really savor the experience I was about to have. I've gotten better and better at being mindful and present. I'm not going to act like I don't still have so much screen time looking on my phone could be a part-time job, but I'm improving.

When I was ready to go, I walked down the staircase, and got the attention of my dad who was waiting on a bench by the door looking at his phone. He stood up when he saw me and for once I think he actually really noticed me. Then he did an astonishing thing. He said words I'd always longed to hear and never thought I would.

"You look lovely," he'd said, and I knew he meant it so it was really touching. "You've done well Maverick, you saw the truth of Suni when everyone around you was blinded by her facade and best of all you found true love. You have something a lot of other people lack, character, and it will take you far."

I was really surprised that he even knew everything that had happened. I mean, I know he follows politics like it's his religion, but he'd mostly stayed away from all the trial proceedings after my time on the stand. It was Brandon and Barbara who I could see staring at me with contempt in court. Boy, am I glad that's all over. They never acknowledged all the ways they stabbed me in the back, Brandon, and Barbara. I guess I never really expected them to, but still it'd be nice if they noticed someday, but I don't hold on long to false hopes.

I'd taken one final look at myself in the long hall mirror, before I turned to my dad. "Thanks," I'd said. "Those words mean more to me than you can ever know. Shall we?" I slipped my arm into his and we'd started to walk.

As soon as we stepped through the French doors out onto the flagstone terrace with its elegant white stairway that led to the aisle strewn with wildflowers, Ryan lifted his cell phone above his head and

206

"In Your Eyes" by Peter Gabriel started to play. It went through speakers that were set up so everyone could hear it, and at that moment I knew without a doubt that everything in my life had led me to that point, to that place, and there was not one thing I would've changed.

Everest flashed me a grin, Saul gave me a thumbs up, Genesis and Bashir smiled brightly, and Jay and Pear beamed at the end. Barbara sitting with Lily surveyed me as I went by, but like tunnel vision all I saw was Ryan, and when I got him I don't even wait for my dad to give me away, because I ran right into Ryan's arms and all my fears evaporated like they'd never been. Everyone cheered, and I cried a bit, and Ryan hugged me so tight, and then we got married.

We danced and ate. We had Greek food for the fare. Barbara was vehemently opposed to it when she heard. She said guests would have falafel rolling down their fancy clothes, and that hummus and gyros had no place at a catered affair. We didn't listen, and everybody loved it. We're still getting raves about the baklava, and stuffed grape leaves. The cake was coconut cream; we made it vegan and gluten-free so it could fit a multitude of diets. It was served with fresh-cut fruit, and people ate it up. Jay and Pear ripped up the dance floor, and even Brandon joined in with moves that can only be described as interesting.

Ryan and I had our first dance to an old classic, "The First Time Ever I Saw Your Face," by Roberta Flack. I got to pick the first dance song, and I picked it because Grandma Prue used to sing it to me when I was sick, or scared, or just couldn't sleep. I hadn't listened to the song since she died so I was a little nervous about having an emotional breakdown in front of everybody, but as soon as the song started to play the words resonated in every fiber of my being and Ryan was my only optic.

Everest told me later watching us made her a little jealous and brought tears to her eyes. So, when I threw the bouquet, I made sure to aim it in her direction. The night ended with everyone gone and Ryan and I, dancing barefoot on the terrace under the stars, to a playlist from his phone. It was all I could have ever wished, hoped, or wanted. It was everything.

We had a fun honeymoon in Hawaii. When we got back, we sent Jay to Space Camp, and she documented the whole experience in video and through journal entries. She says her next book is all about a girl like her, who gets a chance to go to Space Camp and how it changes her life. She definitely came back with a whole new set of ambitions, and where she was mildly interested in astrophysics and math, now she's wildly interested in both. Next summer she says we all have to go to Montana so she can find her inner cowgirl.

She's also started working on starting her own foundation. It turns out she's really good at fundraising, and she's fearless when it comes to calling people up and asking for money. She's a natural salesperson, so the amount she's already raised is nothing short of amazing. She wants to call her foundation *Carlos Kids* in memory of her dad. I think it's great. She's going to help kids in under-served neighborhoods do stuff like participate in STEM programs, earn scholarships to Space Camp, enter robotics contests, and also start businesses. She watched some program on T.V. and now she's determined to own several vending machines.

She's also working on a business plan for a startup she says is going to change the fundamental underpinning of things, whatever that means. It's interesting to watch her be so self-assured, so knowledgeable about what she wants to do with her life, there aren't many people like her. She self-published her book about her adventures with me and Ryan. She marketed it as a *Tween Time Adventure*, and it really took off.

I know she misses her dad a lot, sometimes she tells me different things she remembers about him or little memories that pop up. His grave didn't have a headstone and so we had one put in. Jay wanted it to say that he was the kind of dad every kid could only dare to hope for, and though he was only physically with her for a short time, his spirit was with her for life, it was super touching. Dream and her are still working things out. I think it'll take her time to trust that Dream has really changed, but I think Dream is proving to her that she's trying every day, and that's what it takes.

Overall, I think Jay's happy, and she's going to grow up and lead a fulfilled and fulfilling life. I think she'll give herself to the world and the world will give back to her. Most of it will be good, some of it will be bad, and certain things will be downright hard, but in the end, she'll prevail. It's pretty humbling to watch someone with so much talent bloom, it makes me think a lot about Suni, and all the chances she never had to use her talents in the same way Jay is. But I guess that's the kaleidoscope of life. Every time you turn, you get a new perspective. Both Ryan and I feel lucky and blessed that we get to have Jay and Dream in our lives.

Dream's doing well in her two classes at the local community college and so far, she's enjoying both. I think she's been inspired by all the things Jay is accomplishing and has decided to go for it too. Sister Agnes comes to visit sometimes, and she and Dream have become fast friends. They spend a lot of time talking and drinking tea in the conservatory or wandering in the gardens. I think whatever it is that haunts Dream, that holds her back from believing she can do anything, is soothed when she's in the presence of Sister Agnes. I can tell Sister Agnes loves it too, having someone who needs her counsel, and it's great.

Everest texted me the other day. She said my bouquet must have been lucky because she met a nice guy who hikes on the same trails as she does. He's in the military. He just got stationed in Alaska and he's excited to explore. Everest was relieved when they caught Arezo, and a little scared when I told her it was Suni's twin and not Suni. I didn't tell her to scare her. I just wanted her to be aware that Suni was still out there somewhere, but I also told her I didn't think she had to worry anymore. That it was all over.

I mean I think Suni is right, there will always be someone or something we have to protect our Democracy from, but it'll never be Suni again, and she won't come back to hurt Everest either. I did tell Everest to watch out for The Gus because according to Suni she was a ruthless assassin and Everest was shocked. Apparently though, after everything with Suni, The Gus went around the bend and was placed in a very nice facility. So now Everest is free to live her life without worry, and hopefully this new guy will be the one, and Ryan and I will be going to their Alaskan wedding.

Saul settled back into his Florida life, although he's never stopped searching for Suni. He's taken a couple of trips to Afghanistan, traveled to some European countries where he thought he'd found her trail, but nothing. He always knew Arezo wasn't Suni, and that Suni was still free the whole time the trial was taking place, but no one in the bureaucracy wanted to listen to him either, so he just kind of went rogue. I don't think he'll ever find Suni. I think it's a fruitless mission. She has more resources at her disposal than we could ever imagine, but I understand why he needs to try.

We went back to Cocoa Beach for Dia De Los Muertos, since it was Jack's memorial service. It was lovely, just like Saul said it would be, a fusion of old and new traditions. Saul had the service on the beach with candles burning in the sand, the sound of waves and the smell of salt water. He and Jack's friends told funny stories about Jack, sad stories, heroic stories, and then they released his ashes into the sea accompanied by beautiful flowers in every shade. Jay and Ryan, Dream, and I clustered close, and remembered Jack and supported Saul. Saul's supposed to come for Christmas and we're all really excited about that. Jay loves seeing him. Part of her is also interested in becoming an FBI agent. Although if Dream and I have our druthers, we'd rather see her break through the atmosphere in a rocket ship than chase criminals, but we know whatever she decides to do it will be amazing.

Brandon proposed to Lily a few weeks after Ryan and I got married and they're planning their big day for next summer. Brandon has already hijacked most of the wedding plans and I think him and Barbara are booking appointments to take Lily dress shopping, and I feel for her. I really do, but I generally try to keep my nose out of it.

Not much has changed with my family. My dad said those touching things at our wedding, and he actually comes out of the den for a few minutes to say "Hi" when Ryan and I come over but other than that

210

everything is just the same. Except it's not the same, cause Ryan is my family now, so whenever I'm around Barbara and Brandon their little mean clique doesn't even matter anymore, plus now they have Lily to bully so things are quieter for me.

It's amazing to break off from your family of origin and start your own branch. To look down the line and see yourself with kids, grandkids, the head of a lineage one day. It's really wild, and I'm loving it. Especially since we just found out we're pregnant. I keep telling Ryan it's twins Hazel and Hedley, and for some reason I'm certain of it even though it's too early to know anything.

Ryan's still commuting and working for the DOJ, but lately he's been talking about trying something different, maybe working for the Foreign Service or even a global charity. He wants to travel, to see the world, to live in other countries, and I agree. We would never sell the castle, of course, but Dream and Jay are here to stay so we have people to watch over it if we decide to live abroad for a few years.

Looks like all Beverly's hard work paid off because Pear is a shoe in for the Olympics. Beverly is sending everyone she knows an announcement about it, with a cute picture of Pear on skates in one of her costumes. Barbara just muttered, "That's interesting," when she got hers and then threw it in the trash. I don't think she likes being topped by Beverly.

For some reason after the whole Suni debacle Barbara has gotten it into her head that Brandon would make an excellent president. I think that was part of the push for Brandon to find a wife. Brandon's been talking about running for the House and asking me if I have any ideas for campaign slogans or social media. I just tell him I'm retired from all that and don't get involved, and I am retired from all that.

I never went back to work in the political arena after everything with Suni. I just couldn't do it. Plus, my two books have done pretty well financially, so I've decided to try my hand at writing full time. I haven't completely flushed out the idea yet, but I think I'd like to pick up where Grandma Prue left off, and revive the Lady Ethel Holmes character. Except this time the books won't be about a Biracial girl finding her place in this world, they'll be about a woman who knew her place in this world and made a difference. A woman like Grandma Prue, who believed in herself and her books when no one else did. Those are the stories I intend to tell, stories of perseverance, hope, and love.

Tomorrow is the most important day of the year for America. That's right, it's Election Day. Our country got thrown into a lot of turmoil after Suni was outed as a Russian operative and went to trial. There was so much vitriol and finger pointing I could barely stand to see it, except I couldn't turn away from it because I was directly involved. Things have settled down a little now, but it's still hard for people to pull together. I'm hoping that no matter the outcome of the election, we take the time to find ourselves again after everything settles down. We can't let ideology, or party, tear apart who we were meant to be. I mean everyone says it till they're blue in the face and it sounds so cliché, but it is our motto. *E Pluribus Unum, out of many, one,* and it's so true.

Arezo was being moved to a maximum-security prison earlier in the fall, and a curious thing happened. She disappeared halfway through transport. She was being escorted by tons of guards, but she still managed to slip away. There's a massive search happening, but I know they'll never find either of them, Suni will make sure of that. I know her name's not Suni, but I still call her that because that's who she is and will always be to me.

That's the person I remember when I think of everything that's happened and everything I've learned from it. This picture of Suni and Arezo deep in the mountains of Afghanistan, with a group of girls in their care, always flashes in my head, and I've come to accept it as true. I feel like Suni's stewarding girls who are orphaned or in need, or just have nowhere to go. Girls who are smart, who have potential, who can grow up to do so much good, but are powerless to the circumstance they were born into. Girls that don't have the advantage of being born into freedom, into the right to go to school, or choose who they marry and when, girls who will become our future generation of women. Girls like me, like Suni, and Jay, like all of us, and I know that despite the things that Suni has done, she and I will always have a connection.

Suni helped me see the ways of a world I thought I already knew. She opened my eyes to a struggle that I knew existed outside myself, but could never really see. I'm not going to blow smoke and say that it's suddenly made my life easier, or that I don't have my own unique set of problems, prejudice I encounter for being who I am in this world, but I don't look away from my privilege. And suddenly being an American has even more weight and meaning. Being a person who is endowed with the right of personal liberty is a powerful thing, and I can't reinforce this thought enough. The power lies in the chance we have for opportunity where even the meekest among us can rise to greatness. It makes me realize we can change anything in this country that we want to with the power of our dollars, with our voices, and most of all with our votes.

If Suni would have followed a different path, I have no doubt that things would be different, and that we would still know her name, but it would be with honor and reverence instead of scandal and notoriety. I don't judge her by the life I've had or I lead though. I know that I've never been faced with the decisions she was faced with, or the tragedy that shaped her.

A few weeks ago, I got a postcard with a picture on the front. It was a garden blooming with flowers, a riot of trees, abuzz with bees. The viewpoint stretched back far into the horizon so that all you could see was endless growth. Even though the postcard was blank with a printed label, I knew it was Suni. And I got the message, understood what she was trying to say, and I know she's found peace.

All the news outlets are reporting on how divided our country is on the eve of this Election day, and even though I don't want to admit it, I know it's true. There's just one thing I hope people remember when they vote tomorrow. I hope they remember us. Not the us, of political party, not the us, of affiliation or race, not the us, of gender or class, but us as Americans. Because no matter what divides us the ties that unite us are much stronger, and I can't imagine this world, this life, without our bumbling brand of self-examining, scandalous, grace as we try to execute democracy in a fair way. In a way that will shape the human race, a way that will honor our past, make our present better, and take its place in our history. Like they say, *let the best person win*, and I hope they will. But no matter what happens, I know we will be okay, because I believe in us, and if we all believe in us, if we all refuse to let go, if we all band together instead of pulling apart, we can rise to the greatness we were endowed with at our creation. And I have no doubt we will because we're American, and in America good will always win. And we fade out to the sounds of "Brand New," by Ben Rector, and it's so true.

Maverick's Playlist

"Sunny"
Boney M.

"I Won't Back Down"
Tom Petty

"White Wedding"
Billy Idol

"Truth Hurts"
Lizzo

"bad guy"
Billie Eilish, Justin Bieber

"Bette Davis Eyes"
Kim Carnes

"Danger Zone"
Kenny Loggins

"Push It"
Salt-N-Pepa

"Love Me Olé"
MAJOR., Cierra Ramirez, C-Kan

"Suddenly I See"
KT Tunstall

"What A Man Gotta Do"
Jonas Brothers

"The Obvious Child"
Paul Simon

"Born This Way"
Lady Gaga

"Neon Moon"
Brooks & Dunn

"Easy Love"
Sigala

"My Favorite Things"
Julie Andrews

"Talkin' Bout a Revolution"
Tracy Chapman

"In Your Eyes"
Peter Gabriel

"The First Time Ever I Saw Your Face"
Roberta Flack

"Brand New"
Ben Rector

Like what you read? Then talk about it! Word of mouth is still the best way for authors like me to sell books and trust me, I need all the help I can get! Want more Lloyd Scott? Visit my website or follow me on Instagram, Twitter, or Medium.

Website: https://www.electionyearlloydscott.com

Instagram: https://www.instagram.com/flamingjune86/

Twitter: https://twitter.com/riseupwomankind

Medium: https://medium.com/@lloydscott4america

Spot a mistake? Well, I'm only human and so was my editor! Instead of turning into a grammarhole let me know! Email me at lloydscott4america@gmail.com and I'll do my best to remedy the situation!

Dear America,

This past year as I've written this book, I've been a woman on a mission. A woman with wild ideas, crazy hair, mood swings, a sudden penchant for burning things (don't ask), and shouting out random words…! I've reached the pinnacle of genius (in my own mind, this was during the crazy hair phase) and fallen to the lowest depths and through it all my cheering section has (had some serious concerns but…) believed in me whole heartedly. To them, I'd like to say thanks. It has been the 'Rainbows' in my life who made this book possible. I couldn't have done it without you. Especially my husband, who says he's "writing a book about a woman writing a book, and it's going to be a tale of horror for the ages," — whatever that means! And to my dog Alister Kennet MacRay Von Friedrich IIII, (his royal snoutiness was found wandering the streets of Hollywoof, "Everybody wants to be a star!" We just call him Al. Hearing Paul Simon's, "You Can Call Me Al" as I type!) thank you for mostly letting me work without too many whiny interruptions, barking outbursts, demands for food, walks, scratches, playtime, bite-time, bedtime, but most of all thanks for the love. And to my Bestie who despite my babbling pleas of self-pity never let me give up and set me on the path of steely reserve each time I fell down, a million hugs and lots of love. Thanks to my editor, and all the other team members who made this possible. It has been a joy, an honor, and a pleasure working with you. To my readers, thanks for taking the time to read this far, I sincerely hope you enjoyed the book. Take care of yourselves, America. I'll write soon.

Love,
Lloyd

Made in the USA
Monee, IL
06 July 2020